YOU WOULD HAVE DONE IT TOO

HEATHER CHAMBERS

Cover art and design by Diana Galván Mejía and Nathan Fréchette. Interior design by Deanna Broodhagen. Edited by Shawn Brixi, William Keizer, and Alec Cimeša.

Paperback ISBN: 978-1-990086-78-6
Ebook ISBN: 978-1-990086-81-6

Presses Renaissance Press
pressesrenaissancepress.ca

Renaissance acknowledges that it is hosted on the traditional, unceded land of the Anishinabek, the Kanien'kehá:ka, and the Omàmìwininìwag. We acknowledge the privileges and comforts that colonialism has granted us and vow to use this privilege to disrupt colonialism by lifting up the voices of marginalized humans who continue to suffer the ongoing effects of ongoing colonialism.

Presses Renaissance Press acknowledges the support of the Canada Council for the Arts.

To all the queers battling mental health throughout your education,
may you accept your diplomas while standing proudly on the corpses of
your inner demons.

CONTENT WARNING

Please note that this novel contains depictions of bullying, homophobia, ableism and internalized ableism, violence and murder, and discussions of self-harm.

Body Found at Local College!

Blood pooled underneath him.

"I'm sorry. Your call cannot be completed as dialled. Please check the number and try again."

It seeped through the bottom of the classroom door, crawling over the gritty tiles and staining the grout.

"I'm sorry. Your call cannot be completed as dialled. Please check the number and try again."

"Guh... Guh..."

A few doors down, a professor gathered her things and strolled down the halls that sucked the life out of people's cries.

A trembling hand lifted at the sound of her clicking heels, mustered every ounce of withering strength to slap sticky fingers on the window. The professor didn't see the bloody handprint, didn't hear the rasps. Warm blood slid down cold cheeks. The hand streaked down the glass and fell limp upon the last digit of 9-1-1.

The phone, smudged with red fingerprints, finally connected and began to ring.

"9-1-1, do you need fire, police, or medical?"

The response came as a gurgle.

"I repeat. Fire, police, or medical? ... Hello...?"

The sound of the professor's heels faded. Her figure got smaller. Blurrier.

"Is this a prank? I swear, if this is a prank..."

"Guh..."

"Stupid kids..."

Click!

The phone screen went dark.

Second Body Found at College!

"They say he prowls at night and stabs anyone not in bed. I think that's ridiculous. Felix? For Pete's sake, quit dozing off!" a familiar voice shouted.

Felix's head shot up. His skull collided with Liana's. "Ow!"

All five-foot-two of her sat cross-legged atop his desk, wiggling around in pain. Her long, dark hair was up in a loose ponytail, with a white sport headband to keep the flyaways back. The text on it always made Felix smile, and he thought it was great for this moment.

"Suck it up, Buttercup," he teased, to which she stuck her tongue out and rubbed the sore spot on her forehead.

"You didn't get much sleep last night, did you?" Concern was etched into her pretty face like chiselled stone. "Was it a pillow thing or a sleepwalking thing?"

"Sleepwalking..." he mumbled to the floor. Liana wiped some drool from the corner of his mouth. He flushed and rubbed his face with the hem of his sleeve. His collection of hair ties and bracelets scratched his skin. "How'd you know?"

"Your hair smells. You didn't shower this morning."

"Don't sniff me."

Felix had sleepwalked all his life. He was pretty sure it was the reason he didn't have any siblings, though his parents denied it. It couldn't have been easy to take care of a toddler who could walk off the roof, whilst snoring, the moment you turned your back. His mother could write a book on the many hilarious situations they found themselves in because of his sleepwalking. Of course, no one thought those 2 a.m. stories were funny at the time.

Liana clicked her tongue sympathetically while Felix untied the rope that kept his leg attached to the desk—a precaution that would result in another embarrassing moment to include in the book, but he'd rather trip and fall flat on his face if his unconscious body decided to wander than everyone know the truth.

Though, nowadays, he had another reason to keep himself weighted down in his sleep.

"By the way, did you hear? They've got a new name for our infamous celebrity!" Liana clapped her hands and slowly spread them to imitate one of those retro arched signs, and said in her best announcer voice, "*The Campus Killer*!"

Voilà. Felix had no intention of handing his defenceless, unconscious backside to some rando whose definition of fun was playing doctor with a hammer.

"You really need a new hobby."

"But we may have our own serial killer! How can that not be exciting?"

"Why does everyone assume they're committed by one person? And what part about having to remember to put mace in your bag is 'exciting'? Did you not see the bodies on the web like the rest of us, or was Picasso's *Intestines à la Mode* just not up to your standards?"

"First of all, there was so much wrong with your last sentence I don't even know where to begin. Secondly—" She waved to a cute guy, who she might not even have known, as he walked past the classroom's windows, and whipped back around to finish her sentence, smacking Felix in the face with her hair. "—this place has been so dead it's nice to finally have some action!"

"I thought, hang on..." Felix pointed at a redhead passing the class windows. "I thought he was your action. And her. And him. And—"

She slapped his pointer out of the air.

"Since when did blood and gore replace the warm, living bodies on your literal 'to do' list?" he asked.

"They haven't been replaced by gore, yuck." She pretended to gag. "It's the same thing over and over with them. Flowers, woo the girl, kiss by the lockers, sex. It gets repetitive. But killers? And *serial* killers? You never know what they're going to do next!"

"Murder. It's going to be murder, next."

"Is she still going on about dead people?" said a pleasing voice by Felix's shoulder.

It belonged to a young man whose chestnut brown hair, accentuated by thin blonde highlights, seemed to glow in the classroom's soft lighting. It looked more appealing than Felix's hair, which was dull, overgrown, and always tied back so he wouldn't accidentally eat it.

"Hi, Nikolai." Felix's quiet greeting was drowned out by Liana's wave of complaints.

"Not dead people! Murderers! Honestly, I thought you knew me. By the way, did you hear that he has a name?"

"The Campus Killer, I heard," Nikolai said, giving Felix an amused smile that brought a twinkle to his warm brown eyes.

Nikolai pushed a few desks out of the way to fit his long limbs in the space provided. His height wasn't burdensome to his everyday life, and his stride was no more or less awkward for being gifted a couple extra inches than everyone else. Oh, no. If anything, when he finally settled in and stretched with a happy hum at the pops and cracks in all the right places, he made sitting in a plastic chair look luxurious. Leaning back with his legs crossed, supporting himself with one elbow over the back of the chair, Nikolai could look no more like a king if he wore a crown.

Maybe Felix could steal one from the theatre department...

"If we have one more body, he'll be classified as a serial killer!" Liana said, perhaps a bit too enthusiastically.

"Why can't it be a girl?" Nikolai teased.

"Considering how both victims were men, that's a good possibility."

More classmates had entered while Felix was dozing, all of their heads bowed in hushed conversations.

A group of guys near the back leaned against the wall, laughing. One pointed to some girls in the front and twisted closer to his friend, who sat on a desk, to exaggerate a mocking whisper in his ear. The group cackled. Encouraged, the two boys pretended to faint and catch the other.

Felix's phone buzzed in his sweater pocket. He didn't have to look to know who it was.

"Parents?" Nikolai leaned over to fish it out of Felix's pocket. His long-sleeved shirt twisted against his forearm, hinting at the strength that hid under his deceptively thin body.

"I bet you five bucks it is," Liana said.

"Not a bet I'm taking. I know it is. Our crazy parents are blowing up all our phones. I'm surprised they haven't contacted the board of directors."

"Oh, they have," muttered Felix, snatching back the phone. "The school almost shut down all the extracurricular activities and clubs because of it. Students have started emailing as well."

"That's why Coach was so tense?" marvelled Liana.

Nikolai gave her a look. "Yes. Your coach was 'tense' and stopped the late-night training hours because two people are dead. Why else?"

She shrugged. "We have a volley tournament in two days."
Felix snickered and checked his messages:

```
Hello, Felix! It's Dad! Just checking in to see if
everything is going well with school and your friends!
We know that in times of stress people tend to drink and
take comfort in each other any way they can. Forgetting
everything else is only natural.

Lord knows your mother and I turned to each other many
nights, but you need to make sure that you're taking
precautions. Are you and your friends being safe?
```

Felix choked on his spit.

"Whoa, there!" Nikolai smacked him between the shoulder blades, eyeing the blush creeping up his neck. "What'd they say?"

"They think—we—polyamorous—*sex!*—together—holy—"

Liana barked a laugh and dove for his phone. Felix scrambled to type before she could get her grubby paws on the keyboard and make it worse: *DAD, NO! Yes we're being safe! but no! not with each other! There's nothing between us! No being safe at all!*

Liana snatched the phone and read the texts. She cackled and shoved it in Nikolai's confused face. The horror crawling up his gut was only made worse when Nikolai smirked and sent him an exaggerated wink.

There was a buzz and Liana knelt on the desk out of Felix's reach so she and Nikolai could read the new text first. Whatever it said was worse. So much worse. Liana burst into giggles and Nikolai, well, he tried to hide his laughter. He really did.

As she handed Felix his ticket to Hell, Liana said, "As always, I love your mother."

Uh-oh.

```
SAFE FROM DEATH, CHILD. SAFE. FROM. DEATH. GET YOUR HEAD
OUT OF THE GUTTER! YOUR FATHER AND I WANT TO KNOW IF
YOU'RE LOCKING THE DOORS AND BUYING TASER GUNS.
```

Felix wanted to crawl under the desk and never come out.

DID NOT CARRY YOU FOR NINE MONTHS AND RAISE YOU WITH LOVE AND CARE FOR YOU TO MEET OUR MAKER IN SOME BACK ALLEY WITH YOUR PANTS AROUND YOUR ANKLES!

TASERS.

I am buying you taser guns and using them ON YOU if that's what it takes for you to understand your situation! How could you be thinking of SEX with that sociopath on the loose?

"By the way, she means psychopath," Liana said, grinning. "Fun fact, sociopaths are less likely to kill. Not that all psychopaths are serial killers either. That's the media you've consumed talking."

"I'll be sure to tell her that at the next family dinner," Felix muttered. He sent back a quick apology text and decided it was best to shut his phone off before she called. He shoved it into his binder and hid his heating face in his arms.

If someone looked up "tough love" in the dictionary, they'd get a picture of his mother. If he wanted to complain about a minor scrape or sneak an extra ice cream cone in before bed, he'd go to Dad. Dad was the more sentimental one. He cooed the best. That didn't mean Mom didn't love him. It just meant he got... those kinds of text messages.

"There you are, Felix! You fucking mouse, you were hunkered so much I couldn't see you!" cut in a taunting, grating voice from the back.

It was Michael, one of Emilio's goons. Emilio was a fellow Photojournalism student who thought Felix was delightful. An absolute hoot to pick on.

Felix tried to ignore him, even as the gaggle of boys at the back showed off their innumerable braincells by attempting to mimic mice scrounging for cheese crumbs, which was about as impressive as one would expect, and parroted each other's squawking laughter. If he didn't respond for long enough, they'd find a fire hydrant somewhere to bark at.

"Were you having a wittle nap because you spent all night editing photos that'll never get higher marks than Emilio? Oh wait, or were you crying all night because you miss Trevor so much? You two had such a special bond."

Ah, yes. The second victim. Trevor.

Trevor had liked to remind everyone he had been the star of his high school football team, as if that mattered in college. He had been one of the top business and finance students, a wizard with numbers, the brains and the brawn, the whole package! His most impressive attribute, however, had been his gift for assholery.

Students glanced at Felix and murmured confidence-boosting things like, "*That's the weirdo who Trevor used for target practice, didn't he get his tongue stuck to a frozen pole?*" and "*I still don't get why Nikolai tolerates him,*" to each other.

Trevor and Emilio hadn't been pals, but they hadn't been enemies. As long as one stayed in his business and finance territory and the other in the arts, they'd had no problem with each other. They'd only worried about stepping on Rhett's toes. That guy had ruled the school. Compared to Rhett, guys like Emilio and Trevor were nothing but betas. Wannabees. Rhett could mess with anybody, on anybody's territory, free of charge.

Then Rhett had become this killer's first taste of a whole new world. Like a sample platter at a restaurant.

The hierarchy had crumbled. Now, with Trevor dead, it was open season for Emilio and his underlings.

Felix could never find any real reason for being part of one of the many targets. Perhaps he had "Loser" written on his forehead with an invisible marker. Or he had a strand of loose hair that acted as an antenna, calling all jerks to his vicinity.

"Have some respect, will you?" a student by the window shouted. "A guy is dead!"

A girl in the front scoffed. "Not exactly a loss to the societal gene pool..."

Michael just laughed. "Felix, you should be counting your lucky stars! Weren't you going to test the limits of the human body with him? I think we should complete his research. Y'know, in his honour."

Liana glowered. "You're testing the limits of my patience right now."

Michael wasn't even bothered by Nikolai's icy glare. He rose and extended his arms with a wide grin. "No, really! It would be a wonderful experiment! I tell you what, why don't we tie a rope around your waist and hang you out the window to see how long you can hold on?"

Felix was about to retaliate when Nikolai and Liana jumped to their feet. The only thing that saved Michael was the professor who walked in and paused, examining the whiteboard.

The professor made a face. "Oh, what is that? Algebra? Someone erase it before I puke."

After class Felix booked it out of the building so fast his friends had to jog to keep up. Partially to lure them away from any more fights Michael would pick—he wasn't worth the trouble—but also because he would begin to wither if he didn't get dinner in the next five minutes.

With Liana's gag-worthy flirting distraction, they snuck takeout into the library and spent the evening attempting to be productive members of society. Key word: attempted.

Contrary to what he'd expected, he managed to finish some assignments despite the banter and the good-natured teasing. It wasn't his best work, but it would get him a passing grade and that was all he could ask for. He bid the others goodnight around eleven and walked back to his dorms to submit some projects online, and, for once, on time.

The moment he stepped outside and heard the crunch of loose rocks under his foot, he knew something was amiss. The usual nighttime hustle and bustle of students rushing to finish assignments at the last minute or to catch the library before it closed, or even the nighttime partiers getting together, were gone, replaced by a silence so tense that Felix almost expected it to snap at any moment and to hear somebody screaming for their life.

For a place where no cars waited on the side of the road, where not even a squirrel wrestled with the flimsy branches of a tree, Felix had the distinct impression of being watched.

Don't be silly, he chided himself, *you're just paranoid.*

But was he? The hair rising on the back of his neck told him something different. He could have sworn he heard the soft thumps of feet behind him.

"No need to panic," he said to himself. "It's so quiet that your footsteps are echoing. That's all."

He paused and listened. The second pair of feet stopped. A chill gripped his heart. He began walking again. The feet followed.

Felix spun around to catch his pursuer off-guard, a shout rising from his lungs. All he saw was the rustling leaves.

Maybe walking home alone hadn't been such a smart idea.

"As I walk through the valley of the shadow of death, you bet your ass I feel fear," Felix grumbled to himself, clutching the camera around his neck. He resumed walking.

The dorms were just up ahead. Felix picked up the pace. He ignored the whispers taunting his ears.

It's just the wind, he told himself, it's just the whistle of the wind.

A shadow crept up on him as he passed a streetlamp. Spindly claws reached for him.

Faster. There was someone there. He had to be faster.

The footsteps grew louder, closer.

He could see the building doors. He was almost there!

Crunch!

Felix jumped and tripped over the stairs, tumbling to the cement in a graceless pile of limbs. He curled up on the steps and tossed up his hands to protect himself from the oncoming attack.

Only the stars stared back. They twinkled as if laughing at his foolishness. He glanced at the leaves stuck to his clumsy feet. He'd scared himself. Wow, he needed to pull himself together. At least nobody saw that spectacle.

He cast one last glance at the tree's eerie shadows waving at him, and the wind that whispered for his return. He hurried inside.

It wasn't a grand place, no shining décor to welcome him or lavish rugs to warm his feet like in the movies. The first thing to see upon entering the honeycomb-shaped lobby was the unusable elevator on the back wall, sectioned off with pylons and caution tape. Perfect first impression.

Then there was the empty security station, reminding him more of a serving hatch than a beacon of safety, doorways everywhere leading into a labyrinth of halls and staircases, and the small, dirty glass cabinets with outdated trophies. No doubt plastic. The most exciting part was the bonsai tree by the exit.

Felix was one of the fortunate souls to reside on the ground floor. Ever since the elevators had been closed off, he and the rest of the students living on the ground floor were the subjects of many envious and sour looks. The worst were those carrying grocery bags. Felix thought they might actually throttle him.

However, walking past the bright yellow caution tape X and the ghost of handprints, he thought those living far away from the elevator had gotten a much better deal. He could still see the elevator doors close, then hit an obstruction and open again. Close, and open. Each time with a small squelch. The smell of rotting meat still lingered.

He unlocked his room and stepped inside, shivering at a breeze. Home sweet home. He took off his shoes and locked the door behind him.

It was a quaint little space, shaped like a large upside-down L. It had a tiny bathroom with a toilet, shower cubicle, and sink on the right of the entrance, and a microwave and toaster oven sitting on counters directly to the left of the entrance, sandwiched by cupboards above and below. Next to the makeshift kitchen was a wardrobe for his clothes, a work desk underneath a large open window, and a bed shoved into the nook on the far right of the L for privacy. He placed his camera on the counter.

Of course, he'd personalized the space. The room was filled with candid photos of friends and family strung up like fairy lights from wall to wall. The corners were cluttered with tripods and camera boxes and stacks of books on crates. He could pick up a new film roll or a box of lenses anywhere, find them stashed between piles of laundry, under his bed, behind the cereal boxes in the cupboards, atop the mirror in the bathroom—he had gotten quite creative with his lack of storage space. Anyone else might say it was chaos, but it was his organized chaos. He knew where everything was.

Which meant he knew right away that window was supposed to be locked. He locked everything. All the time. Even before the murders happened. Felix had grown up locking doors behind him so he wouldn't sleepwalk off a balcony. It was the reason he was living on the ground floor, after all. The only way the window would be open was if someone had come in uninvited...

Felix tiptoed over and slowly turned the latch. It made a sharp *click!* in the still quiet.

Had a custodian come in to clean the windows and left, forgetting to lock up after himself? No, whatever messes college students made in the dorms were their own problem. Plus, the door had been locked. If the custodian had remembered the door, he would have remembered the window, especially nowadays.

He rubbed the wristbands and hair ties around his wrists and turned in a circle to inspect his room. No clothes piles disturbed or tripod shifted.

He eyed the expensive cameras and photography equipment, things that would rack up a shiny price if you knew where to sell them. All there. He looked at his knife block. Not all there.

That didn't add up.

He had read enough Sherlock to know you didn't break into somebody's home and leave without their valuables. Or leave your exit wide open for anyone to see. It tipped them off. Let them know that you knew the halls had cameras, but the windows didn't. The only reason someone would leave your exit open was if—Felix's eyes landed on the closed bathroom door—his breath hitched—if they'd never left.

Felix padded to the knife block and grasped a handle with shaking hands. He tried to listen for the intruder, but the rush of blood in his ears made it difficult to hear anything. He crept towards the bathroom, all too aware of the soft creaking his feet made on the wood flooring.

The thought that he should run straight out the front door and get help vaguely passed by, but it vanished when he wrapped his sweaty palm around the doorknob. The cold metal shocked his skin, raising goosebumps up his arm like scuttling spiders.

Should he open it slowly in case there really was someone there? No, if someone was breathing just beyond that door, then he should push it open fast while the element of surprise was still his to wield.

Felix sucked in a sharp breath, steeled his nerves, and shoved open the door. A looming figure in the dark dove down, reaching for his neck. Felix shrieked and slashed the knife. It sliced air. He'd missed!

He slapped the light switch and raised the blade to defend himself against—his reflection. In the mirror.

His legs wobbled. He leaned against the wall before they gave out. He was safe. Nobody was there. He took a deep, shaking breath that bordered on a hysterical sob. He'd probably just forgotten to latch the window this morning, seeing as he hadn't even had time for a shower before getting to his first class.

Felix's stomach dropped to his knees.

The shower.

He whipped around and that time he did fall over, hands slapped against his mouth to muffle a shrill cry of horror.

Dried, watered-down blood tinted the cream floor tiles pink. Various clothing items lay in lumps, torn and suspiciously blotchy: a sweatshirt with his college's name and logo, Trevor's college ID sticking out of the pocket; a t-shirt with streaked handprints; and a black sock with the heel ripped open. All of it, tossed around a once-orange towel that blocked the drain, having soaked up the pool of blood instead of letting it wash away and dry.

Felix scrambled out of there as fast as he could and backed into his kitchen cupboards.

Oh, no. No, no, no.

This was so very bad.

He swallowed back the rising bile in his throat. Those clothes. That was evidence. In his shower. He had *evidence* in his shower!

He needed to tell someone. Felix fell to his knees, barely registering the sparks of pain, and threw open his backpack in such a hurry he nearly pitched his phone across the room. His clammy hands fumbled it onto the floor. It landed by his foot with a clatter. His fingers froze over the lit-up keypad.

Who should he call? The police? What if they thought he was to blame? It was no secret around campus that Trevor had it in for him. It wouldn't exactly look good if he rang up the police and told them he'd found his recently murdered bully's sweatshirt in his shower.

Not the police, then.

But he couldn't keep this a secret for long. He couldn't call his parents. They would notify the cops whether he asked for it or not. What about his friends? That would implicate them as accomplices. What should he do? Destroy the evidence? And how? Wash the blood off? Burn it? It had stained the tiles!

"Hey, Felix, what's up?" His shoe was talking to him. "Hello? Felix?"

It took him a solid five seconds to realize he'd somehow pressed speed dial with his toes.

"Did you just butt-dial me?" Nikolai sighed.

The sound broke his stupor. Screw implicating accomplices. He needed help. He raced to speak before Nikolai hung up, but his voice caught in his throat and everything tumbled out as panicked garbled nonsense.

Nikolai's laugh didn't calm him as it usually did. "Am I supposed to guess what you're eating? Hang on, I'll put you on speaker. Hey, Liana! Felix has a game to play that'll gross you out!"

All he managed to do was croak, "Blood."

A pause.

Liana's muffled voice came through the receiver. "What?"

"Shower. Blood. Trevor."

There was a rustling that he assumed was Liana taking the phone from Nikolai and walking a few steps away, turning off speakerphone. "Are you asleep?" she whispered.

He glanced at the open bathroom door, whimpering. "No."

"Felix. Can you hear me?" Nikolai's voice got louder, like he'd pressed the speaker button again. "What's going on? Is everything okay?"

"Help," he whispered.

He could almost hear their spines going rigid. Nikolai's voice was calm and collected through the receiver, something Felix would be grateful for later, as he was one notch from hysterics. "Where are you?"

"Home."

"Are you okay? Are you hurt?"

He could vaguely hear them telling each other to gather their bags.

"Nuh-no—I'm fine. I'm—there's..." The circles of different wood textures that made up the bathroom door stared back at him, wide-open mouths screaming. "*Blood*."

Nikolai said, "Stay where you are, wait for us. Do you hear me? We're coming to get you. I'm coming."

Body on Campus Identified as Student, Killer at Large

His friends all but kicked the door down. Felix had had just enough time to unlock it and hop on the counter before it slammed open and almost dented the wall. Both of them looked ready for a fight but one look at Felix hugging his knees on the counter swept the violence away. Liana gathered him into a hug and let him bury a relieved sob in her hair.

"Thank God you're okay," she whispered.

"What happened? Where's the blood?" Nikolai asked, frowning at the lack of wounds on Felix's person.

Felix pointed to the bathroom. They glanced at the open door, at each other, and cautiously stepped towards it. They turned to the shower and their expressions morphed into a mixture of horror and disgust.

"I see the cause for concern," whispered Liana.

They walked out of the bathroom. Then paused. They ducked their heads back in just to make sure, just to check, that they hadn't had a group hallucination. Nope. The evidence was still there. Nikolai walked back to Felix and braced himself against the counter. Silence descended upon them.

Finally, Nikolai pulled himself together enough to begin asking questions. "Are they yours?"

He shook his head.

"You mentioned Trevor over the phone. Do you think, maybe, the sweatshirt's his?"

Liana answered from the bathroom doorway. "Seeing how I'm staring at the guy's ID, I'm gonna go with yes."

"Wasn't the first victim missing his shoes?" Nikolai said quietly, sounding like he wanted nothing more than to be wrong.

"Yep. And his sock, too."

"Missing items from the crime scenes... How did they get here?"

Felix motioned towards the window. "When I came back the door was locked, but the window wasn't. And I always lock the window."

"Then..."

A frantic laugh bubbled from Felix's chest. "Does it matter, how? There's nothing we could say that would convince anyone that I didn't do it. As soon as this gets out, everyone will blame me!"

"They won't blame you, no one liked Trevor or Rhett," Nikolai assured, though not well enough to hide the fearful trembling undertone, and that sent Felix's fragile control spiralling.

"He terrorized me, Nikolai! I'm such an easy target that he picked on me all the time! No sane person will believe that a murderer waltzed in here and bestowed bloody tokens upon my shower. It's not like the cops will do a thorough search to prove my innocence, they're as anxious as anyone else out there to put this case to rest!"

Nikolai's knuckles whitened against the counter. "It'll be fine. We can deal with this. We'll just—"

"It's *not* fine. Someone's framing me!"

"You don't know that!"

Liana's deadpan voice cut through like a knife. "Hide everything."

"What?" Felix croaked.

Under the dim bathroom light, she appeared relaxed, as if the answer was easy and they were stupid for not realizing it. But the shadows accentuated the steely look in her eyes. "The evidence. Hide it all. Now."

A shiver rolled down his spine.

"How?" asked Nikolai, baffled.

"You, put the clothes in the sink. Scrub that shower to within an inch of its life with soap and cold water. If you use hot, it'll just set the blood. I'm going to take out the batteries of the fire alarms in here and in the hallway, and then I'll find a lighter and a metal garbage bin. Felix? Search the dorm from top to bottom in case there's anything else stashed and find me a hiding spot for Trevor's ID."

It was like she was back in the courtyard: calm, focused and empowered by cool self-confidence that made everyone else feel like they'd be an idiot to not listen.

"How do you know hot water sets blood?" asked Nikolai, a little green.

"Everyone knows people with uteruses perform monthly sacrifices to the gods. Now, get moving."

They worked fast. Nikolai rolled up his sleeves, snapped on a pair of rubber gloves, and began moving clothes. By the time Liana came back with a box of matches and a metal bin, which she stole from the janitor's closet, he was two inches in bloody foam.

"Where'd you get the matches?" he asked when she walked in.

"Smoker a floor up," she said, taking apart Felix's fire alarm.

"And he just gave them to you?" Felix asked. "They normally don't give those up for anything."

She smirked. "I may have told him the girls' volleyball team are doing a secret risqué calendar photo shoot and we needed the light for ambiance."

She pointed out that the hall's smoke alarm was installed in front of the security camera; if they took it down, people would see and be suspicious, so she gathered all of Felix's towels and blocked every crevice in the front door instead to keep the smoke from seeping out of the room.

She then tossed all the evidence into the metal bin and pulled a half-empty bottle of mouthwash—actually vodka—from Felix's bathroom cabinet. She took a swig, sprinkled some on the clothes and, with the window wide open, struck a match and dropped it inside.

Felix couldn't find anything else hidden in his room, thankfully. Since he couldn't stomach dealing with all the blood in the bathroom, he relieved Liana of her duty directing the smoke out the window so she could help Nikolai instead. When they were finished, they all sat on Felix's bed, staring at the scraps in the metal bin. They'd melted the plastic ID card to make it unrecognizable and hid it behind his wardrobe. Now, all they could do was hope.

"Why would anyone frame you?" Liana asked, rubbing her face. She was hugging one of the throw pillows she'd gifted him on his birthday—a pillow of Nicolas Cage's screaming face photoshopped onto the head of a woman from a movie about to be murdered in the shower. Looking at it now, he wished she'd turn it around.

"I guess I'm just lucky," he mumbled.

"Maybe it's not a frame-job?" Nikolai said, staring at his shoes with his knuckles pressed to his mouth. When they gave him a look he raised his hands in self-defence. "I'm just saying! We haven't thought of all the possibilities!"

"Which are what?" Liana prompted. "That this is the worst prank in history? A warning? A symbol of affection?"

"I don't know... Whatever. You're right." He threw Felix's comforter over his shoulders and rose to double-check all the locks. Some of the warmth left with him.

Liana rubbed the goosebumps from her arms. "That—*this*—is freaky. The fact that you were picked randomly just makes it scarier."

"What do I do? Continue on as normal?" Felix said. It seemed ridiculous to even think about walking the halls with this brewing under his skin.

"You have to, to avoid suspicion. If anyone else finds out..." Nikolai shuddered.

"I'd be arrested. Or killed."

"That, or you'd be getting *them* killed," Liana said. It was her turn to get the *Dude, not helping* look. "I'm serious. Think of literally any slasher fiction. Or, heck, real life murderers! Anyone who finds out something the killer doesn't want known yet gets knifed."

"That's gonna help me sleep tonight," Nikolai muttered.

Nobody was safe, not the sweet guidance counsellor, not his professors, not the students down the hall. Nobody could get wind that anything was wrong.

"I feel sick." Nikolai looked nowhere near ready to step foot back in that bathroom, even if he needed to vomit.

"You know what we need?" Liana jumped off the bed and opened up all of Felix's cupboards until she found what she was looking for: cupcake mix and hot chocolate powder. "A party! I'm scared, and you both look like you're about to throw up your intestines. Let's just hole up together to make each other feel safe!"

"Deal," burped Nikolai, holding his stomach. "But we're using water for the hot chocolate instead of alcohol this time."

They both looked at Felix with wide, hopeful eyes. This scared them as much as it did him, but they didn't run away. A surge of warmth loosened the cramp in his stomach.

"Deal."

Liana did a terrific job getting everyone's minds out of the darkness. They ended up making an absolute mess attempting to bake cupcakes. Nikolai whisked the mixture in a frying pan with a fork, dared Felix to lay on the floor with his mouth open to catch what mixture didn't land in the three hefty pottery mugs, and stood by the toaster oven hoping the mugs wouldn't explode. They watched old comedy shows, poked fun, and didn't go anywhere near the bathroom.

Halfway through their night, someone's phone rang. The melodic yet annoyingly chirpy tune made the three freeze in their seats. They looked at the forgotten mobiles on the floor, drifted to the one that vibrated against the wood. The sound grated on Felix's eardrums.

Bzzzt.

Bzz—

"It's not like it's going to be the cops," said Liana, forcing a laugh.

"Of course not," Felix chuckled. "It's not like they could know what we did!"

They all ignored how his voice warbled.

Bzzzt.

"Is that your phone, Nikolai?" Felix asked.

Nikolai shrugged, perfectly content with letting it go to voicemail.

"I think it is," Liana decided, and promptly kicked Nikolai off the bed.

He squawked, landed with a thump, and scrambled to his feet as if a monster would pull him under the bed. Nobody laughed.

His dancer's feet barely made the floor creak. Felix and Liana held their breath, though he didn't know why.

Bzzzt.

Bzzzt.

Nikolai knelt. His hand hesitated over his phone.

"It can't be the killer. Can it? Like in the movies?" Liana whispered. "*'What's your name? I want to know who I'm looking at.'*"

Nikolai shot her a glare.

"Sorry."

When he picked it up the tension released from his back, and an annoyed twitch set in. "It's my parents."

Felix and Liana sighed and slumped against each other.

"Give me a minute." He walked into the hall.

They turned the comedy show back on, but Felix's attention wasn't on it anymore. Nikolai never got on with his parents, and none of them were in the right headspace for a toxic argument with a relative. Felix's mother might be a bit rough around the edges but compared to the little he'd heard about Nikolai's parents, she was Mary Poppins.

He excused himself to get more hot chocolate and listened in through the mostly closed door. If it got too bad, he'd interrupt and hang up for him. Nikolai would probably be thankful for the getaway.

He could vaguely hear angry foreign snippets and heavy accents from Nikolai's parents. Nikolai was unwavering in his English responses, refusing to utter a single word in what Felix assumed was his mother tongue.

"Home! *Now!*" growled a deep voice between bouts of another language. Felix assumed it was his father.

"There are vowels in my fridge. Would you like me to fetch them for you?" Nikolai said, not a hint of an accent in his voice.

Cue the harsh train of the foreign language. Nikolai sighed. He pressed mute. Scratched his head. Yawned. When he unmuted, his father spat, "There is murderer!"

"Oh, now you care?"

"Wot's that supposed to mean?"

"I thought I wasn't your son anymore?"

Felix's heart seized. He knew it was bad between them, but he'd never expected that. He reached for the doorknob, ready to intervene, but Nikolai had already hung up. His shadow under the door flickered with the hall light, just standing there. Felix shuffled backwards to allow the door the space to open and waited patiently, fiddling with his bracelets.

When Nikolai quietly pushed into the room, rubbing his face, he paused at the sight of Felix handing him his cup of hot chocolate. Pleased to watch the frustration slip, Felix tolerated getting his hair tousled in thanks.

Felix whispered, "Are you okay?"

The cup stilled on his bottom lip. "You heard that, eh?"

"Not all of it. Just the English bits," he mumbled to his swinging feet. He'd just wanted to help, but thinking back, he'd probably overstepped. If Nikolai had wanted him to know, he'd have said something.

Nikolai's mouth twitched into an amused smile. "It's fine. The family wanted me in accounting, is all." The smile dropped. "They didn't see a career waiting for me in dancing. I saw different. We fought. I rebelled. They disowned me."

Felix winced. He shouldn't have pried. "I'm sorry."

"Why should you be sorry? You didn't do anything wrong."

"I know, I just feel bad, you know?"

Nikolai's confused surprise melted into a fondness that left a twinkle in his eyes. Felix ignored how his stomach fluttered. Liana sometimes looked at him like that when he said something less than intelligent. Nikolai steered him back into the room with an arm around his shoulders.

"Don't be. I chose this path. I'd rather be at odds with a conservative family and happy with life than be chummy with them and suffocating. And accounting is the definition of suffocating."

For someone as artistic as you, to be under somebody's thumb and forced to study something so stifling would be hell.

"Besides, they care enough about their heir to tell him off when there's a killer on the loose, so it looks like I'm not completely banished." He joked with ease, but the prominent veins in his neck and his tight jaw hinted at something else. But unless he offered the information, Felix thought it best to leave him alone and continue watching B-rated movies.

It wasn't long before Liana's yawning became contagious, and they were all falling asleep in a massive lump.

"What're you doing?" Nikolai whined to Liana, who fiddled on her phone; he was using her lap as a pillow. "Stop being productive and sleep."

"I'm getting a taxi to take me home. I have some things I need to take care of—oh, get *off* me—before classes start..." She checked the time. "In six and a half hours."

It was Felix's turn to whine around a mouthful of bed sheets, "No!" He slung his arm around her middle. "Why? Just stay. Sleep here. Easier."

"Yes, yes, this is very adorable and all." She pried Nikolai's arms from around her thighs, only to be yanked back down by Felix's legs around her back. "Oh, come on. There is no way I'm getting any shut-eye with you two snoring like congested walruses."

"I don't snore, I purr," Nikolai mumbled back.

"For the love of..."

She pulled out a pair of knuckle dusters from her back pocket. The boys let her go and clung to each other for safety. It was a flat cat face made of solid plastic.. Her fingers slipped through the cat's eyes and the pointy ears stuck out of her knuckles, perfect for stabbing anyone as she punched them.

"This is a My Kitty Self-Defence Knuckle Weapon. My sister mailed them to me after the first murder."

"Have a safe ride home," said Felix.

"Text us when you get there," added Nikolai.

"I love you," said Felix.

"I love you more," said Nikolai.

"Nice try, you're coming with me," she said to Nikolai.

"What? Why?"

She gestured to Felix. "Because we need to let our introvert quiver before he has to socialize again today." When Nikolai wasn't looking, she pointedly glanced to the floor where, to Felix's horror, his shoebox peeked from under the bed.

"Oh! Uh, yeah. I didn't even think about that!" Felix stretched to mask his heel nudging the box back into the shadows.

Bless his soul, Nikolai got off the bed so fast he slipped. "Sorry! Of course you'd want some time. Are you, uhm... Are you sure you'll be alright sleeping here alone though?"

Felix smiled despite the way his stomach turned in on itself. "I'm a lot better now that the ... stuff is gone. Thanks for showing up, guys."

"Of course," Liana said on the way to the door. "Be extra sure to lock up behind us." Liana cast a final glance at the bathroom on the way out.

With them gone the room felt empty and dark. He resisted the temptation to call them back and double checked all the locks. He pulled out the shoebox of restraints and hesitated. What if someone broke in again while he was chained to the bed? How was he supposed to defend himself?

It'd be worse if I sleepwalked straight into the killer's knife, he reminded himself before locking his wrist to the bed post.

Psychopath Or Sociopath? The Public Debates

"Man, morning classes are just Satan!" Liana groaned and buried her sorrows into a bowl of poutine.

"Preaching to the choir. Hang on..." Nikolai reached up and grabbed Felix's favourite sandwich from the top shelf of the school's cafeteria and inspected it before handing it to him.

"Are you checking my food for poison, too?" Felix grumbled.

Nikolai stuck out his tongue. "Hardy har har. I'm just being a good tall friend to my small friend."

"I'm not small. I'm less than a foot shorter than you, you six-foot-three giant."

"Vertically challenged," Liana teased with a mouth full of gravy and cheese curds.

Felix scowled down at her. "If I'm short, what're you?"

"Ridiculously adorable."

They had decided to take their lunch on campus. It had nothing to do with the fact that places off campus had less security, of course. They just liked faster access to food, that's all.

Speaking of...

Felix glared at Nikolai as he grabbed a juice bottle for him as well. Nikolai had been checking up on him either physically or by text all morning. At first, it was nice. Now...

"Seriously. Quit it!" he hissed, snatching away the bottle. "No self-respecting killer is gonna jump out from behind the orange juice!"

"I'm just looking out for you. Someone's got to, since you're such an easy target."

"I'm *not* an easy target."

Nikolai and Liana raised a brow in unison.

"You said it yourself, yesterday," Liana said.

"Yeah, but you're not supposed to agree with me."

The cashier scowled at Liana for eating before paying and they walked out onto the grounds for some sun. It was easy to tell that people felt safer during the daytime, seeing how they were outside sitting on picnic benches, hanging around trees, and soaking up the sunlight like a plot of photosynthesizing plants.

That didn't mean the murders weren't on their minds. He caught murmurs of "*no, that was a high-functioning sociopath,*" and comparisons to trigger happy characters on television between conversations.

His friends were suspiciously quiet.

"Stop thinking about my shower."

"Kind of hard not to," Nikolai mumbled. "I mean, what kind of person does that?" He turned to Liana. "Is he a... What was the term? Psycho?"

"Careful with the association there. Technically, psychopath, yes. Sociopaths are the hot-headed ones, and as brutal as those bodies were, this wasn't a crime of passion." She ticked down her fingers. "The lack of clues at the scene, the evidence dump in the shower, and the connection between the bodies, that's a cool-headed psychopath's work—if it even is one. Not everyone with an antisocial personality disorder is violent and associating them with this is quite damaging. The killer could just be some entitled douchebag."

"Okay. Uninvited-stabby-night-visitor it is, then."

She lowered her voice. "Did you find anything else this morning?"

Felix said, "Nope, and my birthday isn't for another eight months so I hope I don't get any more gifts until then."

Two girls walked hand in hand toward the library. They giggled at inside jokes until they spotted a group of boys loitering in front of the doors. They fell silent and let go of each other's hands. One of Liana's volleyball teammates noticed this as she was trying to leave the library and shouted, "Out of the way, peasants!" When the guys still didn't move, she shoulder checked them on the way down the steps, creating an opening for the girls to gratefully zip through.

She came their way, waving. "Hey Felix! You feeling any better?"

Had she not said his name, he would have stepped out of her path for the person she must have obviously been speaking to. As nice as the team was, being addressed felt more like a courtesy since he was always around Liana. "Fine, why?"

"Oh, Liana and I were supposed to hang out last night but she bailed saying you had some sort of emergency." Her face tightened, as though forcing her smile . "Wasn't anything bad, I hope."

Depends if you like living a crime documentary.

"No, but thanks for the concern," he said, side-eyeing Liana. "Sorry to ruin your guys' plans."

"There's nothing to apologize for." She checked her buzzing phone and sagged before remembering herself and squaring her shoulders.

"How's your sister doing?" Liana asked gently.

A pained expression flickered across her face. "As well as can be expected. I'll tell you about it at practice later when I break your point streak. Gotta go."

Once she was out of earshot, Felix asked, "What'd you say for her to care about me?"

"I didn't have to say anything. Trevor bullied her sister straight out of school and into a mental hospital last month. She's been a bit more... attentive since."

Nikolai shook his head. "That was her? Poor thing. That's messed up."

If there were any justice the bullies responsible would've been punished. In a morbid way he supposed they were in this case. Trevor *was* dead...

Two guys ran past, laughing and shoving each other. One of them stumbled into Felix, knocking his book bag off his shoulder, and barely gave so much as an apology. He opened his mouth to say something and it felt like every pair of eyes turned on him at once. The memory of the blood running down his shower drain clogged his throat.

"Hey! Watch where you're going!" Liana snapped, making him jump. The pair blew a raspberry and disappeared. How did she make standing up and being loud look so easy?

"What's that?" Nikolai said as he helped pick up Felix's things, pointing to a photo that had fallen out of the binder.

"That's my submission to the campus art journal," Felix mumbled, balancing his sandwich in his mouth to free his hands. "Whoever wins the district vote gets featured in the regional magazine. A lot of big names pay attention to the contest. I'm going to hand it in after taking photos for the school's sports page. We've got a meeting later."

He wanted to skip so bad, award or not, but he couldn't let fear rule his life. He had to go on as normal.

Nikolai gingerly held the photo to the light. Liana stole a bite of his sandwich as she took a peek and whistled.

The photograph showed a little boy, barefoot in the grass, with muddy, smudged handprints all over his rumpled hand-me-down clothing, holding onto a balloon string in the dead of night. On the end of the string was a round moon, glowing in the darkness as if to guide the child along his path. The pale light kissed the tip of his nose and accentuated his dimples and the twinkle in his big, round eyes.

"You did this? No photo manipulation?" Liana asked.

Felix smiled and nodded.

"It's beautiful," she whispered.

"How did you make the moon?" Nikolai asked, breathless.

"Papier-mâché balloon, spray paint, an LED light, and an incredible amount of patience."

Nikolai brought the picture up to his face and extended his arms, making little *woah* sounds. Warmth bloomed in Felix's chest. Nikolai always gave the best reactions.

"Does it mean something?"

"It means"—the tips of his ears reddened—"everyone is scared. With the murders. No one feels safe. Everyone is lost, grasping at the air for answers, seeing as the police haven't given us any. They couldn't even keep the students safe; another one of us is dead. There's this fog of questions and fears that are pushing us down. I wanted to remind people that there's hope in the dark."

"That's what the balloon is?" Liana tossed her empty container in the trash and tried to get around Felix's stiff arm keeping her from his food.

"Mhm. People use the phrase 'as black as night' to describe something foreboding, suffocating or, well, dark. But the night isn't completely dark, is it? We have the moon. The moon always shines. It never leaves us unprotected. Even in the darkest time in our lives there's always...."

"Hope," Nikolai finished for him, smiling so brightly the top of his pale cheeks rounded. "I expect nothing less from our brightest photography student!"

Felix looked away with an embarrassed grin, rubbing the back of his neck.

Liana spared her assault on his lunch to squint at the child. "Isn't that Coach's intern's kid? Michone from sports management?"

"Yup. Interesting request it was, though: 'Hey, Michone! Can I dirty up your six-year-old in an abandoned park at midnight? For a school project, you ask? Nope. On my personal time.'"

"Oh good. You didn't just kidnap a child, then. Man, he'd make a great libero one day. If he stopped catching the ball with his face, that is." She spun around and took a large bite of Nikolai's unsuspecting sandwich, dancing away before he could understand what happened. "This is my turnoff. I'll see you two losers in a couple of hours."

Felix laughed at Nikolai's glare.

"And Felix?" Her expression sobered, drying his amusement. "Watch yourself today. You never know who's listening."

It felt like every pair of eyes on the grounds bore into his back. He swallowed thickly and nodded.

After class, Felix leaned against the wall, fiddling with his Polaroid camera as he waited for Nikolai to finish speaking with a professor down the hall so they could accompany each other to their next destinations. They tried to do it whenever possible, even if they had to split up after only a few minutes. Like now, as he was going to hang out with Liana in the gym while Nikolai attended his next class. It wasn't anything special, but Felix cherished their walks.

They'd stopped by the photography department to get the sports camera, and now it lay snug in its case by his feet. He could've been checking the settings to save himself some time when he got to the gym, but his Polaroid was more fun. He enjoyed the instant gratification of pressing the button and holding the captured memory in his hands not ten seconds later. Instant cameras had their cons—an unsteady hand would make a horrible picture and waste film—but if used correctly, they could be much more fulfilling than digital cameras.

He watched the bustling hall through the lens's eye. One student stepped out of class like a prisoner being released from jail. Someone flipped the bird to a poster that read, *R.I.P. RHETT*. One man was curled up in a corner, fast asleep. He didn't even stir at the loud *bang!* a couple of doors down.

Felix peered closer to investigate the sound and spotted none other than Emilio bearing down on some poor student, fingers curled in his shirt like an owl with its talons around a mouse's body. The snarl Emilio let out had his lips curling while the other student cowered backwards into his shirt.

Other students ignored the attack. At least they had the presence of mind to step around the halo of fallen essay papers at their feet. Felix noticed a cracked phone under Emilio's boot.

The instinctual trickle of electricity in his feet urged him to leave quickly. Someone else would help.

Don't be ruled by fear.

With a *click* and a *fizz* Felix captured the scene. "Leave him alone, Emilio," he called, pushing through the crowd.

Emilio looked past the crook of his nose to settle his glare upon him. His large, meaty hands and his big, clumpy boots looked like they could cause some nasty damage. Felix thought it best to keep out of arm's reach.

"Look who it is," Emilio sneered. "The Cowardly Lion. Your courage isn't here. Why don't you search somewhere else before you get hurt?"

"Let the guy go," he said, louder.

Someone look. Someone care.

A couple of people turned to watch. They noticed Emilio and hurried on.

Emilio scoffed. "Or what? You don't scare me."

"But this might." He willed his hand steady and held up the photograph, a clear shot of the bullying. "If you don't back off. I'll bring this to the council."

"A picture? You should know those don't hold up. Everyone knows they can be doctored. And then what are you gonna do? Pull 'witnesses' out of the crowd?" He pulled the other boy into a chokehold by his side, ruffling his hair and laughing as he struggled. "Witnesses to what? We're just playing around!"

"It's fresh off an instant camera, meaning there's no Photoshop involved. No way to fake the image." Felix nodded to the boy who was turning red in the face from asphyxiation. "So let him go, or I'll turn it in."

Emilio growled but slackened his grip. The guy took the chance to duck out. He snatched his phone from under Emilio's boot and ran away, coughing.

"You've gotten bolder," Emilio noted with no small amount of disgust. "You think you can threaten me? You think you're safe with Trevor gone?"

Fantastic. At least he'd helped one person before the cafeteria added "Felix-pancake" to the menu.

"I think you've got this mixed up." Emilio stepped forward. "Rhett isn't here to claim dibs and with Trevor dead, it just means I have you all to myself." He cracked his knuckles. "Maybe I should remind you where you stand in this relationship."

In that moment Felix discovered he knew a lot more curses than he thought he did. He stepped back, looking around for the quickest escape route, and bumped into somebody's chest, nearly jumping out of his skin. Nikolai was holding a bag of chips and carrying Felix's camera bag over his shoulder.

"There you are! I had just gotten a snack since Liana ate mine and when I turned around, you were gone! Here, they're your favourite." Nikolai's voice was kind and pleasant, but the way he kept his eyes on Emilio, who fumed in a pile of papers, told Felix he wasn't as oblivious as he pretended to be. "Oh dear, it looks like you've dropped your essays. Do you want help picking them up?"

Emilio grumbled something Felix thought they should be glad they missed while gathering his papers and left, throwing nasty looks over his shoulder.

Felix sighed in relief. "Thanks. For a second there, I thought he was going to charge. Ooh, salt and vinegar chips!" He pretended to be unaffected, making a show of stuffing a handful into his mouth. "You should go on to class."

Nikolai pursed his lips and the good-natured veil fell away to reveal his concern. "I could always skip, you know. It's just Dance History and Theory. I could get the notes from someone in my class."

Felix knew what he was getting at. While taking on a mountain troll by himself wasn't the smartest idea, he couldn't hide behind Nikolai forever. He took the camera bag with a thankful smile and showed the photograph he took. "I'll be fine. Emilio won't try anything while I've got this."

He did his best to look like he believed himself.

"That just might be the reason he does try again," Nikolai muttered. "But if you say you're okay, fine."

Felix put on a brave smile pocketing the photograph, before tossing Nikolai the bag and backing into the sea of students. "I'll see you later. Don't worry, I left some chips for you!"

He was already turning around when he heard Nikolai's disgruntled shout.

"You thief, there is one chip left! One!"

You Would Have Done It Too

The gymnasium wasn't Felix's favourite place on campus. Sometimes, the shouting and the pounding music gave him a headache that put off his appetite. If it wasn't that, the smell did him in for sure. The heavy, tangy musk clung to the banners and the wood flooring no matter how many times they were washed.

He preferred a good windowsill, one with a view of grassy fields and frost-tinted trees. Maybe with a book or a nice scroll through the internet. Of course, his favourite place on campus was the college darkroom, where there was nothing but dim red lights, quiet background music, and the joy of creation for company.

Alas, even if it wasn't his scene, he enjoyed it for what it meant to Liana. She relished pushing herself until there was no room for thinking. How high she could jump, how fast she could calculate the ball's trajectory and react, they were all barriers she could break.

So, he resolutely ignored the sweat slithering down his back and his frizzy hair and spent his free time doing homework on the bleachers, providing her support as often as he could.

What awaited behind the heavy doors this time was no different. He gagged at the assault of sauna-grade humidity and waved the smell away. He set up his equipment in a corner, carefully setting aside his instant camera, and walked along the sidelines, taking snapshots with the sports camera of anything that caught his eye.

The gymnasium was split into four sections: one for the girls' volleyball team, one for the boys' volleyball team, and two for the all-gender basketball team. Felix winced thinking about how well that discussion must have gone.

He adjusted the camera settings, waving at Liana as he did, and laughed when she almost got hit with the ball because of the distraction.

Something crackled underfoot. Uh-oh. He hoped he didn't just ruin some sort of tiny sports equipment and have to deal with *Coach*. He peeked under his shoe. Saved! It was only a flyer. A ripped, crumpled rainbow-coloured flyer that said *We're here. We're queer. We have no fear!*

Something in his chest twisted as he brushed off the footprints from the once vibrant message. Someone had worked hard on this, only for somebody else to tear it down. He smoothed the creases and propped the flyer up against the coach's windowsill, apologizing under his breath for stepping on it, and got back to work.

When he was satisfied with his shots, he returned to the bench to pack his equipment and spotted his art journal submission poking out of his binder. He took it out. A swell of pride filled him. Truly, he'd outdone himself. The Art Journal Club was going to love it.

Wait a second. Pride. That gave him an idea.

He grabbed his instant camera and hurried to the dirty LGBT flyer. He cleaned it off with his sleeve as best he could. It still looked battered, but for what he had in mind it was in perfect condition.

Liana spiked the volleyball the same way she slammed down trolls in day-to-day conversation. On the other side of the net, her teammate and friend, Riley, skid on her knees across the court, missing the ball by an inch.

It amazed a lot of people how Liana could be accepted on the volleyball team as wing spiker when she was so short, as the position needed players to jump high above the net to slam the ball. Sure, she was cute with her button nose, small face, and those cherubic cheeks that constantly made Felix want to pinch them, but unless the coach had a kink for jail time there was no way Liana had flirted her way onto the team.

Then people saw her play, and all questions went out the window.

"I'll stop it next time! Another!" Riley shouted, blowing a brown lock of hair that'd escaped her long braids out of her eyes and crouching. If anyone could make Liana break a sweat, it was the libero. She was the strongest engineering student he'd ever seen. Her thick, muscular thighs were ready to lunge anywhere at a moment's notice to receive Liana's powerful spikes. It was amusing to watch other people get whiplash seeing the pair do each other's hair on the sidelines and then try to decimate each other on the court.

Liana raised a brow in Felix's direction as she got back into position and, honestly, he couldn't blame her. From her perspective, he was propping up a crumpled piece of paper against some stranger's shoe and wriggling on his stomach like a worm.

It didn't bother him. He'd been caught in far more compromising positions.

He remembered having balanced one foot on a picket fence, the other in a nook inside a tree, hoping he didn't rip a thigh muscle from stretching so far, and pointing the camera directly down. There'd been a pretty caterpillar munching on some leaves in the grass. The sunlight had made the fuzz on its back glow and appear extra fluffy. To anybody walking by, it looked like he'd been taking a very creative crotch shot.

Felix fixed the flyer in the best position and waited. That encapsulated the majority of photography, sadly. Waiting, not scratching that itch, hoping that crawling feeling wasn't a bug.

It was always worth it, because there finally came that moment where everything lined up and *click*—you were rewarded for your troubles.

Felix bounced to his feet and tucked the photo under his shirt to let it develop safely in the dark.

The battered and torn flyer shone clear under the gym lights in the forefront, standing tall off to the left. Behind, on the right, Liana and two girls were caught mid-jump blocking the net as a team, with two more kneeling behind them at the ready. The ball gleamed in the air, just bouncing off Liana's fingertips. As secondary focus, the girls were blurred the right amount, but not too much to obscure the stretch of Liana's smile.

This one was going up on his wall for sure! He couldn't wait to show Liana.

Somebody barrelled into his side, sending him tumbling to the ground. A flare of pain in his elbow and hip told him he landed on his side; the bash and ensuing throb in his cranium told him he did not enjoy it.

The camera!

Thankfully he'd gripped it to his chest when he fell. It remained unharmed. He looked up to find the culprit. He shouldn't have been surprised.

"This is the perfect shot!" Emilio exclaimed, standing right where his face had been.

"Was the bulldozing necessary?"

Emilio looked down and cocked his head in interest, sending a shiver up Felix's spine. "Look what we've got here," he rumbled, sounding like a body being dragged across gravel.

Felix flinched when Emilio reached for his foot, but his fingers never touched his shoes. Emilio held up the picture that had fallen out of Felix's pocket. "I must admit, for a sleazy nobody, you managed to catch my good side!"

It was the bullying picture.

"Wait!"

"Oh no." Emilio tore it into two. "What a pity." Into four. "Whatever will we do?" Into eight. "It looks like you won't be handing this in anytime soon." He dumped the pieces onto Felix's head, singing about confetti.

Felix was about to snap at him when he spotted his submission a few feet away. Emilio could tear up his bullying evidence, fine. But he couldn't get his grubby paws on that!

Felix dove and slapped his palm over the photograph. Just before he could pull it to safety, Emilio stomped on his hand. Felix clenched his teeth against the sharp pain. He tried to pull away. Emilio pressed harder. The tiny bones in his hand shifted.

"And what do you think you're doing?" Emilio said.

"Get off!"

"Not happening. I think I want to see what you're hiding."

"It's mine!"

Felix pulled at his wrist but Emilio dug his heel in until he couldn't stop a cry of pain. A handful of heads turned at the sound, though quickly lost interest. Only one person kept searching the sidelines.

Emilio bent, grinning at Felix's gasp, and slid the photograph from his aching fingers. The stretched skin over his bones felt wet. Had he broken the skin? He couldn't tell.

"Is this what you were going to hand in? You honestly believed *this* would be picked? Over mine? There's no way it can compete."

"Give it back!"

He couldn't destroy it! He couldn't!

"I don't think I like your tone."

Felix watched, helpless, as Emilio ripped the polaroid in half and let it fall to the floor like feathers. All those sleepless nights storyboarding ideas, the countless attempts to create that floating papier-mâché balloon, and the effort he put in working with a grumpy child and a sleepier mother in the dead of night—all of it culminating in a small, beautiful picture, now torn.

Weeks of hard work, gone.

"Let this be a lesson to you, pig, to never—Ow!"

A volleyball hit Emilio in the back of the head with a resounding *thunk!* and down he went like a sack of bricks. Felix gathered his torn photograph, cradling the pieces, and his injured hand, to his chest.

Liana had taken one look at the two, caught the ball, and spiked it with all her strength at Emilio's head. Half the team stared at her, many of them with satisfaction.

"You bitch!" Emilio clutched his head, wobbling when he tried to stand. "You'll pay for that!"

"Will I?" Liana picked up the rock-hard volleyball and rolled it between her hands. "The ball goes out of bounds all the time. You're responsible for watching where you step if you're not playing." Her fingers pressed dents. "And you *did* cross the line."

"I—"

"In fact, what is a photo journalism student doing in the gym, anyway?" She dared turn her back to help Felix to his feet. "Stealing Felix's ideas? Again?"

"Why would I need to steal this loser's ideas?"

"Because you're about as creative as a baked potato."

"Oi!"

"What's going on here?" barked the volleyball coach, marching out of her office with her intern, Michone, in tow. Anyone lazing around scrambled to their feet.

Emilio sent Liana a slimy grin and went to complain to the coach, rubbing his head for show. She walked straight past him.

"I wasn't talking to you. Liana, what's going on?"

Emilio's jaw dropped.

"He got hit in the head by the ball," she said simply.

"Yeah, that you threw!"

The coach didn't even spare him a glance. "Walk it off." Emilio gawked. The team snickered. She nodded to Liana. "You. Keep playing."

"Yes, Coach!"

She patted Felix on the back and jogged off. He turned to get a head start out the doors before Emilio, but the coach's sharp voice stopped him.

"Not so fast, Felix."

He cringed and turned. But there was no anger on her face. She grabbed his hand and inspected the nasty bruise beginning to form across his swelling knuckles and frowned at his wince.

"What happened?"

"Do you want some ice?" Michone asked.

He glanced at Emilio, who was seething behind the coach's shoulder. "I tripped trying to dodge a ball. Sorry for interrupting." He squirmed a little, bunching the hair ties further around his wrist before her sharp eyes spotted the thick skin underneath.

"Nonsense," she said, but let him take his hand back. "Oh, I meant to thank you for helping us last week when our photographer fell sick. Liana said you were flexible and had a good eye. I didn't realize what she meant until you hung upside-down from the goal post." She chuckled. "Anyways, we're going to use that photo to represent us in the tournament. Can I call on you if they spring any more requests on us?" She glanced at his hand. "After you've healed, I guess."

Were he not in danger of getting beaten the moment she turned her back, he would have laughed at the outrage on Emilio's face.

"Of course. I'd be glad to. I've got to go. Good luck with training!"

He scampered out the door with his things before she could ask any more questions.

He looked sadly at the halves of Art Journal Club submission. He hoped they wouldn't be too mad.

They were mad.

Everybody in the small classroom was already on edge, probably because of the sunset casting an eerie glow over the inky *KILLER STILL ROAMS COLLEGE* headline plastered across the newspaper on the table.

"I'm disappointed in you, Felix," the club leader said.

She was a tall girl with beads in her beautifully plaited hair that complimented the warm orange-red undertones in her brown skin. They glistened under the flickering lights and clicked against each other as she shook her head.

Sitting on chairs around her, the Art Journal Club members bore the same frowns. All except for Emilio, lounging in a battered armchair to the side, reading one of the newspapers.

"You promised to submit a photo. You gave your word. Do you know how excited we were?" said another member. His key ring jangled like wind chimes against the newest addition on his belt, an extendable baton. "We've pushed the deadline enough; we can't hold back for you any longer."

"I know." Felix's voice was barely a whisper. He couldn't bring himself to meet anyone's eyes. He stared at the can of mace in one girl's purse and hugged his camera.

"You *know*? That's all you've got for us? We bargained with the council and pleaded with the printer shop to put a hold on the printing for crying out loud! Made ourselves look like fools compared to the other colleges! All you've got to say is, '*I know*?'"

"Do you not realize how many big names are watching this contest? Judging everyone's professionalism through every stage? Do you think this club is a joke?" said the club leader.

At that, he had to look up. "Of course not! I had the submission! It just—" He glanced at Emilio, whose smile dripped dark promises over the edge of the newspaper he lazily flipped through. "It just got damaged."

She scoffed. "How could you be so irresponsible? The real world won't stand for that sort of excuse, you know!"

"It's not an excuse!"

"Even if it isn't, nobody is going to hire a photographer who can't take care of his product!"

The door opened. Nikolai's head poked through. "I hope I'm not interrupting. I was rather hoping to steal Felix from you all. We have a prior engagement, you see."

His voice soothed the nerves like honey cinnamon tea. A collective sigh rolled out. Emilio rolled his eyes.

Felix couldn't blame them for swooning. They'd watched him perform enough to associate his presence with a gooey, tingly feeling that left you gasping for more. His magnetic personality got their attention, his dancing sealed the deal, and it didn't hurt that he was handsome.

While glad the attention was off him, Felix couldn't help feeling uncomfortable with how they regarded his friend.

The club leader shook herself and said to Felix, "You need to pull yourself together. No matter what is going on in your life, or in the world around you, you can't let it distract you from your responsibilities. Your photos are good, but it takes more than that to be a photographer."

Nikolai opened the door wider and offered him his coat. "Put this on, it's been getting colder recently."

Emilio laughed, "How adorable! He brought his little boyfriend a coat!"

"Not my boyfriend," Felix grumbled, pushing past without taking Nikolai's offer.

"Just a little tip for you lovebirds," Emilio called. "Sharing naked body heat is the best way to stay warm!"

"Then you must be cold as ice," Nikolai shot back, his smile never faltering, and followed Felix out.

Felix was more than happy to hide away in one of the performing arts practice rooms, bundled in his, Liana's, and Nikolai's coats like a burrito and studiously ignore his homework.

They'd grabbed dinner near Rhett's old stomping ground because, ironically, it now felt like the safest place on campus to grab food free from harassment.

It wound up being to-go when they saw Emilio and his goons strolling through like they owned the place. They wouldn't have dared cut into lines and take other people's trays a week ago...

The studio grew colder as the seasons progressed. Perhaps that was due to half the practice rooms being underground and the other half having floor to ceiling windows, adjacent to the wall of mirrors overlooking the campus' greenery, that did nothing to prevent the autumn chill from seeping through the glass.

This room was grand enough to accommodate a full class of dancers. In the back corners sat a water cooler, sound equipment, and speakers that blasted Nikolai's music for all to hear, unless you were seated in the hall, where you would be met with silence. The Department of Performing Arts spared no expense for soundproofing.

Yet not for insulation, Felix thought, huffing at another tickling lock of fallen hair.

The temperature was ideal for Nikolai: he wouldn't get heatstroke, his sweat chilled quickly, and the crisp air came easy to his stuffy lungs.

Felix thought his toes might fall off. At least he wasn't in his dorm. The more time he could spend away from there the better.

"If you don't stop blowing your hair out of your face, I'm going to tie it above your forehead and make you look like an apple," Liana said, not looking up from her phone. He tied it into a low bun.

Out the window, tiny people scuttled across the pavement, reminding him of ants. They looked around quickly before dashing under trees and into buildings. Scratch that, not ants, more like skittish deer.

He burrowed deeper into his burrito and sniffled. He got a waft of Nikolai's scent from his coat and couldn't help but smile. Crushed autumn leaves, tart apples, and... a little bit of a sweaty undertone, but surprisingly not that gross.

He stopped himself from taking a deep inhale. Because that would be creepy. And weird. People did not want to be friends with those who sniffed their clothes.

Felix forced his attention back to his binder. One after another, the pages nagged at him with late hour deadlines and big red pen marks. He flipped to his most recent headache: showing versus telling. Take a picture that showed a story, a photo so expressive that there was no explanation needed, and write a report explaining why you know what you're doing.

Tough luck. Nobody ever knew what they were doing. Recent events certainly didn't help his creativity. Would something else await him on his pillow tonight?

No. He needed to ignore those scary thoughts.

He'd wracked his brain for a week, time was running out, and he still couldn't figure out what he was going to submit. He would be in deep academic trouble if he didn't hand *something* in.

Liana had had no trouble with her film studies assignment, lucky thing, and was currently texting her teammates about hanging out later. And Nikolai—the annoying enchanter—was in his zone.

His performing arts group had an upcoming show, so Nikolai spent every free moment he could practicing. Felix didn't mind listening to the same songs on repeat every time he came to hang out because he got to see his friend in his element.

Nikolai's muscles had memorized the routine long ago, allowing him to lose himself in the flow of alluring arcs and twists. But for all the grace he was unafraid to be sharp and powerful.

Singers could tell stories with their voices, photographers could show you a different side of the world, but dancers? Nikolai danced like it was the air he needed to breathe. He gave emotions physical forms: he wore the silk of honesty and dragged the chains of anguish. He became the stories.

As the last breath of music died from the speakers, Felix whipped out his instant camera and snapped a shot before he came back to reality. It would in no way do what he saw justice, but it would capture the memory for later.

He quickly hid the developing photos as Nikolai took a shuddering breath and stumbled to the ground between them. He caught the bottle of water Liana tossed and gulped it all down without pausing to breathe.

"Slow down, it's not going anywhere," she chided.

The dribbling water mixed with his glistening sweat trickled down his golden skin, exploring the pronounced veins in his neck and the dips of his collarbones before it disappeared under the collar of his shirt.

"Did you have something to work out of your system?" she asked. "You went longer than usual."

"I think this whole killer thing is getting to me. Everyone missed steps in class today and tripped over each other. I guess seeing everyone freaked out got under my skin. I just needed to shake it off."

"You did more than shake. I think I felt the floor jump."

He ruffled his sweaty hair like a dog and laughed at her disgusted face. His shirt stuck to his lean body as he twisted.

"Your group should relax. It's not like they found Trevor's body," Liana said. "I don't imagine the language arts professor will return from leave any time soon. But, hey! At least Trevor's head wasn't used as a dartboard like the Co-Ed Butcher's mother's in 1973."

Nikolai rolled his eyes. "For shame our Campus Killer isn't that creative."

She waggled her brows and opened another water bottle.

Noting the lack of sarcasm, he turned to Felix. "Are you still stuck on that project?"

It was better than admitting to staring at the way his best friend's shirt clung to his body. "Yep. I've accepted it. I've used up all my creative juices on my art journal submission. I'm going to flunk."

"You will not!" Liana said.

"I'm serious, I can't come up with anything. There's no story coming to me here." He wiggled his arm out of the coats enough to grab the photo album from his bag. "I can't even pick one of these pictures and bullshit the report."

"Never underestimate the power of bullshit," said Nikolai.

"Easy for you to say! You don't have to. Your dances tell stories!"

"And your pictures don't?"

Nikolai thumbed through the album pages, pointing to pictures as he went.

"I see a bird learning to fly on its own. It's scared of falling, but it knows it's okay if it falls and fails because it's loved. You know how I know that? The mother is right there beside it. The way she's not crowding tells me she trusts the baby bird, providing encouragement to go at his own pace. But you see how she's not too far away? She's not uncaring, she's ready to swoop down after it if need be. I see love and trust."

Felix blinked. "I didn't. I just thought their colours were pretty."

Nikolai grinned and pointed to a picture of an old house flanked by two bigger, shinier modern houses with their sharp corners and large windows.

"I see the struggles against the pressures of society. To conform. To compete."

He pointed to the silhouette of a young barefooted teenager facing the glow of the rising sun on a dirty road with his hands clenched to fists at his sides. The photo was taken from behind, capturing the light orange rays washing the pavement in welcoming light, kissing away the darkness on his scuffed ankles.

"I see a survivor."

Some of those pictures were simply the results of a gnat's attention span and too many beers. How did Nikolai see such beauty everywhere? He'd give anything to experience life the way he did. It must be incredible.

He thought of the rusted houses in the picture, of the light bouncing off the birds' colourful feathers. He stared at the survivor with scraped heels under Nikolai's fingers and flexed his aching hand. Everything clicked into place.

"I need to take a shot with your body."

As soon as the words left his lips, he realized his mistake.

"Wait—no, I mean—"

Liana was already on the floor, clutching her sides. Nikolai looked as though his soul had left his body.

"Wait! You know what I—Liana, stop howling! You know what I mean!"

Liana gasped, "Can I bring my Hakuna Ma'Vodka shot glass?" and sent herself back into laughter.

"A shot! A picture! I want to take a picture!"

"Of that scene? So do I, honey! So do I."

He looked at Nikolai for help but found him gaping like a fish out of water. Felix blushed so hard his ears burned.

"I meant, 'Can I use you as a model?' You just gave me the best idea for the project and if I'm going to hand this in on time, I'll need your help."

It was perfect: Nikolai in the rugged, beat-up part of town wearing subtle pride gear, dancing amongst the torn LGBT flyers. It would scream, 'You can't push us down.'

Liana lounged in Nikolai's lap, still giggling, as he sucked back enough of his soul to chuckle at the situation.

"A model?"

"You sure you don't want to do body shots for the camera and hand that in?" Liana asked, winking. "It'll get you a great mark! Nobody can say they don't know what the story is!"

Felix glared, though it was half-hearted at best because he was too busy swatting away imaginative thoughts with a broom. "No body shots. Just the assignment."

Judging by Nikolai's grin, he enjoyed Felix's discomfort far too much to be healthy. "Let's do it."

"Tomorrow after school?"

"What if the killer attacks us?"

"He won't," Liana said. "The guy's clearly got some plan for Felix. Weird that he's not just putting a strand of your hair at the scene, but I guess he's toying with you. I'm not saying that's much better, but... if he *is* framing you, he needs you alive. Which means you're safe. Also, I have a baseball bat."

"You don't have to if you don't want to," Felix said, toying with a loose thread in the coat.

"Nah, it's a date," Nikolai said with the most devastating smile.

According to his poor heart, that was the wrong thing to say.

Normality in Troubling Times! College Insists on Remaining Open!

Rain crashed against the window. It splashed in puddles and disrupted mischievous shadows. Felix shivered. A chill nipped his toes. He stretched to find warmth and shuddered at a gush of cold. A faraway sound called to him. He hummed a peaceful tune to himself and felt his mind sway pleasantly with the lullaby, soothing him back asleep.

The distant call morphed into his name, but it was distorted, like screaming underwater. He didn't want to acknowledge it. He was far too comfortable, enjoying the feeling of his body rocking. There was no reason to disturb him, thank you. Classes could wait. It was still sleep time.

"*Felix*!"

A hand jerked him backwards and like a bubble popping, a roar of sound exploded all around him. He stumbled into an icy puddle, tearing a gasp from his lungs. He blinked something wet from his face. Rain, he realized. His bedsheets were probably soaked.

A painful tug whirled him around to face Nikolai. Nikolai, who, with his dishevelled hair plastered to his face and his glistening coat clinging to his body like a rag, somehow managed to make scowling look like an art piece.

"What the *hell* are you doing?!"

Felix yanked his arm away. "What am I doing? What are *you* doing?"

"I'm not the one slow dancing in my pyjamas with a cupcake mix box in the rain at two in the morning!"

Felix frowned and looked at himself. He was in an undershirt and boxer shorts. A soggy cupcake mix box floated past his feet. He wiggled his toes in the puddle.

"Oh."

Rain. Rain was very wet. How was it raining in his bedroom? What was Nikolai doing in his bedroom?

Nikolai let out an exasperated groan and shucked off his coat, wrapped it around Felix and dragged the sluggish boy onto a sidewalk. The pavement was cold, and gravel dug into his soles. Water slid down the slick coat and streamed down his bare legs, raising the hairs as it went.

When did they get outside?

"Honestly... A murderer's on the loose and you decide *now* is a good time to start roaming the streets in your frilly undies?"

"They are not frilly," Felix mumbled back indignantly, stumbling along.

"You're lucky he didn't decide killing you would take less effort than framing you, seeing how you're offering yourself on a silver platter!"

Nikolai stomped enough for the both of them along the short walk into the dimly lit dorm lobby, past the shut-down elevator, and into Felix's dorm. He shoved a handful of towels into Felix's arms and pushed him towards his wardrobe. Felix blinked. Nikolai groaned and rummaged around the drawers until he found a pair of sweats and a sweater and laid them on the bed.

"I'm going to be in the hall until you're done. Don't make me wait too long," he said, and grabbed a towel for himself and marched out.

Felix stared at the towels in his hands.

What had they been doing outside? He must have been sleepwalking.

Nikolai had seen him sleepwalking.

He looked down at the droplets falling from his boxers onto his numb feet.

Nikolai had seen him in his boxers.

Oh.

Oh shit!

The fog cleared, and suddenly Felix couldn't get himself dry and covered fast enough. Curse his sleepwalking! He could have sworn he'd fallen asleep clothed! Of all people... Why did it have to be Nikolai to find him? Wait, how did Nikolai find him?

He peeled away the wet clothes and tugged on the dry ones with so much enthusiasm he almost fell flat on his face.

Nikolai heard the struggle and asked through the door, "Are you okay?"

"Perfectly clothed! Absolutely dressed! Nothing to worry about! Come on in!"

The door creaked open. Felix pointedly avoided looking, and busied himself with shucking off all his hair bands and bracelets to dry his arms.

"I might owe you an explanation. Unless you want to, I don't know, forget this whole thing ever happened?"

Nikolai snorted and sat on the messy bed, towelling his hair. "Not likely."

"Right. Thought not."

Being framed for murder must have shaken him so much he'd forgotten to tie himself to the bed before falling asleep. He roughly ran a hand through his hair. Stupid. Nikolai was right, he was lucky the killer hadn't jumped at the opportunity. He should stop making it so easy.

He groaned into his hand. He had never wanted to tell Nikolai about his sleepwalking habit. And if he did, this was not how he wanted it go down. There were many more civilized ways to tell your best friend that you occasionally made a full four-course meal or a nest in the dryer in your sleep. Letting him know by proclaiming your love for cupcake boxes in the rain was not one of them. Felix wished the ground would swallow him whole. Now Nikolai was going to think him a freak and never want to talk to him again!

"Well, you see, it's a bit awkward. Of course. I, uh... I do this thing—actually, it's not exactly a 'thing.' But... You know what? Liana's much better at words. Maybe we could wait for her—uh, Nikolai?"

Nikolai had tears in his eyes. Felix's heart plummeted to his knees. This was it. He'd lost his best friend.

"I messed this up, didn't I?" Felix whispered.

Nikolai slowly got to his feet and reached for Felix's hands, staring at them with so much pain that Felix's knees wobbled at the intensity. Nikolai turned them over and gently, as if holding fragile jewels, pushed up the sleeves. Felix gasped and yanked his arms away, but it was too late. The first tear fell.

"No, no! It's not what you think! I swear!" Felix shouted.

His denial only made it worse.

Nikolai's fingers closed around nothing and his voice cracked. "I'm so sorry—"

"No! There's nothing to be sorry for, you fool! I didn't hurt myself! They're from sleepwalking! I sleepwalk! I tie myself up so I won't pee in your sink in my sleep! That's why I was dancing outside! I was asleep!"

Nikolai's mouth opened and closed like a fish biting bubbles.

"You didn't hurt yourself?"

He never thought he'd be doing this. He took a deep breath and rucked up his sleeves, and for the first time in his life, showed his bare arms to someone. The flesh two inches around his wrists was thicker, calloused to the touch. The creases of his joints were the worst, discoloured and as tough as an elephant's hide.

"It's too weird to be from any blade, right? I've got them on my ankles too. They're from years of rug burns and tugging against restraints."

Instead of sad, Nikolai looked a bit sick. "Restraints?"

Felix frantically searched around the boxes underneath his bed for the black shoebox he kept stashed. He shoved it into Nikolai's hands.

Nikolai examined the array of ropes made from cotton, nylon, and hemp: cloths stripped into bands, weathered leather cuffs. If he hadn't known Felix, he'd have made some racy assumptions. He stared at the contents for a while. Felix watched him slowly absorb the information , trying to control his erratic heart before it leapt out of his ribcage.

"You really do... sleepwalk, then? Out there, you weren't just... being you?"

"What? No. I wasn't. What do you mean, 'being me'?"

"Being... unique. Uniquely you."

Felix wasn't sure whether to laugh or cry. "So, you believe me?"

The fond crinkle in the corner of Nikolai's eyes made something in Felix's chest flutter. He put down the box. "I'll always believe you." He looked from Felix's face to his scars thoughtfully. "Do you mind if I—Is it okay if I... touch them?"

Felix's brain thought this an opportune moment to vacate.

"Touch the... scars. The wrists. My wrists. Yes. Skin. Touch away."

He wanted to slap himself.

With Nikolai so close and his eyes still misty, smelling of pine and fresh rain, Felix had a tough time remembering why he was so scared. Sure, if his nervous stomach squeezed any harder, they might get reacquainted with his supper, or if his fearful pulse rushed any faster, he might faint. But... he was with Nikolai. If he could trust anyone on this planet, it would be him.

He let his friend gingerly turn over his arms again and nudge his sleeves back. Nikolai looked from Felix's tense face to his twitching fingertips for any indication to stop, but Felix never pulled away. Nikolai's palms felt dry and smooth cupping the back of his hands, caresses soothing the minute trembles away. There was no disgust in his movements. He slowly drew his thumbs over the rough flesh, felt the bump of his bone and ghosted circles across the dips and abrasions. Felix barely remembered what the breeze felt like on his forearms, but if he had to imagine, he thought it might've felt like this.

"How long has this been going on?"

"Since childhood..."

His fingers gently curled around the thick, raised skin. His thumb traced the edges. "Who else knows?"

"My parents, the doctor, Mrs. Rosewood, Liana," Felix replied breathily, distracted by the feather-light touches. "Since our moms have been friends forever, we've always lived close by. One night I broke out, crossed the street, and crawled through her open window to play with her toy firetruck. I didn't know until they started screaming."

"You were asleep the whole time?"

"Out cold," he confirmed in a whisper. "How did you find me...?"

"I was walking home from the studio. Got caught in the rain and took the shortcut by the dorms. I didn't expect to find you out there."

Felix frowned. "You were practicing until two in the morning? In these dangerous times?"

He shrugged lightly. "I had a lot of things to work out."

Nikolai held his wrists like they'd shatter into hundreds of tiny pieces at any moment. His fingertips drew patterns along his flesh, almost absentmindedly, and the feeling mesmerized Felix. It reminded him of sitting by the pond and trailing his hand over the water's silken surface.

Finally, Nikolai spoke, so quiet Felix almost missed it. "Why didn't you tell me?"

"Because I didn't want you to be creeped out... and run away."

Nikolai released him and Felix shivered at the cold that replaced his touch. "Why would I run away?" He didn't sound angry, just confused.

"They called me names. In school. Said I was a freak." He rolled the bracelets and hair ties back on to hide the ugly scars and rubbed the goosebumps from his arms. "I didn't want you to have a freak for a friend."

"I got called 'Cossack' growing up," Nikolai admitted, raising Felix's gaze in surprise. "Because we immigrated from Russia when I was a kid and like to dance. Everywhere I went people made fun of me, asking if I knew the Cossack Dance. They didn't know how ridiculous they were being because A: the squatting, arms folded, high-knee kick dance that they're thinking of is actually called 'Hopak,' and B: it's Ukrainian, not Russian. They didn't care when I pointed out the distinction or the fact that my family aren't Cossacks. It was just fun to tease the little Russian. The little foreigner."

Nikolai was bullied, too? But he was so talented, so humble, so... full of life. How could anyone pick on someone so amazing?

"Some geniuses found that if you say 'Cossack' real fast it sounds like another slur and, boy, that one's a lot more fun." Nikolai shook his head at the memory. "It got to the point where I eventually stopped dancing."

He couldn't imagine the thought.

"I hated what made me different, hated my ancestry, hated dancing, all perfectly innocent things. I allowed other people's disapproval to twist them into a personal hell. It took a long time before I broke out of that coffin and figured out locking my happiness and identity in a box and throwing away the key wasn't worth it. Even then, it's difficult to brush away the dirt. Not everyone is 'supportive' of our choices."

"That's why you fight your parents every day," Felix whispered. "Oh, no. I didn't know, I should have..."

Nikolai smiled. "Don't worry. We all hide things to look better in the eyes of those who matter to us."

It would seem not everyone was as they appeared. Felix had dozens of things he wanted to say, but he couldn't pin one down long enough to vocalize before it zipped past, replaced by another. He blurted the first thing he could.

"You're a very nice Russian!"

Nikolai made a sound similar to a honking goose and hung his head. Felix watched his shoulders shake and panicked. Thinking he did something wrong and made his friend cry, he apologized furiously, but stopped mid-word when he realized Nikolai was not biting his lips to hold back tears.

"You're giggling. Why're you giggling? I don't understand. What's wrong with you?"

Nikolai straightened and took a deep, sniggering breath, his moist eyes crinkled from a breathtaking smile. "There's nothing wrong. Nothing at all." He picked up the box of restraints. "Now that we've gotten our feelings out in the open, how's about you show me which of these kinky things we're gonna tie you up with?"

"This is going to be a thing, isn't it?"

"You bet."

Felix used the leather handcuff to chain one of his wrists to the bedpost. Nikolai futzed with the pillows on the opposite end of the bed to give him some privacy and didn't comment on how Felix hid the cuffs under a blanket to fake normalcy.

"Hey, Nikolai?"

Nikolai hummed to let him know he was listening as he got comfortable.

"What're we going to do about the serial killer?"

Nikolai's body tensed up like a coiled spring. He met Felix's wide eyes and relaxed. "We're going to do as we always have. You're going to take photos. I'm going to dance. Liana's going to play volleyball. We're going to live our lives."

Felix nodded and watched him contentedly suffocate himself in the pillow. "One more thing."

Nikolai grunted, too comfortable to move.

Thanks for not running away, he wanted to say. The words lodged in his throat. "Your feet stink," he said instead.

Nikolai chuckled into the cotton and tossed his feet over Felix's shoulder.

Felix groaned. "You are such a royal twat."

He wanted to suffocate himself in his blankets out of embarrassment when he woke.

He was worried Nikolai would change his mind, realize he was friends with a weirdo and run away. Luckily, Nikolai acted as if it were any other morning, whining about a lecture he had to attend later and stealing whatever lonely granola bars were gathering dust in Felix's cupboard.

It was relieving, despite it meaning he had to stop by the convenience store later for snacks. The day was turning out much better than he'd thought it would.

That thought survived up until the lobby.

He spotted a discarded magazine on the security desk.

"This is wrong on so many levels," Nikolai said.

Emilio's smug face smiled back at Felix from the open art journal, stubby fingers pointing at his photograph on the next page: a snail on a leaf before the rain. Admittedly, a very pretty snail with highlights on the swirling pattern of its shell, enhanced to bring out the transparency of its antenna, and a blurred background to focus the attention. But his hard work had been replaced by a *snail*. A snail beat him for the chance at the regional magazine.

His phone buzzed. It was Liana. She'd sent a blurry picture of herself shaking another copy of the art journal, open to Emilio's page. Her comment read in full caps lock, "*This should be you!*"

Nikolai frowned at the publication date. "How did they get this printed already? The submission deadline was yesterday. They couldn't have had the whole journal ready for midnight printing?"

"I guess they really were waiting for me," Felix mumbled with a stab of guilt. His raincloud grew a lot heavier as he replied to Liana, "*I saw. Oh well.*"

"They had so little to say they had to blow up his photo to cover half the page. Talk about making do. They should have picked your photo."

Liana texted again. "*I'm going to write a strongly worded letter! Unacceptable!*"

Felix smiled at their attempts to cheer him up, but it didn't have the staying power. He sent her a quick pacifying message and left the lobby. "What's done is done. There's nothing more to do."

Nikolai jogged after him. "But you've worked too hard for this to be taken from you!"

"It's okay. They had their reasons for going with Emilio. It's my own fault they couldn't choose me."

"What do you mean, couldn't? They're the *Art* Journal Club! They're supposed to have taste! And sense! Your photograph is moving and has far more relevance than Emilio's snail. There shouldn't have been any question who to choose!"

The sunlight cast a glow on Nikolai's curls, bringing out the soft blond strands that waved in the crisp, gentle wind. Felix blinked rapidly to regain focus, but Nikolai's steadfast gaze rooted him to the spot. He cursed his ability to see when there was more to a story, more to a lie. Felix was as transparent to him as that snail's antenna.

Curse him though he may, he wasn't upset at Nikolai for calling him out. He'd never told them how Emilio had destroyed his entry. He probably should have, but he'd seen no point worrying them when the damage was already done.

He noticed as the crease between Nikolai's brows deepened in concern rather than judgment. His tone was sharpened for his defence, not to attack.

Felix tossed the observation aside. Nikolai cared as a friend would, just as Liana did. The twist in his gut at the thought meant nothing.

"The club chose. That's that. I'll see you tonight for the photo shoot, eh?" He started to walk away. He didn't want to endure any more of their sympathies, not when it was his own fault anyway.

But walking away just yet didn't feel right. He lurched to a stop on the last step. "Uhm." He flexed his hands. *Just spit it out!* "Thank you. For last night. I don't want to think about how that could have gone a different direction."

"Of course," Nikolai said, as if it were the most natural thing in the world. As if he hadn't potentially saved Felix's life. As if his normalcy about it all didn't mean the world to him.

Felix hurried off, internally screaming about how awkward he was.

He only had classes in the morning, so he could've worked the afternoon away in his dorm, away from people who'd seen the art journal, and away from Emilio's teasing. Except one thought of his bathroom gave him such a spike of anxiety he broke into a sweat.

So that wasn't happening.

He had a better idea. He made a pitstop to gather everything they'd need for the photo shoot to save time at the end of the day. He carefully packed his camera, lighting equipment, and the outfits in his backpack. After classes, he made his way to his favourite place on campus: the arts building darkrooms.

The college was lucky enough to have three darkrooms, with space for five, twenty, and thirty people. Most students went for the larger rooms, but Felix preferred the smallest. It looked like a closet from the outside, the kind you'd see in a normal classroom, right behind the professor's desk, just another door leading to nowhere. Except for the sign above that lit up red with the words, *DARKROOM IN USE* when you flicked a switch inside.

Felix tied his hair into a low bun and slipped on his reading glasses from their case at the bottom of his backpack. He pulled open the door and pushed away the blackout curtains to finally enter his home away from home. It was generally quiet except for the *whirr* and *click* of the machines. Brushing elbows while working didn't appeal to most people, so they migrated to the larger darkrooms, but Felix had never understood that. Wouldn't they feel crowded with more people around? Oh well. At least it gave him more space for himself.

The room was divided in two: the dry side to the right and the wet side to the left. The dry side had a long counter with plenty of room to work with the enlarger, the paper cutter, and access to the paper safe, used to ensure the materials stayed dry.

The counter formed an upside-down L along the left wall, sectioning off the area to leave a metre-and-a-half gap between the workstations and the drying rack at the back, ensuring the final products weren't tampered with. The wet side consisted of two sinks and low tubs for developer fluid, a stop bath, fixer fluid, and water. A very messy business if handled improperly. To his immediate right and left were standing storage cabinets and shelves that the professors insisted on keeping tidy and clean.

Felix went to unclip his latest assignment from the drying rack and gasped. All of his photographs were littered with splotches! Someone must have accidentally sprayed developer fluid or something on them.

Who was he kidding? There was no way any fluid could be accidentally sprayed in the darkroom—everything was poured into tubs!

Emilio must have done it! He couldn't go one day without sabotaging something of Felix's. Of course, there was no way to prove it. With no surveillance cameras in the darkroom, it would be his word against Emilio's. The thought alone raised the hairs on his arms.

All he could do was use the negatives to redevelop the photographs, and hope he'd meet the professor's deadline. Maybe they'd turn out even better this time? That would be a nice surprise...

Taking a deep breath, he got to work. The room was quiet save for the hum of the machines, the brush of paper and the snip of scissors. Thankfully Emilio hadn't thought to ruin the negatives as well, or else Felix would have been in real trouble. He should have been much angrier about having to redo his project, but the truth was that he didn't mind. After last night, this was exactly where he needed to be.

He flowed through the motions: letting his hands turn the dials, flick the switches, and shift the paper without thought. Slowly, his stress cleared. All there was to think about was the image in front of him.

All too soon, the timer was set for twenty minutes, and his prints were floating in the water basin, ending his time in the darkroom for now. He hung his glasses on his shirt as he closed the curtain and stepped back into the real world to wait.

He filled the time by checking emails and due dates on one of the three classroom computers. As it turned out, he'd forgotten to submit last night's assignments because of the bathroom scare. Marks deducted. He rubbed his temples. He couldn't afford to fall any further behind, not with finals around the corner. He submitted the assignments with a letter of apology.

A new link had been added on the school's webpage. It directed him to a forum titled *Terrified and Lost: How Not to Shit Your Pants* on a social news discussion website. There, many students from his college shared their thoughts on the murders, with the odd helpful comment on how to deal with the anxiety and what hours the counsellor's office was open. Felix scrolled through:

Can we reinstate the Buddy System? I don't want to walk home from classes alone…

I'll walk with you!

Me too!

Anyone else realize how the two dudes were jerks? Both Trevor and Rhett picked on a lot of people.

Can't say I'm sorry to see them go.

Mean!

I'm just stating facts. They were [COMMENT FILTERED]

Do you think that had anything to do with why they were killed? It's got to mean something if both dead guys were… not nice…

Does anyone have any idea how the police investigation is going? The school blocked all links pertaining to the murders.

Did you seriously expect the school to make a page to promote that sociopath? 'We've found two bodies! Join our college today!' As if you'd find gory details here.

Do your research. Sociopathy is not synonymous with killer. You're demonizing mental illness.

I remember reading somewhere that the cops would be patrolling the campus more often.

Hey guys! I've compiled a master list of all the articles I found! Click here if you're interested.

Felix could make pretty good assumptions about the gory details based on the blood in his shower, but perhaps reading an update on the investigation would put him a bit more at ease. It'd be good to know how close they were to catching this guy.

The link opened in a new window. The page was filled with lists of more article links organized by *victims*, subjects grouped by the first and second body, respectively; *police*, all queries about the investigation and updates neatly timelined; and *media*, anything from public opinion to hot scoop rumours about the killer's identity.

This guy had done his homework.

He skipped over the *victims* section and clicked on the most recent link under *police*. It was some reporter's play-by-play of a press conference issued just after Trevor's body was discovered, with colourful opinions mixed in. According to the article, the police had everything under control. They were working hard to follow every lead and were leaving no stone unturned. "No killer leaves a crime scene spotless!" they claimed.

Meaning, they did not have it under control. The killer had left no evidence at the scene. And societal pressure was closing in. They had bupkis. Comforting.

He clicked another link.

The post theorized about the items missing from the bodies. Perhaps the killer had a fetish? It was possible he enjoyed keeping mementos of his victims, like prizes. Felix exited that one quickly.

A link in the *media* section read, *Is He Nice or Too Nice? Five Simple Ways to Find Out if You're Dating a Killer!* He rolled his eyes.

At last, he found an article that provoked his imagination. It drew a connection between the two victims being male, in their early twenties, from the same college, and having a reputation for bullying, therefore making it likely that the crimes had been committed by more than one person. Perhaps a series of bullying victims piggy-backing off each other.

It also pointed out the brutality of the deaths. There was a line between crimes of passion and the barely identifiable corpses they had discovered. The gruesome state of the bodies suggested that the killer had more than a grudge, and that he probably wasn't finished.

"There was a lot more rage broiling under the skin. We should expect another body, and soon," it preached. Then it gave the safety speech, "If you suspect you're being followed, make sure to alert someone, never walk alone..." Blah, blah, blah.

He thought about that fateful morning in the lobby. The wet elevator doors sliding open, then closing. *Squelch*. The screams.

Was he in danger? There were hundreds of young adults in the college, why give him the evidence? What could the killer gain from framing him other than the obvious Get Out of Jail Free card. Maybe he had been picked as the fall guy for his connection to both victims? Was it that simple?

His hand stilled on the mouse. What if Emilio was the killer?

He had everything to gain with Trevor and Rhett out of the way.

What if he'd planted the evidence in his dorm as a warning? To stay out of his way for the art journal award? Or that he was going to be attacked next?

He exited the article, shaking his head. He couldn't assume someone was a criminal just because he disliked them. He had no proof other than his own biased opinions.

The dark room door slammed open with a *BANG* that made him jump out of his seat with a cry for help ready. It was only Emilio and two of his goons by his side.

Emilio scanned the room like a snake looking for a good meal and smirked upon finding Felix in the corner. His goons dispersed upon the flick of his hand. One of them sat near Felix. The other logged into the computer just two down from him. How subtle. He recognized one from the other day: Michael, who taunted him about Trevor. The other, Jackson, was about as pleasant.

The boss himself leisurely strutted towards the darkroom. Every heavy thump of his boot made Felix's heart beat faster. Emilio was a fellow photo journalism student. He told himself there wasn't any problem with him going into the darkroom. But all he could think of were his delicate prints and the grudge the size of the Grand Canyon that Emilio nursed for him. What would he do in there, ruin them again?

The door handle disappeared inside Emilio's meaty hand and Felix blurted, "Haven't you done enough?"

The goons leaned closer. Emilio's glare could've cut stone. "What did you say, brat?"

Was there a roll of duct tape he could silence himself with? What was he doing shouting at a possible killer?!

Possible, he reminded himself. Deal with him like a bully, panic about the possible killer aspect later.

Felix bit his lip to keep it from trembling and crossed the room to enter the darkroom first. "I said," he repeated, a bit stronger this time, "haven't you done enough? Destroying my project? I won't let you go in there and do it again."

Emilio's lips curled into a twisted smirk. The way his skin stretched like melted plastic made Felix's bones shiver. "Wow, Your Majesty. I didn't realize everything is about you." He shouldered his way past and turned on the enlarger. "I'm here to work. Don't bother me and stay out of my way."

"Not a problem," Felix muttered under his breath, slipping his glasses back on as he followed.

Everything would be fine. He was just forced to work in the same tiny room as one of the worst people on earth. No biggie.

He made it his mission to get his work done and leave as fast as possible. Emilio was relatively harmless in the darkroom because of the expensive equipment, and Felix took full advantage.

So did his goons. They barged in and out randomly, startling Felix with loud noises and guffaws of laughter. The only thing that saved the developing photos, both Felix's and Emilio's, was the floor-to-ceiling blackout curtain by the entrance. They might've been careful with the light per Emilio's instructions, or by fear of God if they messed up his work.

Those two were never bored. They played music obnoxiously loud, fiddled with every button and switch, pretended to drink the chemicals, and bumped into everything. Felix thought he'd have a heart attack every time one would play with a machine or trip him on his way to fetch something. Emilio watched with a smile, occasionally joining in on the fun when he had to wait for something. When the boys finally tired themselves out, they splayed out like starfish on the floor. That was when they really started to mess with him.

Felix put down his tongs to hang up a photo, and when he turned back they were gone. He took out another set of tongs and moved his photographs from one basin to another, thankfully before they oversaturated, and then the towel was gone.

Jackson tripped him. "As graceful as ever, I see."

The clothes pins were across the room. "Misplaced again!" Michael said.

Emilio shoulder checked him into the edge of a counter. "Didn't I say to get out of my way?"

A shoe goosed him and that was the end of his fuse. "Would you *quit it?!*"

"Ooh, it's the glasses and the furious!" laughed Michael.

Emilio skulked up to him and gave a less than playful nudge, hissing foul breath. "Go on. Give me a reason."

In a surge of frustrated bravery that erased his sense of self-preservation, Felix sneered. "I didn't realize you needed one."

Emilio was on him in an instant, shoving him out the door by the collar and into the brick wall with a painful *crunch!* A gasp tore from his strangled lungs. Bad. This was bad. The hands pulled him back and slammed him against the wall again. Pain cracked along his skull.

The goons cheered and laughed. When his head hit the wall again, his vision sparked, and his head lolled, too dizzy to lift it back up. The hands tightened again. He panicked.

"You'll be next!" he shouted.

Emilio glared, though now the anger edged on confusion. Felix gripped his bear paws to alleviate some of the pressure on his throat, forced his bobbing head up and continued while he still had breath.

"Don't you realize it's a pattern?" he rasped. "Everyone else does. It's bullies! The bullies get killed. If you don't stop, he'll come for you too."

If he wasn't the killer, surely that'd scare him off. If he *was* the killer? Well, maybe he'd get confused long enough for Felix to come up with *literally any other plan.*

Emilio's grip loosened and tightened like he was battling an internal conflict. Then his nostrils flared and Felix suddenly felt like there was a very large boulder rolling his way and things were about to get very uncomfortable, very fast.

A hand tapped Emilio's shoulder. "Excuse me, did you drop this?"

Emilio glanced back to see Nikolai. Nikolai smiled brightly. And then decked him in the face.

Emilio gasped and crashed to the ground by his goons' feet. He clutched his nose. Blood dribbled between his fingers.

Felix barely caught himself before he also fell, mouth agape. Nikolai had actually dared to raise a hand. Nobody had ever done that. He wasn't sure whether to cheer or to hide.

Michael and Jackson rushed to pull Emilio to his feet. He roared and shoved them off. Felix flinched at the sound. Emilio took a threatening step forward and accidentally got blocked by his futzing goons. Nikolai just stood there, rocking on his heels with his thumbs in his pockets. Emilio elbowed Jackson aside and tried again, but almost tripped over Michael this time. He settled for a snarl that weakened Felix's knees and marched out, the two trailing behind him clamouring about ice packs and bandages.

Felix slumped against the wall. He couldn't believe they'd gotten out of that unscathed. "Thanks," he said, massaging his throat.

"I didn't do anything, you were holding your own pretty well."

He almost laughed. "Will you be okay, though? Emilio will come after you for that." Possibly with a knife. His apartment had good security, right?

Something dark flashed across Nikolai's face. His lips curved into a devilishly handsome smirk. "I'd like to see them try." Before Felix could make anything of it, the look was gone, and Nikolai's full attention had zeroed onto something on his face.

At first, he thought there might be food on his cheek, but remembered he'd tied his hair in a messy bun and now his glasses hung crookedly off his nose. He looked ridiculous! He fumbled the glasses into his pocket and futzed with the knot that had become his hair.

Nikolai chuckled. "What did those glasses ever do to you?"

"Made me look like a third-grader," he mumbled. Darn it, he was blushing wasn't he?

Nikolai climbed onto one of the desks and crossed his long legs, tilting his head thoughtfully. "You need them to see, don't you?"

"In the darkroom, yeah. Our only light is a red light, makes things difficult."

An affectionate smile softened his features. "Then don't let me stop you. They're cute, anyways."

Felix choked on his saliva. He pointed to his hair. "And this rat's nest?"

"It's artsy. It suits you."

Felix swallowed his leaping heart and spun around to tidy an already organized shelf to hide his flustered face—immediately regretting the movement when the bump at the back of his head tingled. Curse best friends and their infinite teasing.

"Why are you here? Don't you have an essay to write on contemporary dance?" He hoped to sound nonchalant but had a sneaking suspicion he sounded more like he had swallowed the desert.

He heard Nikolai sigh and shift on the desk. "I'm procrastinating, and when you didn't text back, I thought I should come find you."

Felix frowned and pulled his phone from his back pocket. Lo-and-behold, six unread text messages glared back. "Oh. Sorry you came all this way."

"Don't worry about it!" Nikolai pulled out a ruler and practiced balancing it on his finger. "You always hang out in the gym or the studio for us, so I thought I'd explore your domain this time."

That didn't get his heart pounding. Nope. He was fine.

"I'm afraid you might get a little bored, here. There's not much going on."

Nikolai dropped the ruler and propped his chin on his fists. "Sometimes a little quiet is just what the doctor ordered. What're you working on?"

"I'm, uh, re-doing my project because Emilio sabotaged it. Again."

Nikolai winced sympathetically.

"Wanna see?"

Introducing his world to Nikolai was nerve-wracking, but he made all the appropriate "ooh" and "ahh" sounds. He was careful not to disturb anything, bending at awkward angles to get a better look at the machines and buttons with the wide eyes of a child. Watching him created a fizzing, sparking ball of excited nervousness in Felix's stomach. Did he like it? Was it interesting enough?

Nikolai inched towards the drying pictures in the back, and with a swell of pride, Felix noticed the pictures he paid the most attention to were his.

"Some of these are for the project; others are just for my enjoyment," Felix said, motioning to each in turn. "Emilio's are on the right."

Nikolai crouched to inspect a photo on the bottom rung: one of Felix's, sadly overexposed and unusable thanks to Emilio's shenanigans.

"I don't get how messing with others is so fun. Either he's just too full of himself or he must not have gotten enough love as a child—" He cut himself off with a curse. "Sorry."

"Why're you sorry?"

He felt like a real tool. "Your parents..."

"Eh, who cares? It's fine." Nikolai cocked his head to better appreciate the photograph and mumbled under his breath, "One day that guy will get what's coming to him..."

"You mean the council stepping up? They've got their hands full at the moment. Besides, nobody did anything about the reports on Rhett and Trevor. I doubt they'd care about a small fry like Emilio without some serious proof."

Nikolai gave a noncommittal hum and pointed to a portrait. "What assignment is this one for?"

They spent some more time in the darkroom talking. Nikolai wanted to know the story behind every photograph and Felix's plans for his assignment. All the attention made him feel fuzzy and warm. He took back his earlier curse. There was a reason he enjoyed being around Nikolai. Pretty soon he completely forgot about Emilio's bullying and the throb in the back of his head.

Nikolai eventually let Felix get back to work and shuffled back into the classroom to do his own thing. He turned off the lights and drew the window curtains, so Felix could keep the blackout curtain closed but the door open so they could still talk.

It was peaceful, just the two of them. Felix didn't realize just how peaceful it was until he'd finished his work and asked a question, getting no response. Nikolai was fast asleep at a desk.

Felix stacked the binders and pencils out of his way so he could lounge more freely. Nikolai didn't stir. Locks of his drooping chestnut brown hair floated and dipped with his soft breathing, like feathers in the breeze.

He looked so calm, so happy. Felix had to take a picture. Perfect blackmail material, he thought with a giggle.

When Nikolai shivered, he pocketed the picture and draped Nikolai's discarded jacket back over his shoulders. Nikolai wiggled his nose like a hamster and happily tucked himself into the crook of his elbow. *I'm just being a good friend*, Felix told himself. Friends didn't let friends sleep cold.

It was entirely normal to notice the little things, like how dark and thick his lashes were, or how his cheeks looked as soft as bread dough. Nikolai had pleasingly pokeable cheeks.

Of course he would notice his friend's attractive points. Felix was man enough to admit Nikolai was a handsome human being. That didn't mean Felix was attracted to him. It just meant he had eyes and was able to see what might appeal to other people. Besides, Nikolai was straight. Heterosexual. Into women. And so was Felix. They were just friends.

An incoming text from Liana saved him from further torture. He snorted at the message and shook Nikolai awake.

"Up you get, sleepy head. Liana texted saying she's finished her test and wants copious amounts of love to replenish her fried brain cells."

Nikolai smacked his lips and stretched. "Well, we mustn't keep the lady waiting, should we?"

"No," Felix agreed, tearing his eyes away from a sliver of skin peeking from under Nikolai's sweater. "Let's go meet the bear."

Police Advise All Students to Remain Indoors After Dark

Liana almost forgot to park the truck before jumping out of the driver's seat and tackling Felix and Nikolai in a hug.

"Where'd you get this beast?" Felix gasped, stumbling under her weight and marvelling at the new vehicle.

"Owen down the hall from me said he wasn't going anywhere tonight, so he lent me the keys! It's perfect for the photo shoot, right?"

"Remind me to thank your newest conquest," Nikolai said, touching the shiny pickup.

"And to apologize when you inevitably crash us into a tree," joked Felix. He ducked a playful cuff to the ear.

Felix sat in the passenger's seat beside Liana to direct her. Nikolai, bending his long legs to fit, sat in the back beside the metal baseball bat, making sure none of the equipment got too badly rattled by the potholes and sharp turns.

"Why're we heading west?" Liana asked, slowing down as the conditions of the road got worse. "Isn't the demolition site close by?"

"I need a background that's in ruins. The more destroyed the background is, the more powerful the message."

"You could have just used Nikolai's room." Nikolai punched her shoulder. "Oi! I'm driving here!"

Felix interrupted before the two could spiral into an argument and send them into a ditch. "It's just up ahead. If you could park us around the most broken-down building, that'd be great."

It was the oldest part of the city, the place with the most history, about twenty minutes outside the city by car through a beautiful swath of forest. But it was also one decade too old for the city council and condemned. People had fought for the area at first, mainly those who had family that used to live in the dilapidated houses. The protests ceased once they'd seen the zeros on the cheques for the land underneath.

Now, rubble lay scattered all over the streets. Many of the houses were missing walls or entire floors thanks to the demolition crew's hard work—the props department for an apocalypse film would be out of work if they filmed here. Support beams groaned, the wooden floors rotted dangerously, and the only beings that lived in those buildings anymore were the homeless and the ghosts of laughter carried by the wind.

Liana and Felix set up on a lot that overlooked a cluster of trees while Nikolai got changed in the truck. Felix recalled a grocery store once stood proud in this exact spot. All that remained was its rickety skeletal structure. He could see the darkening sky looming over the trees through the gaping holes. He knew he could turn them into a forest with the proper angles.

"Where'd you get these colourful things?" Nikolai asked, climbing out of the truck.

He wore a white tank top with the shimmering words *Still Standing* across the chest, alongside a worn hooded cotton vest on top that read *Don't Need Your Approval* on the back. His baggy pants hung dangerously low on his hips, bunched at the ankles above his sneakers. But that wasn't what he was referring to.

Bracelets of every colour covered his wrists, similar to the ones that hid Felix's scars. Nikolai's were much louder: some were beaded, while others were tied into patterns with cords, leather, and even rubber. The best was the choker around his neck: a cord made from strands of different colours weaved through a river of black. It wrapped around his neck a couple of times and seamlessly knotted so that it hung past his collarbone and the metal beads at the ends rested against his broad chest.

Felix gulped. "Theatre department," he lied.

Liana wolf-whistled. "Look at them arms!"

Nikolai laughed and rubbed the back of his neck sheepishly. He snuck a glance Felix's way, as if seeking approval. Felix nodded stiffly, ignoring how it bloomed a smile across Nikolai's face.

Felix had purposefully chosen battered clothes that still held their colours. It worked. Nikolai looked like a comfortable guy on the streets. But anyone who looked closer would see the rainbow stitch up the pant legs and along the hips, the bracelets purposefully arranged into specific patterns of colours; the subtle designs in the vest, the words shimmering in different colours under different lights.

"We're doing a colourful theme, are we?" Liana asked.

"Uh, yeah." Emilio's voice taunted him from the shadows. He shrugged it off. There was a reason he'd chosen this theme. He needed to go through with it. "There's one more detail we're missing." He pulled out a long sleek cloth from his coat pocket.

Nikolai said, "You want me to dance blindfolded? Not that I can't, I'm just curious why."

Felix took a deep breath. "The blindfold, like the battered clothes and the buildings in ruins under the night sky, would symbolize the oppression that people face and the attempts to silence voices and destroy identity. I need you to dance like you refuse to give up. Not your home. Not who you are. No matter what they do, they can't take it away." He braced himself for judgement. "Is it an okay idea? Do you think you can do that, maybe?"

Nikolai and Liana shared a sly look. He snatched the blindfold. "I think I can do that."

Liana took charge of the music and blasted everything up to eleven. Felix was thankful there was no one around for kilometres. Nikolai tied the cloth around his head and started dancing.

It was exactly as Felix had pictured. The clothes were just loose enough to ripple like beach waves without getting in Nikolai's way. The cluster of trees appeared thick and expansive through the holes in the building. The sun set at just the right height to cast a glow on it all. He had to jerk himself out of a trance twice to continue snapping photos.

Nikolai got into it too. His movements were sharp, as though struggling from within against a suffocating weight. He fought back, straining to keep his head above the water and clawing out of the anguish that threatened to consume him. Felix felt like he was watching prey struggle to survive.

Then Nikolai ripped off the blindfold and everything changed. He gasped like it was his first breath of fresh air in years. The light streamed from the cracks in the wood and reflected off the words on his clothes and the sweat on his brow. It highlighted the clarity in his eyes, the determination in the set of his jaw. He snapped the silk high in the air in an arc, the light bouncing off it. He caught it between his teeth. Felix almost dropped his camera.

There were no words to describe him. The prey had won. His jumps and spins became fluid, yet strong and unwavering. His white teeth glistened against the dark cloth that trailed down his chest. Nikolai did not hesitate. He kicked up dust, shook the ground with his power, and used the very earth to be reborn from the rubble and ashes.

With the sunset gliding through the leaves and illuminating every crooked nail and broken plank with an ethereal light, he finished gracefully.

Something beeped in the background. Liana beamed and tucked away her phone.

"Were you filming me?" Nikolai asked, panting.

"Of course I was. Do you know how much money I could make auctioning this off to your fans?"

"I do not have fans."

"That was well done," Felix interrupted, still reeling. "I'm going to check what I've got."

He sat on a rock and reviewed the photos while Liana showed Nikolai the video. Felix laughed to himself when he noticed none of them would need much digital editing. "Of course he doesn't need any extra lighting, he's perfect."

Did I just say that? he thought to himself.

When he looked back up Liana was hanging upside-down from a railing, demonstrating something she'd seen in a movie.

"Hey, quit drooling over your camera and come play with us!" she shouted.

"I'm not drooling!" He ignored how he definitely was and switched to his instant camera to commemorate the sheer ridiculousness that was her hair.

"You don't have to shoot anything more, do you?" Nikolai asked.

"No," he said cautiously, grinning. "I've got plenty to work with."

"Then come and dance with us!"

Liana turned the music back on and Nikolai dragged him from his rock. The performance had got them both riled up, and they decided to expel it by singing loudly in his ears and twirling him around until they all got dizzy. It was wonderful to let loose and enjoy the moment. Felix laughed, watching Nikolai try to teach Liana some dance moves, but poor Liana only managed to resemble a drunk goat. They danced and chased each other for hours, climbing the structures and making silly poses for Felix's camera.

There were no corpses. No killers. Just three people playing in an abandoned neighbourhood.

A spatter of rain broke up the party. They squealed and scrambled to pack the equipment in the truck and toppled over each other trying to get in.

Nikolai climbed over Felix's lap to get to the back seat, giggling over their close call. "I'll use some of those shots in my portfolio, eh?"

He was positively tingling. "It would be my honour!"

Liana drove them to Felix's dorm to drop off the equipment. They sang and poked fun at each other the whole way. For a blissful moment, they all forgot why they'd brought the metal bat.

As the thrum of the truck and the pounding of music gave way to the spatter of rain in the otherwise desolate campus, their laughter died out. They finally heard the bat rolling against the back of the driver's seat. Felix picked it up to stop the clanging. It was so cold.

Each dip and jerk from the potholes startled them. They tried to tease each other for jumping or gasping in fright, but they all had the bat in their sights, now. The trees waved as they passed. Felix hugged his instant camera as twigs scraped against the windows, sounding like nails: like someone trying to get in.

The truck rolled into the parking lot. Felix wasn't the only one to shiver. He felt the tires grind against the gravel. He was vividly aware of every tiny rock cracking under the weight. Crushed. Like his hand under Emilio's boot. Like bones.

"Let's get this over with," Liana murmured and unlocked the doors.

They gathered the bags and dashed through the wet parking lot. Felix kept his eyes locked onto the gloomy lobby. They skirted inside, circled the taped-off elevator, and crossed the carpeted hall to his door without slowing down.

His trembling hands made it difficult to stick the key in the lock. He pictured the blood in the shower. The missing knife in his knife block. Would the window be wide open again? Or would something worse await him, like organs under his pillow?

"Go on," Liana said. "We're right here. It's okay."

Felix steeled himself and unlocked the door. Liana and Nikolai dumped their stuff by the entrance and checked the place out. They deemed it safe enough to raid Felix's cupboards, but he hesitated.

Something gnawed at him, but he couldn't figure out what. Nothing was misplaced, nor was any bloody message hanging from the ceiling fan to greet him. His pictures strung up like fairy lights across the walls and ceiling remained untouched. What was it?

He checked the window latch. Locked. He nudged his pillows. No entrails. He glanced at the bathroom.

He was being silly. But ever since discovering those pieces of bloody evidence, his room hadn't felt the same. Nobody could blame him, but—no, he was being paranoid.

Felix opened his laptop and downloaded the pictures from his camera for later. They'd done a great job. He imagined printing some for himself and hang them on his walls. Nikolai's phone buzzed and he stepped to the door to answer. Liana sat on Felix's desk with a granola bar to give him some space.

"Nikolai!" barked a gruff voice from the receiver.

Felix's skin chilled. They knew immediately who that was.

"Mama and I found great school! Not far! You transfer now, yes?"

Nikolai grumbled something, got yelled at for it, and said, louder, "No. For the last time, I'm not leaving."

Cue the agitated licks of what were most likely swears. Liana and Felix did their best not to listen while sorting the photographs, pointing at the pretty ones.

"You would rather prance around like rabbit and get killed? Bouncing on tippy-toes is worth death?" said Nikolai's father from the receiver.

"I rather like that one," Liana murmured, pointing at a picture. "The colours pop."

"You cannot defend yourself! I have seen goats with bigger arms than you!"

"Oh, go back one. That was a pretty rock," Liana said.

"You enjoy smell of rot? That is why you stay? I did not raise you with ox brain!"

Rhythmic thumps told them Nikolai was banging his head against the wall.

"Join numbers classes! Numbers are safe! 'Not leaving.' Psh! My ears are wilting."

"You kicked me out, remember?" Nikolai whispered. "You told me I could starve on my own and get mugged in a ditch for all you cared. You don't get to just—you don't get to call me now that two people are dead and pretend like it never happened."

"Eh. You survive well enough."

Liana winced. Felix couldn't believe his ears. How could a parent say such a thing to their own child?

"You don't get to do this. Not after what you did," Nikolai said. Felix worried he might crush the phone with his bare hands. Nikolai dipped into the bathroom, out of sight. It didn't muffle the snarky Russian from the receiver.

"I was *sixteen*!" Nikolai snapped.

Liana and Felix looked at each other in horror.

"You know what? No. This isn't worth it. You aren't worth it." Nikolai hung up. It rang again. He didn't answer. They all listened to it echo against the tiles.

Felix felt nauseated just thinking about the implications of what he'd said. He didn't think he and Liana could ignore it. Should he say something? Or would that make things worse?

Nikolai stepped out of the bathroom, sighing heavily. He looked tired, a little disgusted, but not too bad. "I feel like I got slimed on by a ghost." The joke was a relief. Felix wasn't sure what he'd do if Nikolai broke down on his toilet.

"I know what you need—what we all need. To go drinking!" Liana said.

"What?" Nikolai and Felix said in unison.

"We deserve it! I just passed a big test and have a volley tournament tomorrow, Nikolai probably wants to forget both his parents, and Felix most likely wants to forget the last forty-eight hours!"

"I mean, she's not wrong," Nikolai mumbled.

"Forgetting it would be kind of nice," Felix agreed cautiously. "I haven't pissed in that bathroom for two days now."

"That settles it!" Liana grinned. "We're getting drunk!"

Felix raised a brow. "Are you paying the tab?"

"I said we're getting drunk. Not that we're getting sugar daddies."

"Will it be safe?" Nikolai said. "Coming back to campus so late was risky enough. But to stay out and return inebriated at three in the morning? That would be handing Felix over to the killer."

She waved her free hand as if physically brushing his concerns away. "You act like I'm taking you to some monster's dungeon to be poisoned. It's this cool place Riley and some of the girls are going to quell pre-game jitters. Anyways, remember: the killer wants to frame Felix, and to do that he needs him alive. Ergo, he won't go after him."

"For some reason that's not at all comforting," Felix muttered.

Nikolai snorted at her slightly offended look. "And if he comes after us two?"

She clapped him on the back. "At least we won't have to submit our finals!"

Felix downed the last shot on the table and shivered at the bitter taste. Liana and Nikolai laughed at his disgusted face on the couch beside him.

"How did you both finish so quickly?" Felix pointed to their empty lines of shot glasses, coughing.

"Practice!" Liana yelled over the music. "You'll get it one day, youngling!"

"It helps when you don't have a gag reflex!" chortled Nikolai, nudging Liana.

"*Control over* the gag reflex!" she corrected, shoving him back and grinning at Felix's cringe. "I'm talented with my throat muscles."

Felix threw up his hands before she could go into any more detail. "Okay! I get it! I suck at swallowing!"

They looked at each other and burst into laughter. Felix blushed and kicked them off the couch. "Oh, go and dance you drunk, hormonal fiends! You know what I meant!"

He relaxed into the cushions to watch his two best friends merge and twirl into the sea of dancing bodies. Their massive smiles shone as bright as the strobe lights. They were perfectly content to make utter fools of themselves, head-banging and flailing their arms. To be fair, almost everybody here jumped around like pogo sticks.

He'd never seen a room so packed. It might have been an illusion made by the walls of mirrors on either side turning the place into a maze, or the electric fog of alcohol was beginning to infect his brain. Either way, it wasn't long before he lost sight of them.

He huffed. They were supposed to be unwinding together! Where had they gone? Why had they left him?

He got up to find them. Gravity and a shift in his centre of balance had other plans and dragged him unceremoniously back onto the cushions. Wow. He normally didn't get this drunk until after a few hours. They couldn't have been here that long.

His gut sank. Had someone spiked his drink?

He whirled on the spot to search for the exits. He blinked the swimming dance floor back into focus. His head bobbed. He stared at the shot glasses. Maybe he'd drank too much too fast. Yeah, that was it. He hadn't done this "loosening up" thing in a while. He was just rusty. There was no way a killer would sneak into a club.

Plus, even if he did, what damage could he possibly inflict? Killing Felix was off the list, as Liana pointed out. So, what was he gonna do? Bludgeon someone in a densely populated room with no blind spots, shove the weapon in Felix's hands, and jump gracefully off the balcony before the cops came? And if it *was* Emilio, he was nowhere to be seen! The club was, ironically, the safest place Felix could be.

He smacked himself in the face. That line of thought was the whole reason he was drinking. *Loosen up!* He forced himself to take a deep breath. He smelled salty sweat and fruity drinks mixed with the leather couch. He let his head fall back on the cool cushion and finally allowed himself to revel in the buzz that washed over his tired body.

The music took over: every pound of the beat resonated in his chest loud and clear. Every hit of the drums felt like a defibrillator shock reviving his heart, casting away the negativity of the past couple days. The cymbals exploded through his veins, striking his limbs with electricity before evaporating and repeating. The melody flowed through his whole body, creating pictures in his mind, caressing his heart, drifting through his extremities, and exiting through his fingertips and toes—only to return and repeat the entrancing process.

He opened his eyes again. He spotted Liana dancing with a tall man who had glistening brown skin and striking eyes. Some of the volleyball team had shown up and were drunkenly cheering her. Nikolai had been swept away by a group who were excited to have him join their circle.

The women all wore a skirt or dress that flattered their forms beautifully. Their hair and makeup were flawless, even as their foreheads began to glisten. The men dressed simply: jeans, T-shirts, and hair swept back or sweat-curled. They didn't try to impress anyone and yet, because they were having such a good time, they were the most fun to watch. It was the lack of effort that made them shine. The colourful lights reflecting off the rise of their cheekbones and the gleam of alcohol on their wet, bitten lips only enhanced what was already there.

Liana twisted her hips in ways that turned a couple of the men's heads and locked them in. Felix watched her move, wondering what had stolen their attention. He wasn't an idiot—his friend was a beautiful lady; there was no doubt about that. She didn't have to wear a cocktail dress to be lovely. He didn't understand what turned those gazes hungry. Men regarded her as something to be devoured or worshipped.

Every other guy dancing with a partner had the same captivated look, as though the woman losing herself to the music were a goddess. Why didn't Felix feel the same? He appreciated their beauty, sure, but wasn't interested. Was something wrong with him?

"Nobody should be thinking that much in a club," shouted someone to his right over the music.

The voice belonged to a young man with his hands in his pockets, slouching lazily as he watched Felix with an amused grin.

He belatedly realized he'd been gawking and shut his mouth. "I'm sorry. Do I know you?"

The man looked out the window to hide an embarrassed snicker, giving Felix a good view of his sharp angular jawline and bronze skin under the soft moonlight. "I probably should have started with my name... Oops." He extended his lean hand. "My name is Sergio. You kind of, uh, saved me from Emilio yesterday. You took a photo?"

Felix hadn't been paying much attention to the man at the time, so it took him a couple of awkward moments to recognize him. "Oh! By the lockers! The essays on the ground! Sorry, I, uh, I didn't..." He gave up explaining and settled for shaking Sergio's calloused hand. "I'm Felix."

Sergio gave him a relieved white-toothed smile. "I just thought I should come over and thank you. I think I would have escaped that encounter with a dislocated shoulder if it weren't for you."

Felix remembered how Emilio had turned on him after Sergio had run away and shuddered. He glanced towards Nikolai, bouncing happily among his circle. "Me too."

Sergio cupped his ear. "What?"

Felix shook his head.

Sergio leaned in so he didn't have to raise his voice as much. "Hey. Before, you looked like you were thinking hard. Is something the matter?"

Felix rubbed his face as if that would get rid of the nagging feeling. "Just an observation that decided to rear its ugly head."

Sergio bit his lip. The tips of his ears flushed. "Maybe I could help you forget?"

"How?"

"Dance with me."

Felix looked at Sergio's worn, fitted sneakers and to his own two left feet before pointing to the empty shot glasses with a laugh. "I'm afraid I won't be much on my feet. If I get up I'll just fall right back down."

"Nonsense!" Sergio pulled him up and steadied him with a strong hand on his back. "I'd never let you fall."

Felix blamed the heat that rose up his neck on the booze. Sergio's hand was so warm on the base of his spine, solid yet light. If he wanted to sit back down, Sergio would respect his decision. That was clear by the gentleness with which he held him. But if the hopeful look on his face told Felix anything, he would be missing out on something hilariously adorable if he chose the couch.

"Lead the way."

Indeed, Sergio did stop him from falling on his face a couple of times on the way to the dance floor, and they laughed together when he wobbled.

"I'm warning you, drunk or not, I don't know how to dance," Felix cautioned for the sake of Sergio's toes.

Sergio only laughed and pulled him closer to say in his ear, "Wanna know a secret?" His breath tickled his hair. "Nobody here does."

"I doubt that."

"It's true!" Sergio pulled back to shine a happy smile. "Nobody comes to a club to show off proper dancing. It's all just fun! Here, I'll show you."

Felix ignored how the cold quickly replaced Sergio's touch when he stepped back. He slapped a hand over his mouth to hide his laugh as Sergio flailed like a panicked goose and performed some uncoordinated disco moves. People around paused to hoot and shout encouragements. They squealed when he blew a kiss.

"I can't believe you just did that!" Felix shouted, catching Sergio's arms as he stumbled back.

Sergio gently slid his wrists back so they held hands instead, sending goosebumps up Felix's arm. "See? Nothing to it! No judgement here. Only fun!"

He guided Felix along until he could move by himself, and soon they were dancing like fools. They shouted lyrics, made up sounds to the words they didn't know, and tried their hand at pogo-stick bouncing until Felix felt like throwing up.

It felt magical. The music pulsed through his limbs and sparked out the end of his fingers and toes. The colours merged into rainbows. How long had they been dancing? Minutes or hours? All he knew was his head felt light, his body thrummed, and whenever he lost his balance Sergio was right there to catch him, squealing the entire time.

One instance had them giggling into each other's shoulders: Felix tripped, and Sergio was there to catch him. But Felix's momentum propelled them into a wall, leaving Sergio holding him safely against his body the entire fall. Sergio's shoulder blades slammed into one of the mirrors, and Felix's weight crushed his front in what must have been a painful impact. But Sergio's grip never faltered. They looked up at each other, nose-to-nose, and burst into laughter.

"You're very strong!"

"You're very determined to lie on the floor," Sergio teased back, his arms around his middle no longer holding him upright but simply holding him. Felix wasn't in any rush to leave them.

"No, gravity loves me, is all! Who am I to deny gravity a hug?"

Fingers dug deep into Felix's shoulder and whirled him around. He stumbled with the rush of dizziness. Two pairs of hands grabbed him to keep him upright, one much more careful than the other. Felix blinked the scene into focus and followed the fist in the front of his shirt up to the elbow that it belonged to, to the familiar hooded vest, the tank top, and finally to Nikolai's face.

Sergio shouted something, tugging Felix backwards. Nikolai didn't let go. He glared at Felix and held him upright until he got his feet back under him, then dropped him.

"What's wrong?" Felix asked.

He drunkenly reached up to touch his frown, but Nikolai caught his wrist, hissing, "What do you think you're doing?"

"Oi! Let him go!" Sergio ducked around and shoved Nikolai away. Nikolai didn't spare him so much as a glance.

"You and Liana were with other people, so Sergio asked me to dance. We were having fun."

"Fun?" Nikolai scoffed. "If you-know-who's after you, don't you think you're being irresponsible partnering yourself up? They could become the next target! You're not having fun, you're endangering everyone!"

Sergio looked from hackles-raised Nikolai to deflating-balloon Felix in utter confusion. People around gave them a little more space because of the angry tones but didn't pay enough attention to listen to their words.

"You think crowding up against the mirrors with someone you just met is a good idea? A guy, no less?" Nikolai said.

That struck a chord. Nikolai was upset with him. Not only was that, he was upset Felix was with a guy. But Felix wasn't gay. So, why was he so mad? And why did it hurt so much?

Sergio stepped between them. "Don't you think that was a bit harsh? What does it matter who Felix pairs up with?"

At the sound of Felix's name coming from the stranger's mouth, Nikolai finally shifted his attention. "Because you're not a girl. And because of that, you attract attention. Felix has enough attention on him at the moment."

Deep in his chest, something cracked. Nikolai didn't want him to be with a guy. Because that would be gay. And having a gay friend would be weird. Something to hide. Hot tears burned his eyes. He dashed for the exit. The room tilted and he stumbled. He dodged their reaching hands. He didn't want to hear anymore.

A freak. Nikolai wanted to hide the freak.

Felix gripped the bracelets around his calloused wrist.

Liana bumped into him dancing with Riley by the DJ. Her large smile evaporated when she saw his tears. "What happened?"

"I need to go."

She stopped him from brushing past and cupped his face. She thumbed away the wetness under his eyes. "Okay, that's fine. How're you getting home?"

"Cab."

"Do you have enough money on you?"

"I don't—I think? Yes?"

He felt her plastic card slip into his back pocket and choked on a new sob.

"Use my account. You know the code. Text me when you get there, okay?"

Felix gave her hand a thankful squeeze and hurried out of the club into the rain.

It was one of the most awkward cab rides he'd ever had. The poor cabbie didn't know whether to offer a tissue or a towel. At least Nikolai's reaction had sobered him up for the drive.

His dorm welcomed him home with a chill. The bathroom door creaked as if waving. He locked the door behind him and stumbled to his desk chair. He put his head in his hands to stifle a snivel and his clothes squelched uncomfortably. He wasn't sure whether what bubbled past his lips was a laugh or another sob.

What had gotten into Nikolai? He couldn't even blame the alcohol because they'd gotten drunk together countless times and he'd never behaved like that! He'd never given any hint that he'd be bothered if Felix were...

He should change. The only thing more pathetic than crying in the rain was crying while soaked indoors. He reached for the nearest towel on the floor and realized it was the one Nikolai had dried him with when he'd sleepwalked in the rain. He hiccupped and threw it across the room.

Maybe he should work to get his mind off it. Yeah, that would help. A little distraction should do him good. He texted Liana that he'd arrived home safe and opened his laptop. The first thing he saw was the *College News* page.

PSYCHOPATH ON THE LOOSE!

Are you locking your doors? Are you checking them twice? Be home by seven and read today's issue for tips on how to stay safe. Don't miss the feature from our psychology department's greatest, debating who could be the entity behind these grisly murders!

The comments section was filled with accounts arguing about the damaging term in the title, people genuinely asking for information, and ignorant trolls fanning the flames.

Nikolai's voice hissed in his ear hissed, *"You're not having fun, you're endangering everyone!"*

He sniffled and closed the tab. The digital copies of Nikolai's photo shoot popped up.

What does it matter who Felix pairs up with?

Because you're not a girl.

He gave up and turned off his laptop.

He double-checked the locks, changed, and curled into bed, tying his wrist to the bedframe with thick nylon rope. *It would be better in the morning*, he told himself. He hugged his fluffiest pillow and cried himself to sleep.

Third Body Discovered! Police Baffled!

Felix and Liana walked to class together. Without Nikolai. When he didn't offer an explanation about last night, she didn't press, and he was thankful. Instead, she filled the silence by talking about her tournament that afternoon and the teams she was up against.

"Imagine being trapped in a hot, sweaty gym with that team! That's the only part I'm not looking forward to. It's like it comes with the package! For every win, you must go three months without showering! Be the Number One hotshot and give off the stink of—of—" She sniffed and made a face. "—of whatever candy meatloaf the kitchens burnt this morning."

As he listened, Felix fiddled with his camera and pondered how he could avoid Nikolai today. He wasn't ready to face him. He didn't have enough duct tape to seal the fissure in his chest just yet.

He couldn't afford to skip the classes they had together, but he could sit across the room. Lunch and dinner were easy; he just had to spend them away from the performing arts buildings. Asking to tag along with his new friend Sergio was out of the question. Not only did he not have his number or any idea how to find him, but Nikolai had probably scared him off permanently. He could spend the time between classes in his dorm with the door locked.

But plan as he might, nothing could have prepared him for what they walked into.

"Was there some sort of celebrity appearance happening today that I don't know about?" Liana asked.

"Hm? Not that I know of, why?"

"Then what's with the mob?"

Students were crowded around the edge of the sidewalk. Blue and red lights flashed around the corner of the arts and science building. Officers on the grass urged students to move on.

Yellow tape peaked from between the backpacks.

Liana gripped his hand as the same thought crossed their minds.

"Did you hear from Nikolai today?" he whispered.

She shook her head, wide-eyed.

They dove into the crowd. They shoved between students to scan faces, not bothering to apologize. No matter how much Nikolai had hurt him, no matter how scared he was of being near him right now, the thought that it could be him beyond that yellow tape was far more terrifying.

The further into the crowd they got, the more potent the smell Liana mentioned became. Dread twisted his gut. Felix swung people around. He elbowed into groups and knocked over backpacks. *No, please, no.* Somebody growled and pushed back. An invisible hand squeezed his lungs. People cursed him for shoving, but their anger quickly fizzled as the flashing blue and red lights snared their attention again.

He couldn't find him. He couldn't see Nikolai.

"Felix!" Liana shouldered towards him and pointed to a head of brown hair near the yellow tape. The hand squeezing his chest relaxed a bit.

Nikolai was rubbing his face, looking sick. He spotted Felix and the nauseated twist of his frown changed into panic. He leapt through the sea of students, hand up as if to block Felix's view. It was too late. He caught a glimpse of what lay beyond the tape.

"They aren't here for a celebrity, Liana..."

No amount of rain could wash away that much blood. Mushy red soil tainted the dip in the lawn between the arts and science building and the theatre. In the middle lay Emilio's crooked body. Felix saw the mangled corpse in cinematic flashes, like the early camera prototypes that used controlled flash powder explosions to light up the scene right before taking a picture.

FLASH!

The white of Emilio's broken bones protruded from his ripped jeans.

FLASH!

One of his mud-caked hands still clutched his abdomen, trying to hold his intestines in, the other hand extended ahead towards safety.

FLASH!

The back of his caved-in head glistened.

FLASH!

A bloody branch lay a couple of feet away.

FLASH!

The rest of the world drowned out.

He stared at the slime coating Emilio's ripped muscle tissue, mind blank. What was he supposed to think? Was there a book on *What to Feel When Looking at Your Bully's Dead Body*? Was there a proper reaction?

Nikolai had said Emilio would get what was coming to him. Was this what he meant? Did he know? He couldn't have... could he?

Memories of his interactions with Emilio leading up to his death zoomed past like a flipbook. He saw the same anger, same conceit, and same scowl on his corpse, but now twisted in distress—rigor mortis assuring it wouldn't fade anytime soon.

He pictured himself in Emilio's place. Cold, but burning from his injuries. Throat raw from screaming. Or maybe he'd never had a chance. His stomach slammed against his belly as if trying to leap out and join Emilio's in the grass. He must have been so scared. The pain must have been excruciating.

Did it make him an awful person to wish Emilio had died after the first injury—after his legs were destroyed or after he'd been hit in the back of the head—instead of suffering through the will to live that had kept him awake through the next torture? That kept him hopeful with the chance of survival across the grass? That kept him dragging his mutilated body through the dirt?

His eyes were still open. He'd felt it all.

"Felix Griffiths?"

Felix tore his eyes away from the mangled body to address the police officer walking towards him. The crowd pointed and murmured in his direction. "That's me."

The officer towered over him in both height and breadth. If that weren't enough, his vests and coats bulged under his utility belts and radios, making him twice his size. He had a straight nose, perfect for looking down at people, and trigger-happy fingers that twitched when tucked into his belt. Liana grabbed Felix's hand.

His gruff voice matched his build. "I've been told you knew the victim."

"Not by choice."

He blamed his lack of filter on the shock.

"What can you tell me about this—" The officer squinted at his notepad. "—Emilio Varela?"

"He, uh, was a dude. Another photojournalism student. Talented. Currently dead. Uh..."

Liana gave him a look.

Before the officer could say more, or Felix make an even bigger fool out of himself, Nikolai shoved the last person aside and shouted, "He didn't do it!"

Felix cringed.

The officer raised a bushy brow. "And you are?"

"Felix Griffiths's alibi. He, Liana, and I were out late doing a photo shoot for class and then went to the club until early in the morning."

"Your friends are your alibi." The officer jotted something down. "How convenient. Thank you for offering that bit of information to me."

It was Nikolai's turn to receive a look from Liana. Part of Felix was glad his friends were stepping in to speak on his behalf, being too tongue-tied to do it himself. Another part wished they'd been a bit smarter about it.

"It's obvious, isn't it?" a crowd member interjected. "They hated each other! Emilio bullied him worse than Trevor!"

Liana glared into the crowd and the person stopped talking. Felix hung his head.

The officer flipped through his notebook. "Trevor was the... second victim. You knew both of them?"

"All three!" another person corrected.

"Interesting," hummed the officer.

"Emilio took his place in the art journal, too!"

"He always messes with Felix's assignments! I knew they were jealous of each other."

"Emilio got top marks instead!"

What was this? The Salem witch trials?

Nikolai crossed his arms and glared at them all. "I recognize you. For people who also got pushed around by Emilio, you sure are defensive of him."

"We are *not* defensive!" shouted one.

"Emilio was horrible, yeah, but he didn't deserve to go like that!" cried another.

"Would you all shut up?!" Liana snapped.

The crowd fell silent.

The officer raised a brow. "Why should they? Would they tell me something you don't want me to know?"

Liana's glare was so angry even Felix felt the heat. "The only thing you'll find out is that all three boys were horrible bullies, and nobody liked them. Yes, they picked on Felix. Do you know who else they picked on?

Everybody shorter than them. So, instead of harassing my friend, who you *know* has an alibi, how about you go find the real killer?"

With that, she marched Felix out of the crowd and out of sight.

Not even halfway through the day, the killer had a new name: the Executioner. The shock had rooted enough by then that Felix became aware of the whispers that nipped at his heels wherever he went. He did his best to ignore them, but it was all the Cinema of Horror class would talk about despite the professor's best efforts.

"Following our discussion last week on the relationship between famous movies and the historical context of their time and why that made them so terrifying, today we will review its effects on society."

A girl with short curly hair put up her hand. "Sir?"

"Yes, Miss Robinson?"

"What do you think about the recent murders?"

"I think they are entirely irrelevant. Now, as I was saying, last week we watched—"

This time, a young man with a buzzcut that looked like it had got far too close to the skin put up his hand. "Sir?"

"Yes, Mister Helman?"

"Is it true Emilio's legs were so broken you could see his bones?"

"It's true that you won't pass this course without a grade above sixty." He turned back to the chalkboard. "In the 70s, the Church—"

"Sir?"

The professor sighed. "Has it got to do with the 70s?"

"No."

He smiled over his shoulder. "Then be quiet."

"Sir, I have a question relating to last week's movie!"

He threw his hands in the air. "Finally!"

"Do you think the townsfolk gave the demon child as ridiculous a name as the *Executioner*?"

The professor put his face in his hands. The class giggled. Liana rolled her eyes, barely looking up from doodling in her notebook.

Felix leaned closer and whispered teasingly, "What happened to the girl who was fascinated by killers?"

She elbowed his ribs gently. "It becomes a lot less fun when your best friend is targeted by one."

He hummed and picked up his pencil to help her colour in her ladybug. This wasn't a conversation he wanted to listen to anyway.

The professor rested his elbows on his podium and placed his chin in his hands. "Fine, if you're all so determined, send me your questions so we can get on with the lecture. Why you all are so fixated on this is beyond me."

"Oh, my! The Cinema of Horror class wants to talk about murder!" moaned a student sarcastically, earning a couple of Snickers. "What a shock."

The professor glared and waved his fingers for the questions to begin.

"Have the police found a suspect?" asked one girl.

"I am not privy to that information and even if I was, I wouldn't tell you. We would like to avoid mob justice. Next?"

"Is it true all the victims were jerks?"

That question received a judging frown. "How blunt of you. I suppose there is a pattern to be found now that we have more than two bodies to speculate upon. Such a pattern could be found in the unfortunate way the three men decided to live their lives, yes."

"Why were they killed?"

"If we knew that, the police would be well on their way to finding the culprit, wouldn't they?" He paused for thought. "I suppose there is something I can tell you..."

Everybody eagerly leaned forward in their seats. Felix's pencil stilled.

He waggled his index at them all with a small smirk. "You're very lucky I'm married to a criminal psychologist."

"What a match made in heaven!"

A wave of the professor's hand hushed the laughter that followed. "According to my wife, motives for murder can be boiled down to a few categories. Keep in mind I was reading a good book at the time and have forgotten some." The class snickered. "There's love, revenge, greed, and survival. Murderers kill for themselves or others."

Liana finally looked up, brows furrowed in a pensive frown. "The Seven Deadly Sins, then?"

The professor chuckled but acknowledged her point by tipping his head to her. "I highly doubt someone would kill for Gluttony or Sloth."

A girl in the front piped up, "I dunno, have you seen some of the guys that barge into fast food restaurants? Death be unto all that gets in the way of him and his cheeseburger."

People laughed. Liana clutched her pencil and made a threatening throwing motion at the girl for turning her serious question into a joke. Felix made her sit on her hands.

A boy gulped his coffee and added, "Ever heard the phrase, 'I'd kill for a couple more hours of sleep'?"

The professor raised a teasing brow. "From you? All the time. Now, in our last assignment we studied a classic movie where the killer had an exaggerated case of dissociative identity disorder. The protective, motherly personality would kill out of greed and love. She loved the host to the point of murderous jealousy and wanted him all to herself. In the host's mind, at least."

He circled his podium and walked through the aisles. "I say exaggerated because, for one, it's a movie. Despite what fiction likes to portray for the thrill factor, mentally ill people are not generally dangerous. In fact, they're disproportionately at higher risk of being victims of violence than being its perpetrators."

Felix hadn't thought about how villainized mental illness was in the media before. How much common knowledge was fuelled by inaccurate depictions ?

The profession continued, "You may recognize one murderer's name who inspired numerous classic horror movies unfortunately absent from our syllabus: Ed Gein. The man who lived in a farmhouse fashioning clothes, masks and furniture out of corpses."

"That guy was gross!" a girl exclaimed. "You're telling us someone that sick in the head *wasn't* a psychopath?"

"Not in the term you're thinking of," Liana cut in. "While their actions are sick, the vast majority of killers are not mentally ill. Psychopathy and sociopathy aren't medical diagnoses. Yes, they're often associated with antisocial personality disorder, but only a tiny percentage of people with the personality disorder have violent tendencies that rise to 'psychopathy' levels."

The professor blinked. "That is... correct. How do you know that?"

She beamed and shrugged. "Some people can name every player's stats on a football team..."

He looked pleasantly impressed and resumed his stroll. He stole one kid's coffee as he walked by. "We could debate all class which category

Ed Gein truly belongs to when looking at his history—ew, this coffee is terrible. Take it back. Does the not-so-mysterious death of his brother, who didn't share Ed's unhealthy worship of their mother and had openly criticized her abusive behaviour, put Ed in the revenge and love categories? Or does he belong solely in love as his victims were most notably women who resembled his late mother? But then what of the mementos? The slaughtered victims' family members?"

He sighed sadly and sat on the desk of a student who was too enraptured in his phone to notice. "Alas, we don't have all class for Ed Gein. But we do for last week's movie." At the sound of the professor's voice suddenly so close, the student jumped and banged his knees on his desk. The professor grinned at his pained groan.

Robinson lifted her hand. "If every murderer fits into a category, what's the Executioner's motive?"

Before the professor could steer the conversation back to their lesson, the entire class buzzed with ideas, talking over each other as if volume gave your opinion backbone.

"Maybe it's money!" cried one boy.

The girl beside him flicked his shoulder. "It can't be greed. There was nothing of value taken off the bodies."

Liana and Felix shared a look. Neither of them had thought to check if Emilio's body was missing anything. Both previous victims had items unaccounted for: a sock, an ID card. They'd better figure out if Emilio was missing a shoe before it turned up in Felix's dorm.

A girl with long black hair spoke around the end of her pen. "He could have been paid, like a hitman!"

"A hitman for college students?" scoffed someone up front. "Unless their daddies were CEOs or had ties to the mafia, it's unlikely."

Liana muttered about idiots and went back to her notebook.

"Survival?" proposed another.

"I could understand survival for one murder. But three?"

"What if he's in love with the idea that he's protecting the bullies' victims?"

Liana dropped her pen. Emilio's wide, soured milky eyes stared back at Felix from the swirl of pencilled ladybugs.

The professor's clapping surprised them all into silence. When had he gotten back to his podium? "Yes, yes, those are all good theories. And while all learning is good learning, we still have a lesson to continue."

Everybody groaned.

"But if you're so determined, write me a paper on different kinds of killers for extra credit."

They cheered louder.

Liana looked like she'd had a very uncomfortable revelation and glanced at the splotchy bruise on the back of Felix's hand left from Emilio's boot. He gave her a worried look.

She tried to smile. "Ignore it. Focus on studying."

He buried his head in his books and that was the last of the lesson he heard.

When class ended, everyone continued chattering excitedly amongst themselves while filing out. Liana and Felix slipped into the crowd behind a group of plotting boys.

"I'm going to prove to the prof that someone can kill through Sloth!" one of them gushed too enthusiastically for their topic. "Babies can die of neglect if a parent is too lazy to get up and feed them!"

One of his friends gave him a high five. "And I can write about Gluttony! Overconsumption kills, dude!"

A couple girls broke away from the crowd, looking over their shoulders in disgust. "I can't believe these people," one of them said. "Three people are dead. They should be shutting down the college and sending us home."

Another girl rolled her eyes. "You've got to be kidding me. There could be a worldwide pandemic and we'd still be forced back to school."

A third blanched looking at her phone. "My friend in engineering just got back to me. The police are questioning her professors about anyone showing an interest in security cameras lately. The ones around Emilio weren't working, just like the other murders." Liana rolled her eyes as they passed, though pulled out her own phone to frown at Riley's contact info. "Nice critical thinking, police. It's not like there are numerous sub-fields within each branch. Really gonna narrow it down."

His back pocket buzzed halfway to his locker. It was a text from his parents. Emilio's death had hit the news. Liana peered over his shoulder. "Is that your parents? If so, mine will be calling in three... two... Hi, Mom." She balanced her phone between her shoulder and ear so she could mouth, "Gonna go calm her down. See you later!" He didn't comment on how she glanced at his bruises before scurrying somewhere quieter.

He had an hour before his next class, so he found a nice nook in the walls of a calmer hallway and settled in for the storm. His parents didn't blow up his phone often. Even then, it was mainly "concerned parent" texts: wanting to know if he'd heard the news, if not they'd sent him article links, asking how he was holding up, all very worried but loving messages.

He wished he could tell them the truth. He wished he could tell them how scared he was, how much he wanted to hide behind their skirts until the danger crept away. He could put up with the bullying, but this? He couldn't tell them. The truth was too dangerous.

So, he settled for calming them down and answering what rapid-fire questions he could:

Yes. He was locking his doors.

No. He didn't want to go home.

Yes. He tied himself up before going to bed.

No. He wasn't friends with the victim.

Yes. He'd be careful not to sleepwalk into the killer's path.

Yes. He could borrow Liana's bat for protection.

He paused. His phone buzzed with a new text. He didn't hear.

Protection.

One of his classmates suggested the Executioner was in love with the idea that he was protecting the bullies' victims. These weren't crimes of anger; they were crimes of loving passion. If that were the case, he would think of himself as a hero to the people. If he was so proud, why frame Felix for it? The wrong person would get the credit.

He glanced at his bruised hand. What if the evidence in his shower wasn't a frame job but a "Look what I did for you" sort of deal? What if he didn't see himself as a hero to the people, but to one person? All three victims had been kings of the halls. And all three had been sovereign of Felix's Hell.

A frost settled deep into his marrow. The Executioner wasn't framing him; he was *protecting* him. The echo of Liana's voice told him to put it out of his head, but he could feel the idea burrowing into the darkest crack in his skull. It would sit. It would fester. It would fester. It would wait for the right time.

A pair of birds squawked at each other outside the window and took off to the south. He snapped a quick photo with his instant camera before they got out of sight and shivered into his coat.

"I just want to pass my classes..."

He watched the white of the small card develop into blurry flying birds.

Hang on. If the killer was after those that hurt me, what would happen to Nikolai?

Public Names Recent Terror the Work of Executioner

The police's interest in Felix spread around campus like wildfire. His photojournalism classmates looked between him and Emilio's empty desk with suspicion. Some began speculating what had started their "rivalry." The most popular theory, and the one that got him the most disgusted looks, was a love confession gone wrong. The name of last night's club caught between murmurs answered where that idea had come from.

They weren't the only ones.

The coffee shop on campus went silent the moment he walked in. The cashiers fought amongst themselves for two minutes—nobody wanted to take his order. Then, after he finally got his drink, somebody walking past bumped into him, spilling it all over his shoes. They didn't even apologize. Just muttered a slur and kept walking.

Figuring the cafeteria wouldn't be any more pleasant than the rest of campus, he stopped by his dorm to rinse his shoes and eat lunch. There, he found an angry letter shoved under his door from one of Rhett's friends. After shoving the letter into his bag, he realized he was late for his next lecture. He barely made it.

He took the professor's light scolding for barging into the lecture hall without complaint and slid into a seat. He hid behind his binder and kept his wet sneakers still as to not have them squeak, hoping nobody smelled the coffee he hadn't had the time to wash out. Or hear his queasy stomach that suspected the ramen he'd eaten for lunch had been expired. At least the professor hadn't marked him late.

Thankfully, a text from Liana told him she'd be waiting for him outside the building. All he had to do was get through this hour without shrivelling under everyone's growing hostility. He'd scoot down the halls before they decided to act on their fear and be home free with Liana. Nikolai texted too. A lot. Felix wondered why people thought sending texts until the recipient's butt went numb would make them more inclined to read the first ignored text. It didn't.

Eventually, the texts subsided, but he felt no better for it. After this morning's scare had him believing Nikolai would be the Executioner's next victim, he could admit his fingers twitched to pull out his phone and take comfort in the fact his friend was still alive.

But, thinking back to the club and how angry Nikolai was, the snarl in his words crushed any lingering temptations. He knew what the messages would entail. More anger. More disgust. He sniffed and buried his face in his arms.

He couldn't tell what made him more upset: the hatred toward gays, Nikolai being mad at him, or the insinuation Felix was something he was not?

All were valid reasons for his misery, but he couldn't pinpoint which one was sinking its jaws into his heart and giving it a good shake. It wasn't fair to attack him with those remarks like everyone else. It wasn't fair.

Someone kicked his chair on the way to the trash bin. He clenched his teeth.

It didn't matter what he felt. If the Executioner really was after anyone who upset him, he couldn't let on about his feelings about Nikolai. So he held his chin up, ignored the accusatory looks and did his best to look unbothered during the lecture.

Sit still, look pretty, he thought bitterly to himself. *Keep your mouth shut and they'll live.*

Not twenty minutes later, his phone buzzed.

He removed it from his pocket to give his bum a break and spotted the message. It read, "Share this with everyone you know! Once in a lifetime opportunity!" He chuckled dryly to himself. Wasn't that how all scams started? The professor had his back turned, writing something on the board Felix had long since given up trying to understand. Desperate for an escape, he clicked.

It was a poll of people the student body wanted the Executioner to kill next.

How sick could people be? Just yesterday everyone had been terrified of being caught alone. But after another death, they'd gotten comfortable? Excited by the idea? Did they believe, because it was *Emilio's* entrails falling out of his corpse, this was okay? Did they think, "They were all bullies, it's not so scary anymore"?

Appalled, Felix scrolled through the list. Students. Professors.

Landlords. Thankfully none of his friends. He could tell some people thought this poll to be a joke and had entered perfectly harmless, friendly people to it as a gag. Others—Felix recognized most of their names. If you agreed with the proposed name and clicked "Upvote" it would move higher on the list. Some of the joke names were near the top. He prayed the Executioner would never find this.

Another notification came from his social media page. And another. And another. All links to the poll.

"You're the Executioner, right? Kill him for me. He's hitting me," one message read.

"Help me, too!" another commented.

"Hey. Executioner. Get him out of the way. I want top marks."

Felix's hands trembled so hard that it got hard to read. They wanted him to kill. They *wanted* more death. The messages kept coming. The more this poll spread its reach, the more innocent pleas and sinful begging filled his inbox.

"*Stop sending this to me!*" he wanted to scream. He wanted to throw his phone. He wanted to leave.

Instead, he took a deep, shaking breath and put away his phone. He hugged his camera and faced the board without registering it. He felt like puking.

Finally, the agonizing hour ended. Felix waited for everyone to leave before he did. He slung his backpack over his shoulders and peeked around the doorframe to check if Nikolai was hovering around.

"Looking for someone?"

The college counsellor, Mrs. Rosewood, smiled at him with all the warmth of a hearth on a winter's night. She wore a purple and blue dress that swirled around her voluptuous figure and complimented her cool brown skin. The bracelets around her wrists twinkled where they rested atop her round middle. Her dark hair was soft, like her laugh, and bounced when she skipped. One would think she smelled of roses, just as her name suggested, but her hugs reminded Felix of wood smoke and marshmallows.

"No, I just—I just wanted to look out. In case. People. In case I bumped into people." He fidgeted with the bands on his wrists, forcing a smile. He knew she didn't buy it when she followed the motion and examined his face.

"Have you been getting much sleep lately?"

"Did the police want you to ask me that?"

"No, honey. Your parents," she said gently. "They asked me to keep an eye on you when you were accepted here, remember? We've been worried."

"We?" He leaned against the wall and grazed the plastic of his camera with his fingertips to fake nonchalance. "Why *we*? Aren't you just supposed to make sure I don't sleepwalk off the premises or something?"

"Adding extra locks to your doors and windows is part of my responsibility, yes. But another is your mental health." Her amusement melted away into concern. "Your grades have gone down, my boy. Your photos aren't as good. Your writing is grade-school level. The faculty is getting worried."

"So am I," he murmured. Considering his worries had bled into his class time, the last of which he'd barely paid attention to, he was in big academic trouble.

"Do you know why you're having difficulties?"

"People *have* just died, Mrs. Rosewood."

Her smile wilted. "I know. It's terribly frightening, isn't it? We're aware it'll have an impact on all students, which is why we're ramping up our efforts. Everyone copes in their own way. I'm here to make sure it's a healthy way. So, is there something I can do for you?"

Felix almost laughed in the poor woman's face. Help him? Half the school, including his best friend, thought he was a gay freak. The other thought he was a murderer and asking him to kill people. And a serial killer might've been in love with him. If she could help, he was all ears because he was barely holding it together.

He opened his mouth, but nothing came out. His thin grasp on control weakened. He could be weak, just for a second. No one would get killed if he took a second, right?

"A hug?" he croaked.

Mrs. Rosewood cooed and scampered over without hesitation. She flung out her arms and buried him in the squishiest, warmest hug. It was just what he needed. She rocked him side to side, stroked the back of his head and let him hold onto her like a child because, really, what else was he?

"I know this is scary, sweetie," she murmured sympathetically.

It was terrifying.

"Everybody's feeling the same."

Oh, he doubted that.

"But you just let me know what I can do to make life a little bit easier, and I'll do it in a jiffy!" Her bright eyes were full of hope and promise, twinkling just like her bracelets. "It's tough right now, but it'll all be over soon. The police will catch him, just you wait." Whether he believed her or not, it was nice to hear.

"Thanks, Mrs. Rosewood."

Her eyes crinkled with her smile, and she gave him one last rib-crushing squeeze before letting go. "Now you scurry off to your classes or your room, you hear? I don't want no lolly-gagging on the grounds, especially at night!"

She patted his cheek and walked back to her office with a skip in her step. Felix touched his cheek with a chuckle and turned to walk back to his dorms as instructed, only to stop cold. Michael, Jackson, and a couple of Emilio's other friends burst open through the exit doors and charged at him.

One day. Could he not be left alone for one day?

"You!"

Felix was off his feet, in the air, and rammed into the wall before he could run. Pain rippled down his back. His backpack crashed to the ground. He gasped for air as he clawed at Michael's arms holding him on his tiptoes. His head thrummed where it slammed into the bricks.

Fear sparkled through his veins as Michael snarled in his face, fanning foul breath into his nostrils and pushing him harder into the wall. Felix groaned as his bones ground into the concrete.

"How did you do it, huh?! You're a nobody! Not even important enough to make it into the art journal!"

"I didn't realize you had feelings that needed to be expressed," wheezed Felix.

Jackson growled and kicked his shin. Felix clenched his teeth against the sharp pain.

Jackson and the other goons stood at Michael's sides, ready to lunge if he managed, by some miracle, to wiggle away. They bore varying shades of rage, fists twitching at their sides. Felix's eyes widened.

This was different from usual. He wouldn't get away with a few bruises this time. He considered screaming for Mrs. Rosewood, but she was long gone. His friends weren't around. He was alone.

Months of pent-up frustration broiled in his gut. What did he ever do to them to deserve their relentless torment?

"What do you—" Felix feebly kicked Michael's leg. "—want from me?"

Michael's rage contorted his face into something monstrous. Felix tried to jerk away but had nowhere to look other than Michael as he leaned in. All he could see were his pores, the paleness of his complexion, and the danger thrumming under his skin. This close, Felix spotted the faintest tremble in his jaw. It couldn't be—no, he didn't see it wrong. He glanced around. Flickering eyes. Feral fear. Twitchy fingers palming the outline of something in pockets. They weren't just angry. Something had scared them so bad that the restraints of rationality had disappeared. And that was chilling.

"You said he'd be next and he was! Emilio is *dead*! What the hell!?"

He wasn't sure if it was Michael's shaking hands twisting his shirt, but he missed a breath.

"What did you do?!" Michael screamed.

Shit. If he didn't do something fast, he'd end up in the hospital.

A repulsive thought gave him a flicker of hope. If he played his cards right, he might escape without broken bones.

No, he couldn't do it! He might be sentencing them to death!

One of the goons took out a switchblade. Terror loosened his tongue.

"That's right, I'm being protected by a serial killer. I dare you to touch me now."

Some flinched. Others took a half step back.

"You don't want to end up like the others, do you? Like Rhett, with the elevator closing on your head? Or Trevor, choking on your own blood? His eye had been stabbed so many times it turned to soup in its socket."

He was breathless, partially in horror at himself. He wasn't sure where this was coming from; the words tumbled out of their own accord! But the hand on his shirt was loosening, and the guys were slowly pulling away. So he kept going.

"Surely, Emilio's fate would be the worst? You saw the pictures. His legs were so broken he had to drag his body to safety with his hands. Or rather, one hand. The other was busy trying to keep his intestines from falling out of his stomach."

Michael turned a little green.

"Leave me alone and nothing will happen to you."

Michael stared at him for a moment. Then, dropped him. Felix coughed, leaning against the wall for support, and rubbed his neck. *Yes!* For once, something was going his way.

"You psycho!"

Jackson launched past Michael and punched Felix across the face, sending him sprawling to the ground. Pain blinded him for a moment. Bloody saliva dribbled past his lips.

"You're a freak!" Jackson reared back and kicked him in the stomach. "You hear me? A *freak*!"

Felix cried out and curled around his camera. Another kick. Pain spread from his ribs. Michael extended a hand to stop Jackson, but it went ignored under the other goons' encouragements. Another kick. Another wave of pain wracked his body. Michael yelled at Jackson. The goons yelled back. Tears pricked Felix's eyes. Michael finally pulled Jackson away just as his foot connected with Felix's face hard enough to flip him like a pancake, and that was incentive enough for the others to follow. Felix didn't bother to rise to see them off. Michael pushed them through the exit doors and paused to look back, wide-eyed. He hesitated for a heartbeat, then left.

Felix gasped for air. He shook from the paralyzing pain. Was this what the boys had felt like, lying on the ground in so much pain they couldn't move, only with their worst nightmare staring them down with its foot on their throat?

Emilio's eyes had been open. What had his last thoughts been? Regret? Had he wished for his parents? What was the last thing he'd seen? His murderer's face? Or the teasing sight of safety only a few yards away?

Felix inhaled and convulsed from the exploding chain reaction in his muscles.

Three people: Rhett, Trevor, Emilio. What had it been like for them before the Executioner forced them off the playing field? Had he given them a speech like in the movies? Revealed his motives after capturing them, making them regret ever even looking at Felix? Or had he slaughtered them without any explanation?

The room morphed into a mirror of the rancid crime scenes. He had a feeling there hadn't been any talking involved. No maniacal laughter. Just cold fury. Felix lay there until the shooting pain died to a throb and didn't feel like he was breathing acid steam .

People think I'm capable of murder, huh? I wonder what they'd think if they could see me now.

He coughed and took his time dragging himself to his feet. The room wobbled with him. He wiped his mouth with the back of his hand. Blood. He sighed and checked his nose. Despite what it felt like, it wasn't broken, just swollen and wet. He carefully dragged his backpack outside to meet Liana.

She was giggling with Riley, comparing the bruises from practice. You could get concussed taking a volleyball to the head, and they regularly and voluntarily took them to the body. He imagined they walked out of the gym feeling similar to how he did.

Liana wore the same face she did when checking in on him after a bad sleepwalking episode. She'd probably called Riley out to see how she was handling everything. The murders were getting more attention than her sister's bullying case ever did. That had to sting. Liana was a good friend. He cursed himself for not being like her, even if they were only acquaintances.

At the creak of the door, Riley lifted her hand to wave. Her eyes nearly bulged out of their sockets. "What happened to you?"

Liana spun around and gasped. She ran over and fluttered her hands all over his body to check for more injuries. He winced when she touched his side, and she recoiled.

"It's nothing," he murmured, wrapping an arm around himself and over his camera.

"It is not nothing! You're bleeding!" Riley exclaimed.

He spat blood onto the grass and walked ahead. "I'm allergic to the outdoors."

She squawked in dismay. Liana scoffed and caught up with him in two strides. She took his backpack so he'd stop dragging it and took Riley's offered packet of tissues to dab the blood from his face. He didn't protest but he did take over when she was less than gentle around his nose.

"And your ribs are bruised because you fell down the stairs, is that it?" she said.

"Yep."

"On the ground floor?"

"They bite, you know."

"I'll take it from here, don't worry," she said to Riley, who looked like she was three seconds from calling an ambulance. Or grabbing a baseball bat.

"Did someone do that to you?"

"I've got this," Liana insisted gently, giving her a meaningful look. Riley's nostrils flared. He felt bad for worrying her or possibly triggering memories of her sister—hopefully she'd never been injured—but she didn't need to be so dramatic. He was only...

He looked at his blood-covered T-shirt. He zipped up his jacket.

Riley left only when they promised to visit the campus infirmary. Liana said nothing about how Felix's fingers were crossed behind his back or how they headed in the wrong direction.

At the mouth of the path Emilio died on, they passed signs of the three murdered boys' faces with the letters "R.I.P." underneath. There were flowers, notes weighed down by rocks, and arrayed mementos. Most were ripped, with protests spray-painted across their faces. Liana gently urged him forward with a hand on his lower back .

"Hey, Felix! Liana!" Nikolai hopped down the arts building steps and jogged towards them. Felix's breath caught in his throat. This wasn't his day, was it? He turned the other way and walked faster.

Nikolai slowed, shoulders sagging when he noticed he was unwanted. He looked heartbroken and guilty at first, but spotted the bloody lip and bruising nose and motioned his question to Liana. She could only shrug helplessly and jog after Felix.

"Okay, what was that?" she demanded.

"What was what?"

"Don't play innocent with me," she snapped. There was a minute flinch in Felix's step. She went on, softer, "You're avoiding Nikolai. Does it have something to do with last night? And are you—is that? Are you crying?"

He wiped his eyes. "No."

"Okay. Just stop."

She grabbed his arms. All five-foot-nothing of her held him in place with so much care and concern that he felt guilty for worrying her. He should have made up an excuse to avoid her and only showed his face when the bruises faded...

"You gotta talk to me. We're in this together, remember?"

His heart cracked a little more. He couldn't say it. The Executioner would get wind. He could picture it clearly. Another part of the campus sectioned off. Another son a mother would never see again.

"I, uh... I'm just falling behind, you know? With everything going on, I think I'm gonna fail my classes."

Her eyes narrowed, but thankfully she took what he offered. "We can deal with that. Follow me."

She led him to the library and situated them in one of the soundproof rooms on the top floor. People checking out books pointed, and those on the stairs turned right back around and fled upon seeing Felix. He ducked his head and masked his busted face with a tissue. Liana glared at the ones who stared too long.

The soundproof room's only window was the glass door. The room was small, with white walls and wooden floors, but large enough to fit a dozen people elbow-to-elbow around the round table in the centre. Liana drew the curtains over the glass door and hung an "OCCUPIED" sign on the handle.

"What're we doing here?" Felix asked, folding the wet tissue under his nose.

She dumped the contents of his backpack on the table and divvied up the binders and loose papers. "It's obvious, isn't it? I'm helping you do your homework. I'm not graduating this year without you."

Felix smiled bashfully and lowered himself onto a chair.

"Besides—" She pulled out a couple of cleaner tissues from the packet in her pocket and handed them over. "—I thought you'd like the privacy here in case homework isn't the only thing you wanted to talk about." When he didn't offer anything else and pressed the tissue to his nostrils, she took out a laptop and snuggled into the chair beside him with the college's login page displayed. "Let's see how far behind you really are, shall we?"

They stayed there for the rest of the morning. Liana went through his list of homework to make sure he remembered it all, proofread his essays, pointed out inconsistencies, submitted one paper as he worked on another, and upped the overall quality of his work. They both ignored their buzzing phones. His more so. It buzzed every other minute with a new text. Neither had to guess to know who it was from. He could only imagine how many more poll links he'd been sent between Nikolai's pestering. With Liana's help, he got more done that morning than he had in weeks. By the time noon rolled around he felt comfortable enough to just sit and breathe.

Liana scrolled through blogs and hummed about possible dinner options. She'd tied up both of their hair to get it out of their faces and now her ponytail was slipping. As he watched her dawdle, he wondered how to voice his concerns. Should he be blunt and get it over with? Maybe it was better to explain first...

"Liana?"

She hummed and pressed the like button on a photo of people playing volleyball with a giant white chocolate ball.

You know what? He should let her have a normal life, go to her tournament without worry and deal with this himself.

He blew his nose and winced at the shooting pain through his sinuses. He stared at the splatter of blood mixed with the mucus. He glanced at Liana's smooth, unmarked button nose and crumpled the tissue in his fist. No, if this was true, she was in danger by simply associating with him.

"About this Executioner guy killing people." She hummed again to tell him she was listening and muttered about Thai food. "Do you remember in the Cinema of Horror class, one girl said he could be in love with the idea that he's protecting the victims of the bullies?"

She stopped scrolling.

"I think whoever this is... is protecting me."

Liana closed the laptop. She was quiet for a concerning amount of time. "You know, that doesn't sound too ridiculous."

"It doesn't?"

"No." She sat back in her chair and scratched her chin. "I mean, it makes a strange amount of sense. Answers some questions. Why take odd socks and IDs off the bodies at all? There are faster ways to frame you. Lugging a bunch of bloody items into your bathroom is just asking for trouble."

His phone buzzed. Nikolai's name appeared on the screen. Liana raised a brow when he turned it over.

"Only he wasn't asking for trouble," she continued slowly. "He gave you that stuff to show that the murders were for you."

Felix crossed his arms on the table and rested his head against them. "Do psychopaths normally do that?"

"No, psychopaths can't form emotional attachment. They learn emotions by mimicry. They have a substantial if not complete lack of empathy. Mind you, there are different severity levels of psychopathy, and ninety-nine percent of them are just talented businesspeople or career driven. But we're talking about a minor percentage of this small group of people: remorseless predators who use charm and manipulation to get what they want. And a study could come out in a few years on empathy levels that will drive a wedge in the apathy fact. Anyways, a psychopath wouldn't care enough to do this sort of thing."

She suckled her bottom lip in thought. "Sociopaths on the other hand... I remember reading that it's difficult, though not impossible, to form a bond with select individuals. While it might not be comforting, that does de-escalate the situation in a sense. As long as you're okay, nothing else should happen. I wouldn't be surprised if you found something of Emilio's in your dorm tomorrow, though."

"I don't want to find his stuff anywhere," he muttered, poking a pen. "People call me 'freak' enough as it is. If anyone finds out I'm getting love letters from the Executioner..."

She leaned on her elbows to get a better look at his forming bruises. "Is that what your swelling face is about? Who called you a freak and used you as a punching bag?"

He waved the question away. "You have a volleyball tournament this afternoon, right?"

"Yeah. Coach is worried about one of the teams' nasty liberos, but I'll spike through all of her receives. There's no way she's as tough as Riley. What's that got to do with anything?"

"You don't want to go beating up a bunch of people before a big tournament."

"A *bunch* of people? Felix, who hurt you?"

He swatted her worrying hands. "Look, the point is, I'm fine. I'm not even that hurt; it looks worse than it is. So don't pop a blood vessel and focus on your tournament."

As long as the Executioner didn't get wind of his recent fight, they shouldn't have to worry. Based on the mildly fearful look on Liana's face, she came to the same thought as well.

He took her hands in his and lowered them to the table, rubbing his thumbs along her knuckles. "What do you say we play some video games and watch too many movies after you win?"

She hesitated, looking at his split lip. "I shouldn't go. Not if someone came after you. The team can do fine without me. What if this wasn't the last of it? What if they come back?"

Felix gave a broken smile and half-joked, "Don't worry, I've got a killer guardian angel."

Friend or Foe? Students Begin to Side With Killer!

Felix saw Liana off and waved until the bus was out of sight. He wasn't sure what he'd do for the rest of the day. He had no classes. Nowhere to be. He had an essay demanding his attention, but he'd worked so hard with Liana earlier that his brain was fried. At least he'd stopped bleeding.

A couple got out of their car and made a wide circle around him to get to the doors. The woman glared the entire way, sneaking glances at her boyfriend as if yelling at Felix, *"Why haven't you killed him yet?"* Felix shoved his hands in his pockets to avoid sending her a rude gesture. The man looked at him in disdain, like a bug that had inconvenienced him. Felix thought that he should turn that scowl to the conniving liar hanging onto his arm, batting her lashes innocently.

"She's the one you should be worried about, not me," he grumbled, kicking a rock.

He decided to spend his time taking pictures and avoiding the world, just like a healthy, functioning adult. Except his phone kept buzzing.

Nikolai could text all he wanted about the bruises he saw until his fingers bled for all Felix cared. He wasn't going to pick up the phone. It hurt to think about him and the things he said. And with Liana gone, Felix had no more distractions from the hole in his chest and the ache in his ribs—and he should turn that darned thing off already!

He retrieved his phone from the depths of his pockets and paused at the name of the newest text message. An unknown number. It read,

> I promise this isn't from some sock-sniffing weirdo. It's Sergio, from the club. I hope you remember me, or else this is going to be very awkward. I'll be on campus today and wanted to know if you'd like to hang out? Or not. That's fine too. Let me know!

Then,

> Or you could not do that. If that's what you want. That's
> fine too. If I don't hear from you in like three hours,
> I'll assume you've deleted this text and no hard feelings
> will be kept!

When had Sergio gotten his number? He didn't remember giving it to him. Nikolai sure wouldn't have. It was probably Liana.

He sent a quick reply informing Sergio where he'd be taking pictures. What else was he going to do today? Mope alone? Having some form of non-judgmental company wouldn't kill him.

He saved Sergio's number as "Sock Sniffer."

Sergio arrived at the tree line within half an hour, looking flustered and out of breath. His curled hair poked out beneath a pale, worn, knitted beanie. He wiggled his face out of his thick, also knitted, beige scarf to grin. His red nose shone in greeting. He didn't bring up Felix's busted lip, nose, or bruising jaw. He didn't give it so much as a look, as if he were too excited.

"Did you run here?" Felix eyed his open coat and the mitts sticking out of his pockets.

"What?" Sergio panted, bracing himself with his hands on his lower back. "No. No, of course not. Jogged, maybe. Run? Nah."

Felix motioned to the empty space on the rock beside him. He looked around through the lens of his camera as Sergio all but purred like a happy cat settling in. It was a half-buried boulder a couple of yards from a mass of tall, bushy trees on the edge of the college grounds. It stretched far enough with tightly-knit branches that mimicked a forest, despite only being two kilometres long.

Once he caught his breath, Sergio spoke. "Don't all the English students have an essay to write?"

"Yep."

Felix took a picture of the sun shining through the trees.

"You aren't going to go do it right now, are you?"

"Nope." He took another picture. "It's a stress reliever."

Sergio gingerly picked up the polaroid picture from the absolute corner, afraid that his fingerprints would damage it, and gaped. "*Wow.* It's really shiny, like some sort of magic. The sunlight is just—" He tilted his head and wiggled his fingers like a magician. "It's reaching out to you. Are there some ethereal beings doing some hanky-panky beyond those trees that I don't know about? Because wow, that's some shine!"

Felix laughed out loud at that, raising a proud smile to Sergio's face.

"There's that smile. You were stone cold when I got here, it's nice to see you haven't lost your glow."

He sputtered, "My glow?"

Now it was Sergio's turn to laugh. Felix rubbed his neck, hoping to quell the rising blush. "*Glow* sounds weird," he agreed, "but it is nice to see you smile. And the picture? It's good. I mean it."

Felix huffed in amusement and pocketed the photograph for his wall later. "Thanks. By the way, how'd you get my number?"

"Your cute short friend Liana sought me out of the crowd last night and gave it to me. I hope that was okay?"

Felix shrugged and went back to looking through his pictures.

"She told me you should have more than two friends."

"That sounds like her."

He wondered if she knew about the fight on the dance floor but dismissed it soon after. She would have said something. On that note, he was surprised Sergio had sought him out after Nikolai insulted them. Felix was prepared to never see him again. But here he was, sitting not with his friends but with a boy who had caused him trouble.

"No offence, but don't you have friends to hang out with?" Felix asked, trying his best to not sound mean.

"Their parents moved them back home because of the murders. What about you? Why're you sitting on a rock away from civilization?"

"I'm not avoiding them or anything," he stammered, then realized he hadn't asked that. "They're, uh, busy." It wasn't a complete lie.

Thankfully, Sergio moved on. "So you decided it was a good idea to voluntarily spend your time in a place where nobody can hear you scream? Aren't you worried about the psycho on the loose?"

"Sociopath," Felix corrected, remembering Liana's lectures. "If they even are one. And no, I'm not." Not when said potential sociopath was looking out for him in his morbid way.

"Don't you find this all a bit hard to swallow?" Sergio shivered under a breeze and zipped up his coat. He ducked his chin into his scarf, resembling a marshmallow. "Murders. Psychopaths. That name, the *Executioner*, for crying out loud! It's all stuff from comic books!"

"Preaching to the choir," muttered Felix, taking another picture of the trees' spindly shadows.

"Did you see the poll online?"

He tried to gauge where this was going by Sergio's tone but couldn't tell. Sergio appeared calm, pensive. But an underlying tension made his jaw twitch as if he was working something over.

He didn't seem like a bad guy. What side would he take? He wouldn't agree with the hundreds already using the poll, right?

"I did."

"Did you vote on a name?"

"No."

"Do you want to?"

"I think there's been enough bloodshed for a lifetime."

Sergio sighed in relief. "Thank heavens you aren't like the others. It's all the debate team would talk about! Mind you, it was three to nine, but still!"

"For or against?" Felix asked.

"Three for the serial killer, nine against."

"At least there are still some people who want him behind bars. I've been getting messages from supporters."

Sergio shook his head. "Yeah, I saw your profile. It's flooded. Don't check it. But don't worry, I swear if they were ever to come face to face with the Executioner, they'd be running with their tails between their legs."

At least Sergio didn't agree with them. That felt good.

Sergio put on his mitts and rubbed his hands together. "I also, sort of, wanted to hang out with you because of Emilio. I feel so weird. He's dead. Actually dead. "I still expect him to be lurking around some corner." His nerves reminded Felix of being in high school, where there was nowhere to escape. He tried to imagine a younger Emilio shoving Sergio into a locker but the image didn't fit. Sergio was too big, too strong. But then he recalled how small and scared Sergio had been when they first met, with essays scattered around and Emilio yanking the neck of his shirt. He must not have had a reprieve, unlike Felix. "I thought you might want to hang out for the same reason, you know?" Sergio continued. "Sit with someone else Emilio picked on. Try to come to terms with the fact this is real."

"How did you know he picked on me, too?"

He bumped his shoulder. "It's not exactly a secret. The whole campus knows Emilio wants you out of the way. Even more so when you stand up to him." He cleared his throat. "Or, stood up to him..."

Felix put down his camera to look at him properly. "You aren't in Photojournalism. Why'd he pick on you?"

"Because I'm gay."

"Ah! So you *are* gay!" The confirmation pleased him so much he didn't realize what he'd said until he heard it. He covered his mouth, gut in his knees. "I am so sorry, that came out wrong."

Sergio smirked. "Did you have your suspicions?"

Felix cursed himself and his red ears. "I—it's just—you asked me to dance, and there were so many other pretty women. Nikolai yelled at you, but you're still here. Sorry..."

Sergio laughed, and the sound loosened the grip on his nerves. "No reason to apologize, I get it. I don't fit the stereotypes from the movies or go out of my way to advertise it. I don't think sexuality should be the first thing someone uses to judge you. So I just act like me, and whoever figures it out figures it out. If they don't, they don't. It's usually not a problem."

"But then Emilio found out."

"Yeah." Sergio laid down with his hands behind his head. "When the murders started, I thought I'd be next, and Emilio would've done the stabbing. It's not uncommon. It happens all over the world. Anti-gay crimes went up eighty-six percent America-wide in 2017. Near the end of 2017, the UK stated attacks on LGBT people had surged eighty percent over the last four years. Want to know how it's doing now? I'll give you a hint: thirty-eight people were murdered in the first six days of 2018 in Jamaica. And those are just the statistics I found in the library. So many more are hidden from the public."

"That's horrible," he whispered.

"And I'm not even going to touch 2016." Sergio shivered. "It's a bit surreal. The guy who threatened to kill me if he saw me again was murdered. I don't think it'll sink in for a few days."

Felix plucked at a loose string on his coat. "If you want, you can spend those days with me."

Sergio visibly perked up and flashed him a brilliant smile. "I'd love that."

The two fell into a comfortable silence. Sergio watched the clouds while Felix marvelled at his courage. He was bullied, hated for being different, and scared for his life. Yet he didn't stop being who he was. He kept loving himself and those around him. Felix admired how he didn't fall apart.

"Do you want to go on a date with me?" Sergio asked.

Felix choked on his tongue. Sergio hit him between the shoulders to reboot his lungs. Felix winced and clutched his tender ribs. "I, uh, I'm sorry, I wasn't expecting that." He smoothed out his breathing and tried again. "I like you as a person. I think you're incredibly brave and funny. But I'm not in a position to give you the attention you deserve as a partner."

Sergio just smiled and went back to watching the clouds. "Ah, it was worth a try. Do you already have someone in mind?"

Felix's thoughts went straight to Nikolai, and his heart ached worse than his ribs. Why did his heart hurt? He wasn't in love with him. Just upset. He'd probably gotten kicked there, too. Maybe he should see a doctor.

Sergio grinned teasingly. "It's the guy from the club, isn't it?"

"No! No, I respect him a lot, is all. I'm not gay, nor is he. We've just been friends for a long time."

He snickered. "I wish my friends would rush to my side like knights in shining armour when they saw me dancing with strangers."

"He doesn't rush to my side. Not to Liana's, either. And she's got a new guy every week!"

"Maybe he doesn't look at Liana like that."

Felix remembered the turning heads at the club. The men's eyes tracking the women's every move, ready to drop to their knees at any moment.

"I think there's something wrong with me," he whispered. "I don't look at them like that. I'm not gay, yet when I look at women, I'm not as interested as other men are. They're beautiful, strong people, but they don't grab my attention. Liana can change in front of me, and I don't feel anything! And she attracts a lot of attention!"

"So, you're not interested in women." Sergio turned on his side to watch him play with his bracelets. "I'm not either. Would you say there's something wrong with me for that?"

"Of course not!"

"Then why should there be something wrong with you?"

That made him bite his tongue. Sergio's eyes crinkled fondly, and he said, "You don't get 'gay points' for every woman you ignore until you accumulate enough to evolve from heterosexual to homosexual. It isn't something you contract. You are who you are. And despite what society says, you're not broken for thinking differently."

Felix nibbled his lip and regretted it immediately. He spat out the taste of blood from his re-opened wound. Sergio winced for him.

"If you find yourself appreciating the sight of a hunk instead of the woman beside him, why fight it? Men are gorgeous! We're nice to look at! Ogle away!" Sergio sighed happily. "*I* certainly appreciate them."

Felix couldn't help laughing. With every new breath, a weight melted off his shoulders and left him a little freer. Sergio grinned along with him and watched a cloud shaped like a dragon sweep overhead.

"You don't have to label it," he added. "You can just *be*. That's the best part, in my opinion. You don't have to shout it to the stars or carry around an ugly neon sign so everyone else knows who they're dealing with. It doesn't have to define you. You can be *Felix*. And if Felix decides he likes men, that's great! If not, that's also great! Until then, you can just be you and be what may come from that."

Felix decided he rather liked this man.

They kept each other company a long time after that, and Felix felt better for it. He wasn't gay, nor was he completely straight. But he was what he was, whatever that was. And that was good enough for that afternoon.

They filled the afternoon with gloriously benign chatter, just basking in the comfort of a friend who *understood*. Only when the sun began to set did they say goodbye and promise to text later.

Felix went to the darkroom to develop his photos. He told himself it was for classes, but he knew it was an excuse to develop his own pictures, have some fun, and clear his mind of the day's events. He felt a giddy rush when he poked his head inside and saw no one inside.

He played music on his phone and went about his process. He took out the film, placed the negatives in the enlarger, focused and positioned the photo, made test strips, and moved onto the developer. One photo after another, into the developer fluid, into the stop bath, then into the fixer and up to dry.

He hummed to the music and twirled from station to station. There were no police, no dead bodies, or slurs thrown at him here. He bobbed and weaved his way to the drying test strips, to determine the length of time he should expose the full photograph and what grade filter he should use, and stared at the tests.

He hadn't taken those pictures.

He brought a red light closer and examined them again. He couldn't even figure out what they were, as he'd segmented the pictures into five-centimetre strips, as usual, and each of those segments progressed from having nearly no colour to so much colour that the end was foggy with shades of grey. The shadows were either too dark or too bright to tell what anything was.

Had Emilio or his goons stolen his camera when he wasn't looking to play some sort of prank? When could they have taken it? All of his cameras were always either with him or locked in his dorm. The only way they might have snuck it away was when he was working in the darkroom. Even then, he couldn't figure out when his things might have been taken.

He thought about trashing the test strips and going through the film to find his pictures, and focus on developing them.

But he couldn't peel his gaze away.

It was such an odd shape: one thing wrapped around another, yet it had sharp edges. He had to fully develop the photo, if only to satisfy his curiosity.

He chose which grade filter and time he thought would bring out a proper image and repeated the process. It was still too light on the paper, but he reminded himself the shapes would get dark enough to distinguish once in the developer fluid.

He waited beside the basins this time and watched the timer like a hawk.

Two minutes...

What could it be? Knowing Michael and Jackson, it had probably been shot down their pants. He shuddered.

Three minutes...

Maybe they filled all his film with silly faces so he couldn't use it for homework. That sounded like them.

Five minutes...

It was probably their shoe.

Seven minutes...

Just a boatload of wannabe sneaker promotions.

Eight minutes...

He tapped his foot.

Ten minutes...

His stomach began cramping. He winced as it made his bruised organs spark.

Thirteen minutes...

Could this thing take any longer? He chewed his nails.

Fifteen minutes...

He was beginning to doubt it was a shoe.

It didn't need more than eighteen minutes.

He almost knocked over the basin. He flailed to the edge of the counter to brace himself against a wave of nausea. That wasn't a shoe.

That. *Wasn't*. A shoe.

He gulped air. It had to be the fumes. He'd gotten too close to the chemicals, and the fumes were messing with him. There was no way...

He inched back to the developer basin, plucked the photograph from the liquid with a pair of tongs, and dipped it into the stopper bath. His brain was playing tricks. There was only dim light, after all. He swished it around in the fixer liquid and used the tongs to carry it from the darkroom to view it properly.

That was a foot. That was an elbow. And that was *a lot* of blood.

The picture showed the inside of his dorm elevator and a boy face down on the ground. His head—Felix yacked.

Clumps of hair clung to the drying blood along the edges of the elevator doors. Brain matter bulged in the cracks at the bottom of the doors as they closed around what used to be a skull, now only shards of bone and chunky stew. This was a prank. It *had* to be a prank. Emilio had got Michael and Jackson to recreate the scene to scare him and—Felix gagged. That hair still had skin attached to it.

He ran back inside the darkroom and developed the rest of the film. His stomach knotted more and more with every innocent hillside and forestry scene. He should've been relieved by every normal picture, but all he could feel was his heart throwing itself against his ribcage in fear that the next one might not be. The next one might have captured someone else's last gasp of agony.

The suspense was tearing him apart. Hot tears rolled down his cheeks. His fingers shook on the knobs.

He reached into the tub of developer fluid for the next photo. His tongs dipped into lumpy intestines, slimy with watery blood. He screeched and flung the utensils away. The gore was gone, replaced by another beautiful photo of someone lounging in a river.

He slapped his hands against the counter before his legs gave out. It wasn't real. It couldn't be. A small gathering of liquid on the countertop tickled the hairs along his skin. He glanced down at the blood curling around his digits and screamed. He stumbled backwards, wildly shaking it off his hands. As he moved away from the red lights the blood turned clear and dripped down his wrists into his bracelets as water. He choked on a disbelieving whimper and turned on his heel for the door.

He ran home as fast as he could. He burst open the lobby doors and almost fell to his knees seeing the elevator. He saw the body in his mind's eye. He saw the elevator doors opening. Closing. Opening. Closing. Each time with a stomach-churning *squelch*. Some people turned around in concern at the noise he was making, but upon recognizing him, turned up their noses.

Felix crashed into his dorm door and fumbled his keys. His vision was gradually becoming a blurry mess of tears. White-hot panic burned him from the inside out.

Get inside! Hurry up! I need to get away! I need to hide!

He pushed open the door and somehow kicked it closed behind him in his flailing. The strung-up photographs of friends and family chortled at him. The threads brushed through his hair like sticky spiderwebs. He tripped trying to bat them away and knocked over one of his crates, sending boxes and books crashing to the floor with him. The Polaroid around his neck clattered by his stomach.

Felix crouched there on his dirty floor for a while, head on his forearms, trembling. A few crumbs and dead bugs dug into his arms. Rhett's corpse in the photograph hung before his eyes.

"Go away! Leave me alone!"

He could imagine it turning its head to the side, mushy brain seeping out of the crater in its skull. A cackle floated past his hanging jaw.

How did it get on his camera? Who had taken that picture?

Emilio would never go that far, and Michael and Jackson would never do anything without his permission. He dug his fingers into his scalp to get the image of Emilio's twisted body and the look of terror on Michael and Jackson's face when he'd mentioned the Executioner. That madman had stolen his camera and taken that photo.

What should I do? There was no one to tell; Liana was gone, and he couldn't endanger Sergio...

He sat on his heels with a weak curse. That was when he saw what he'd knocked over trying to get into his room: his memory shoebox. Pictures from the past year were scattered around, chronicling the landscapes of places he'd visited and friends. A lot of them were shots of Nikolai. He had pictures of him smiling, laughing, and making silly faces while eating and dancing. All the happy times he'd wanted to look back on when he graduated and made it as a real photographer.

He picked up a photo he'd taken sitting high up in a tree upon noticing Nikolai below. Nikolai was looking up at him like he'd hung the moon and the stars. His heart stuttered. He turned it over. A bloody fingerprint smudged the date. The photo fell from his fingers.

The cold hand of dread gripped the base of his spine. He peered inside the memory box.

The Executioner hadn't gifted him a shoe or a student ID this time. Atop pictures of Nikolai and Liana's giggling faces were polaroids of Emilio's corpse. Up-close shots of his white bones jutting from his legs, covered in dried worms of blood. Of Trevor's soupy eye. Of the stab wounds that littered his body like holes in Swiss cheese. Of the fear, forever etched into their faces: the ghost of their last screams on their breath.

Felix overturned the box and let slip a hysterical cry. Happy pictures and memories were stained with bloody handprints, and streaks as if someone had petted their faces. How many nights had the Executioner broken in while Felix slept and taken the time to look through the box, painstakingly stash another bloody memento, and put everything away so nobody ever knew he was there?

Felix kicked the box. He crumpled up the polaroids and threw them across the room as he choked on a fresh wave of tears. He didn't want *this*!

A picture of Emilio stared up at him from under his shoe, his face contorted with the wild terror of an animal as he reached through wet grass like Felix had across the gym floor. His stomach acid curdled. That was taken while he'd been still alive.

That monster hadn't just killed those boys, he'd butchered them! *Slaughtered* them!

And then he'd brought the evidence to Felix like a cat dropping a dead bird at its owner's feet. The worst part: it wasn't even in cold blood.

When he'd toyed with their lives, it hadn't been for his sick enjoyment, it had been for Felix. All of it was for Felix.

He didn't want to be protected. Not like this.

He ran out of his room. Students pointed and yelped as he shoved through the lobby. One boy jumped in his way and shouldered him so hard he skidded down the front steps onto the pavement. He gritted his teeth against the pain that clawed up his arm and knee and exploded around his hips.

Their laughter echoed in his head. He couldn't stay down. He had to run. He clambered to his feet and spotted the bloody scrapes on his palms. A rush of nausea almost sent him back to the ground. He pictured the handprints on the photographs, the care in which the bloody hands held the silky paper.

It was all for him.

He wanted to scream. He could feel it searing his lungs and burning its way up his throat. It came out as a distressed sob. The students burst back into laughter—it mixed with the murdered boys' shrieks ringing in his eardrums and sent him running again.

He sprinted through slippery grass and potholes that threatened to steal his footing. The crisp autumn air shocked his burning lungs and nipped his tear-stained cheeks.

They were dead because of him. It was all his fault.

People, trees, and buildings flew by in a blur of colours. He didn't know where he was running to. All he knew was that he had to get away.

Felix recognized one of the buildings on the opposite end of campus, and before he knew it, he was through the doors, up the stairs and pounding his fists on one of the apartment doors so hard the skin on his hands split.

"Open up! Please, please open up!"

There was a scattering of feet. The door flung open so suddenly Felix almost fell through, but Nikolai was there to catch him.

"Felix?" He gasped, hair sleep-tousled and voice sluggish, but certainly alert. "What are you—what's wrong?"

Felix grasped fistfuls of his pyjama shirt collar, swaying. "I'm sorry. But Liana's gone. And I—The *photos*—it—"

Nikolai steadied him with warm hands on his shoulders. "Slow down. You're not making any sense."

"The photos!" he shrieked, coughing around more lung-wracking tears.

"The darkroom—the photos—dozens of them—I can't—"

"*Felix*!" Nikolai slid his hands up to cup his jaw and the curve of his neck. "You have to breathe, okay? Breathe for me."

Felix tried; he really did. It was choppy and panic-stricken, but he tried. Nikolai's thumb stroked along his cheekbone. His lips formed soothing sounds.

"I'm sorry," Felix hiccupped, staring up at those wide, concerned eyes. "I'm sorry. I know you're mad. I didn't—I didn't know where else to go. I didn't know what to do. I'm sorry."

"Breathe and tell me what's going on. I can't help unless you tell me what's going on."

"The Executioner," he whispered. "He killed them all for me."

The colour drained from Nikolai's face. Every muscle in his lean body stiffened. "Maybe you should come inside."

Felix was already rambling before Nikolai had even locked the door behind them. "You're not going to believe me. *I* hardly believe me, but it's true. I swear. I'm not making this up!"

"It's okay. Take it from the top."

Felix told him about developing evidence in the darkroom, finding more gag-inducing pictures in his memory box, the blood on the polaroids, how the killer had visited his room: everything. He was surprised Nikolai understood him through his snotty breathing and stutters.

Nikolai got increasingly paler, but he just kept stroking the back of Felix's neck and wiping away the tears. When he finished, Nikolai just exhaled shakily.

"I'm sorry! I know I shouldn't have come here but Liana's gone, and I panicked, and I know you hate me, but I just—" He was trembling now, and when Nikolai's hand stopped stroking his hair and he just stared at the bruise stretching across Felix's cheekbone with those wide eyes, his heart plummeted to the ground. "I'm scared."

Nikolai pulled him into his broad chest. All Felix could feel was the soft cotton shirt, his strong arms, and the solid muscle against his cheek. He could hear Nikolai's heartbeat pounding as if he'd danced for hours in the few minutes since Felix arrived. He smelled of laundry detergent, autumn apples, and *safety*, leading Felix to burst into tears again.

Nikolai squeezed him tighter than ever before and ran his hands through his hair. Felix was probably rubbing snot all over his shirt, and the cut on his lip felt like it had opened again—great, now there was blood smudged on the cotton too—but Nikolai didn't seem to care.

"I don't hate you." He cocooned Felix with his body like a shield and kneaded away the trembles wracking his spine. "I could never hate you."

"But at the bar...?"

Nikolai tensed momentarily, then relaxed and tucked him in even closer. "I was an ass and... out of line. When I saw you and that guy so close, it rubbed me the wrong way and all I knew was I'd left you alone, and you'd found someone else, and anyone could come up and hurt you or put something in your drink." This time it was he who shivered. "I got scared and I took it out on you. Everything came out wrong. I'm sorry."

"You don't hate me?"

"Never."

"You don't care that I danced with a guy?"

"All I could think of in that moment was that the Executioner killed men around you. A woman would have probably been safe. I was just worried about the guy being killed next and said some crappy things."

Felix sniffed and rubbed his sore nose on Nikolai's shirt. All this crying had aggravated his injuries, and now his nose was vigorously complaining about its treatment.

"Did you just wipe your snot on me?"

"Yes. You deserve it."

He chuckled. "I suppose I do." He leaned away enough to look Felix in the eye. "We'll figure this out. I promise. But right now..." He gently placed his smooth hand on Felix's cheek and thumbed away some dirt. "Right now, you're safe. You're with me. I won't let anything happen to you. No one can hurt you here."

Felix thought that was a monumental lie but smiled a bit anyway. Nikolai twisted to get a better look at Felix's scuffs and beatings and pursed his lips.

"How's about we get you cleaned up, and in the morning, when we're awake and not running on day-old-brain cells, we figure out what to do about the Executioner. Does that sound good?"

"Sounds like a plan," Felix croaked, the corner of his lips twitching upwards.

Nikolai led him into his bedroom and handed him an extra pair of sweatpants and a sweater.

He'd been in Nikolai's bedroom before. So often, it felt just as much like home as his dorms. More so, now.

The apartment was as dingy as you'd expect a cheap college apartment to be. The floorboards creaked; you could hear the neighbours at all hours of the night; the hot water came out of the cold knob and the cold water came from the hot knob; and the edges between the walls, floors and ceiling were littered with cracks, stuffed with caulk that seeped out in nasty bubbles. But Nikolai had shoved flimsy bookcases in strategic spots, covered the odd stain in the small living room with a couch he'd got off the side of the road, softened the creaky floorboards with rugs, and relabelled the faucet knobs. He made it work.

So when Felix walked into the bedroom, he didn't see the boring cream walls that the landlord refused to let anyone nail pictures into or paint over to make it feel less like a prison. Instead, he saw colourful posters of famous dancers taped between furniture like artistic spider webs. He saw inviting, happy bed sheets and the messy chair where Nikolai wrote essays while sitting on a throw cushion Liana gifted him.

Nikolai left to the bathroom to let Felix change in peace but kept the door open, just in case. When he returned, he had a washcloth and a large plastic bowl that they usually used for popcorn on movie nights filled with warm water.

Nikolai kicked his bed a few feet from the wall to avoid the leak in the ceiling and nudged an oddly thriving plant from the hallway to catch the water drips. He gently pushed Felix to sit on the bed and kneeled at his feet, soaked the washcloth and held out his hand.

"Show me your palms."

Felix turned his hands over and hissed as the cloth brushed his ripped skin.

"Sorry. I need to get the gravel out."

Nikolai was as gentle as he could be. He cradled Felix's palm with one hand and dug out the dirt and gravel with the other. He soothed the angry skin by carefully blowing on it. He used the cloth like it was delicate silk and Felix's hands were as precious as a prince's. As if he could read his mind, Nikolai pulled out some cream and childish Band-Aids from his pockets, grinning sheepishly at the ridiculousness of it.

"Sorry, it's all I've got."

Felix couldn't help but notice the dim lighting cast soft shadows along the sides of Nikolai's nose, making it longer and the bridge brighter. It accentuated his cheekbones and slimmed his cheeks. If their roles were reversed, Felix was certain he'd look sickly and starved under such lighting.

Nikolai tilted his head up with two fingers on his chin, and Felix was unprepared for the intensity of his gaze. Nikolai scanned every inch of skin on display. His eyes widened with every wound he saw, and if Felix wasn't mistaken, he got a little misty-eyed. His fingers hovered over his ribs as if he knew they were red and purple, and his hands began to shake.

Nikolai wasn't just concerned, he was pissed. He hid it very well, but they'd been friends too long for Felix to miss it. He could see the anger at those who'd delivered the blows by the minute flex of the muscles in his arms, the veins in his neck. He could see the anger with himself for not being there every time his face would twitch in the beginning of a scowl when he accidentally grazed an injury the wrong way.

Nikolai tilted Felix's jaw to get a better look at his busted lip. He let out a small, horrified exhale. "Who did this to you?"

"Emilio's friends, Michael and Jackson."

Nikolai's whole demeanour changed. His hands remained as gentle as they'd be with a porcelain doll, but the rest of him tensed with a lip-curling rage.

Before he could storm out and kick down their doors, Felix continued dryly, "Don't worry about it. As soon as the Executioner gets wind of it, he'll take care of them."

An odd flash of satisfaction crossed Nikolai's face before it was shaken off. "You shouldn't hope—"

"You think I'm hoping two more bodies get added to the list? For more blood on my hands? I'm just stating facts. The moment the Executioner finds out, they're dead men walking. And there's *nothing* anybody can do about it."

Nikolai's face twisted in guilt. "No, you're right. I know you didn't mean that, I'm sorry. I'm not saying there shouldn't be retribution—"

"You think I am? They could have put me in the hospital! I want justice more than anybody but a weakling like me can't get it by myself. And with these rumours, nobody is going to stick their neck out for me! My only option is this murderous asshole, and do you really think they deserve that?"

His harsh panting hung in the air. The ceiling dripped.

"They deserve..." Nikolai's jaw worked, eyes locked on a weep of blood Felix could taste on the corner of his mouth. "Punishment." He shook his head and gently pressed the cloth to the reopened injury. "I'm sorry. All that came out wrong. It seems to be a theme for me, eh? First the bar, now here. I sure am good at digging myself into ditches."

The self-deprecating smile and hopeful wide eyes nearly did Felix in.

He relented and hung his head with a weak apology for being snappy. Nikolai continued to pet his hair.

"We'll warn Michael and Jackson tomorrow, how about that?" He tilted Felix's head back up to flash him that knee-wobbling smile. "If they believe us, great. If they don't, we'll warn the cops—or," he corrected, upon seeing the wave of panic on Felix's face, "we'll keep warning them until they take us seriously."

Felix nodded. He could still picture Michael's terrified face, trying desperately to hold Jackson back.

"Hey." Nikolai thumbed his temple to get his attention. "Hot chocolate and a movie before bed? You can fall asleep halfway through, I promise."

Felix gave a weak chuckle. "That sounds nice."

They settled on an all-time classic British sitcom from the 70s that always had them in stitches, no matter how many times they watched it. Nikolai propped up his computer on his chair and loaded some online episodes while Felix made the hot chocolate.

This time, lying next to each other under the covers, sipping the hot drinks, the crazy acts on the screen didn't make them laugh. A chuckle was the most the on-screen hotel manager got for barking orders to get two dead pigeons out of the water tank.

Felix's mind wandered: going from what caused the slow drip in the ceiling behind them, to what kinds of positions people might find Michael and Jackson's corpses in, to the body heat radiating off Nikolai, and the possibility that no one might even find Michael and Jackson's bodies. Maybe they wouldn't be found for a long time. People would think the two had skipped town. There was a chance no one would question it. Until the attic started smelling funny, that was.

After the day Felix had, it was no surprise that sleep was already pulling him into its quicksand grip. He was so comfortable with the warm taste of chocolate on his tongue, tucked under Nikolai's duvet, and swaddled in the autumn and tart apple scents. It must be a shampoo, he wondered distantly. It was woven quite deeply into the pillow.

He forcefully blinked his eyes open and tapped Nikolai's arm urgently. Nikolai hummed in response and patted the back of Felix's hand.

"Rope," Felix grumbled. Boy, he was falling asleep fast. "I need rope to tie myself up."

Nikolai gingerly plucked Felix's nearly empty cup from his fingers and placed it next to his on the floor. He came back up with a tie. Nikolai didn't wear ties.

"When I found out about your sleepwalking habit, I bought some things to tie you up in case you wanted to sleep over and forgot your... cuffs and stuff."

A warm feeling washed over Felix's limbs, leaving a light tingly sensation behind.

"I got this because it'd be the least conspicuous thing to buy. I couldn't exactly go to a sex shop and get cuffs." The tips of his ears flushed a deeper red. "On second thought, maybe I should have just thrown dignity out the window and bought you cuffs. They'd be safer, right? Less likely to cut your circulation during the night. Hang on, I'm going to call an Uber and buy some handcuffs."

Felix grabbed his arm before he could leap out of bed. "It's fine," he murmured drowsily. "The tie is perfect."

Nikolai froze halfway out of the duvet. He cleared his throat and shoved the tie over. Felix grinned at his embarrassment and knotted it around his wrist. He fell back into the pillow and offered his wrist to Nikolai lazily, who looked at the joint like it'd started growing mould.

"Tie it for me? I'm too tired."

Behind them, a droplet of water splashed into the plant. On the show, the hotel manager stared in despair at a senile hotel guest casually walking into the bar with a loaded shotgun, muttering about rats.

Looking like he would have rather spared himself by going into a sex shop to buy handcuffs, Nikolai tied the end of the cloth to the box spring, leaving about a foot of room between the metal and Felix's wrist for comfort.

"What's making your ceiling leak?" Felix asked.

"Wha—Oh, the plumbing for the toilet."

"Toilet water is leaking into your bedroom?" Felix yawned. "Shouldn't your landlord do something about that?"

Nikolai tugged on the tie and made a satisfied sound. He caught Felix's eye and quickly let go. "I've been pestering him for four months now. I might have to take drastic measures soon."

"Sic Liana on him."

Nikolai laughed softly and wiggled back under the blanket to face him. "He's too young for grey hair. Let's not scar the man for life until he's done something truly despicable. Like not giving out candy for Halloween."

He could feel himself drifting, floating on a river, and let the stream carry him away. "Let's flood his room. Just a little. See how he likes it."

"Just a little."

He fell asleep to the sound of the sitcom manager screeching and the feeling of Nikolai stroking his jaw.

Public Hounds Police for Information

The first thing Felix thought when he woke up was that he felt terribly cold. He must have kicked the blankets off during the night. The second thought asked if he'd been hit by a truck. Because the more brain cells awoke, the more his body informed him how everything hurt. His head buzzed like a thousand bees had partied the night away in his skull. Body parts argued against moving, and his lungs could only suck so much air before complaining as well. It took him a second to remember why he felt like he'd been beaten with a bag of doorknobs.

Right. He *had* been beaten. Yesterday. With feet. Glorious.

Felix peeled his eyes open, and the third thought of the morning slapped him across the face.

Oh, *shit*.

Underneath him, Nikolai slept. The sunlight peeking from the window kissed his skin and made his cheeks look so cushiony that Felix had to refrain from touching them. Nikolai pouted in his sleep, his lips so soft and pillowy. But Felix couldn't think about that. Not when he was—why was he holding a mug over his head?

He was clutching one of the mugs that had been out of reach on the floor so tight his fingers were turning white. He shook his head, winced at the stabbing pain behind his eyes, and checked again. The hot chocolate-stained ceramic glimmered back at him. He looked at the tie, which should have stopped him. It was unravelled, hanging loosely on his wrist. That was when he fully noticed his position; straddling Nikolai's waist, about to swing a mug into his skull.

Everything clicked into place. Felix screamed.

He pushed away so violently that he fell off the bed. It felt like a bomb went off in his ribs. Nikolai shot awake and reached instinctively for Felix's side of the bed, frowning when he found it empty.

"Don't come any closer!"

Nikolai turned towards the voice and stared, slack-jawed, at the sight of Felix on the ground, waving his hands to ward him off. "Did you have a nightmare?" His hand brushed the fallen mug.

Felix sucked in a breath. He couldn't even make an excuse or yell, "It's not what you think!" because it was exactly what he thought, and it tore a chasm in his chest.

"No, no, no," Felix moaned. "Not you. Anyone but you."

He could still feel the cool ceramic in his palm: a solid, comfortable weight. He blinked, and his mind's eye soaked the bedsheets with sticky blood. What remained of Nikolai's lips were blueish in hue. His brain oozed against the pillow. There was a sickeningly sweet, rusted iron smell mixed with rank feces. He blinked again, and the hallucination vanished. Had he not woken when he did, it could've been real. He could have... to Nikolai...

Nikolai kicked the covers off to join him, but Felix out stuck his hand and scooted further back. "Stop!" He hated the way Nikolai flinched but hated that he needed him to even more. "Don't come near me!"

Nikolai slid onto the floor to be on the same level but obeyed his wish. "Something happened, and it scared you a lot. But you can talk to me. You know that, right?"

His voice—oh, his voice—it was honeyed with concern and comforting in all the right ways and the sound made Felix's heart break.

"I could have hurt you," he whispered. "I could have *killed* you."

"That doesn't make any sense." Nikolai reached for his foot, but Felix scrambled to his feet and dove for the door. "Felix, wait!"

Felix backed into the hallway. The rancid odor of uncooked meat clung inside his nostrils. "You have to stay as far away from me as possible."

Nikolai followed slowly, keeping a metre between them as promised. Felix backed into the couch's arm and almost toppled over. Nikolai tensed as if to jump forward and help, but Felix snapped, "I said *back*!" and he kept the distance.

Felix swore being stabbed a hundred times would hurt less than seeing the wounded look on his face.

"Don't you understand?" he croaked. "I killed them. All of them. *I'm* the Executioner! I murdered them!"

Nikolai missed a breath. Hot tears spilled down Felix's face.

"I can't do that to you. Not you. I'd rather die than hurt you."

The words were pulled from deep in his chest, a dark corner covered in dust and cobwebs he had barricaded long ago. Now a spotlight shone over it, leaving no place to hide. There was nothing he could do but face it.

"Oh, God. I'm in love with him," Felix said under his breath. He'd almost killed the man he loved.

"What're you—"

It was too late. Felix was out the door before Nikolai could finish his question.

Felix locked himself in his dorm. His heart pounded too fast. He gagged back rising stomach acid and hot chocolate. He was a fool. The answers had stared him in the face the entire time, but he'd been too blind to see. He paced, clutching his aching ribs. Sure, it wouldn't have been his first idea, but he was so... pent up. Angry. If he wasn't hindered by his consciousness' restraints of morals and responsibility, and his body missed the memo to paralyze—which was exactly what allowed him to sleepwalk—it wouldn't be such a farfetched idea that he would act on it.

He'd go to jail. No question. Once the police caught wind of what he'd almost done to Nikolai, they'd connect him to the previous murders and lock him up! He thought back to the morning he and the other residents had discovered Rhett's body in the elevator. Maybe it wasn't a bad idea to keep him in chains if it kept him from wandering.

He gripped the dirty kitchen counter. Who was he kidding? He couldn't go to jail for murders he didn't even remember! He didn't feel like he'd committed them at all! He couldn't be the only one going through this. There had to be others. Maybe even somebody who could tell him what to do?

He ran to his computer, typed 'Sleepwalk Murder' into his browser and clicked the first link he saw: an encyclopedia article.

"'Homicidal somnambulism, better known as sleepwalking murder, is the act of killing someone during a bout of sleepwalking.' Great. At least there's a technical term for it."

He went back to the browser and searched for real life cases.

Jury finds man guilty of murder in alleged sleepwalking homicide.
Florida man who claimed sleepwalking during murder is sentenced to life in prison.
Killer's sleepwalking defence fails to convince Jury.

There were over a dozen cases of homicidal sleepwalking. One man had driven twenty kilometres to his in-laws and used a tire-iron to bludgeon his mother-in-law to death. Another man had smashed his infant's skull on the wall, believing nightmarish beasts were attacking him. Some had been set free after trial, but most hadn't. All in all, he learned nothing that could help him.

He pulled at his hair. This was *ridiculous*! He didn't want anybody to die! He just wanted to graduate! He didn't hate his bullies enough to want to murder them so brutally.

Darkness filled his stomach and infected his body with slimy despair. This morning was proof enough.

He'd taken care of those who hurt him. Made the problem go away. Nikolai had broken his heart, and he almost made Nikolai go away. No matter what Felix thought while conscious, he couldn't be trusted unconscious. It wouldn't matter who he was when awake in the eyes of the law. All they would see was the murderer when he slept.

Rap! Rap! Rap!

Someone was pounding on his door. How did the police get to him so quickly?

Rap! Rap! Rap!

Should he let them arrest him? He didn't want to spend the rest of his life in prison! Should he jump out the window? He could live as a fugitive. Plenty of people had done it. He'd skip town, travel somewhere nobody knew him, and start over. But wait, he couldn't live in civilization. No matter where he went, he'd be a danger to those around him once night fell.

"Oh, quit it. You aren't a werewolf," he grumbled to himself.

His phone buzzed with a text from "Sock Sniffer." Sergio. Felix almost laughed. *Sorry*, he thought, *can't talk. About to be arrested for murder. Rain check on coffee?*

Rap! Rap! Rap!

Perhaps he should run away from society and live in the forest until he grew old. He could live off of berries and wild game.

"Felix, you limp noodle! Open this door!"

Liana. Not the police. He didn't have to live as a wild animal just yet. There was still time to figure out what to do.

He sighed in relief and unlocked the door. Liana stood, nearly engulfed in her poofy winter coat, her hip cocked, and her arms crossed with a grocery bag hanging off her elbow.

"I just spoke to Nikolai," she said, tossing her stuff on his bed and ignoring how every bone in his body locked up at the name. "He told me all about your little scare last night and the freak-out this morning. I can't believe you think you're this horrible person who murders college students. I brought you cookies."

She dumped a grocery bag full of cookies onto his sheets.

"We're both in agreement we should hide this from the police and the thousands of eyes on campus. It would be inconvenient if they found out and spread it around like the plague. Nosy little twerps. By the way..." She pulled a lighter from her pocket, flicked it on, and smirked. "I won the tournament. Now, let's burn some evidence."

"What?" Felix squeaked.

She crouched to gather the scattered photographs from his memory box. "Hand me that metal garbage bin."

He handed it over, stammering many confused words that couldn't quite string a sentence.

"Take your time, dear." She flipped through a stack and tossed the bloody photos into the garbage. "Thinking is painful."

"You spoke to Nikolai and you're still helping me?"

She gave him a funny look. "Of course."

"Why? I killed three people—*butchered* three people—and almost attacked Nikolai... I almost..."

She took his trembling hand, giving it a hard squeeze. "Because, whether this is somebody's twisted way of protecting you or not, you're still my best friend." She gave him a bright smile. "I don't care if you've cracked somebody's skull open, as long as I'm the one you call to help hide the body."

He laughed in disbelief. What had he done to deserve her?

She gave his hand a final squeeze and pointed to the memory box. "Now, grab a cookie and help me pick out anything that might be evidence. Can you check under the bed? I think I saw one under the bedpost."

After finding all the fallen photographs together, Liana had to take over checking his cameras when he found pictures of intestines. He turned away and retched as she deleted them. "Oh, gross," she commented offhand. "This one's got grass sticking to it."

"I really don't need the commentary."

"Sorry."

He stuffed clothes around the cracks in the door once again to keep the fire alarm from going off while she burned the binned photographs and directed the fumes out the window. *We should be concerned about how easy it's become to get rid of evidence*, he thought.

He hugged his knees in a corner by the cupboards and watched the smoke dance before vanishing in the crisp wind. It reminded him of the tricks smokers would perform to impress each other.

"You said you spoke to Nikolai," he said, eventually. "Is he mad?"

Liana coughed and tilted the bin a bit more out the window. "No, he's not. Well, maybe a little because you two fought. It's mainly what you said before you left that confused him."

Once the ashes burnt out, she put them in the plastic grocery bag for the trash across campus.

He swallowed around a lump. He felt like an army was charging at him from all sides with their weapons raised and their battle cries echoing against the stars.

He said in a small voice, "I'm in love with Nikolai."

Liana took in his tiny form, his chin on his knees and his fear-filled eyes. "I know," she said softly before walking over to hug him.

"We're Doing Everything in Our Power!" Police Vow to Solve Three Slayings

Felix took multiple days off. He spent the time locked in his room, staring at the walls and thinking. The first day, Liana agreed he should stay home to process. She alerted his teachers that he wouldn't be attending class and took notes for him. The second day, she understood he was still shaken and didn't press. She cooked him dinner, reminded him to eat, and left him to his thoughts. He didn't tell her what he was thinking about, nor did he tell her how his mind was unravelling.

The once-happy faces in his strung-up pictures now snarled at him.

"Murderer!" they shouted. "Monster!"

He didn't fight them. He had three bodies under his belt. If he'd woken up a moment later, there would have been a fourth. He would have been responsible for the death of the most important person in his life. If Nikolai died, Felix wouldn't be able to live with himself.

He thought long and hard about his next move as he stared at the wall's haphazard old paint job. It warped into images of his victims' twisted bodies. He couldn't bring himself to look away. It didn't matter if he managed to peel his gaze away from the contours in the paint that morphed into the curve of Rhett's bruised back or the bumpy texture that mimicked Emilio's torn muscle tissue. They were screaming at him anyways.

He pressed his hands to his ears. Now that he was aware of his crimes, he couldn't keep the protective walls his subconscious put up from crumbling. The wet suction of pulling a hammer from soft flesh played on a loop. The victims' shrill, pleading voices echoed against his eardrums and marked their words upon his flesh. He couldn't have Nikolai's voice join theirs. He was too important.

In the end, he was left with only one option.

Felix gave Liana his key after he'd failed to hear her shouting and kicking his door for ten minutes.

"Have you got cotton in your ears?" she scolded when he'd finally opened the door, her glare hot enough to melt iron. Felix blinked a couple of times, unaffected, and mumbled an apology.

"I brought your lecture notes from today." She had placed her backpack on his desk and pulled out folders. "I told your teachers you were feeling under the weather. They send many happy thoughts and good regards and blah, blah, blah. How you sit through those droning classes is beyond me. You have the patience of a thousand-year-old monk. Oh, Sergio says hi."

She'd turned back to begin explaining his assignments and faltered. Felix stood behind her with his arm outstretched, a key in his open palm. She looked like he'd lodged a javelin through her chest, and though his stare was as hard and cold as an emerald gem, it was plain to see what he wanted.

"I'm not locking you up."

"Yes, you are."

"The door locks from both sides. Giving this to me won't stop you from leaving if you want to."

Felix's smile was as hearty as a cracked doll. "I won't be leaving. I'm going to chain myself up. Properly."

She scoffed. "Don't be ridiculous, Felix! You aren't an animal!"

"Just do it."

She threw up her hands. "What about classes? Think about your future! If you don't show up to classes, you'll never graduate! Lock yourself up in the evenings or—or go home and let your parents take care of you if you're so worried!"

"I can't risk falling asleep in the middle of class or while waiting for a bus. I can do my assignments here until I get this under control. Going home will just put my parents in danger. This is what's safest for everybody."

"Don't do this—"

"Take the key, and—" He imagined Rhett's tiny gasps and saw his body twitch with each blow, the only action he could make on that cold metal floor. "And don't let Nikolai inside. Use it if you need something, but promise me—" His outstretched hand shook. "—promise me you won't let Nikolai inside."

Liana stared at the key. Finally, she deflated and slowly placed her palm over his, holding his hand. "Fine," she whispered, not looking up. "What do you plan on doing by yourself?"

"Stay awake."

She looked pained by his answer. "You can't stay awake forever."

He smiled sadly and pulled away, leaving the key in her hand.

Day after day, Liana checked on him to make sure he was eating and taking care of himself. Most of the time, he was so out of it that he didn't know she was there. She cooked simple snacks and small meals and left them on the counter.

They were starting to pile up.

"All I have to do is stay awake," he mumbled to the night. "He'll be safe if I stay awake."

Liana threw away the food containers. She stopped cooking. She switched to coaxing him to drink water after he cried, and actively feeding him nibbles of anything she could get past his lips.

All Felix could do was stare. Sometimes he cried, silently. He sat on the floor in a growing pile of empty cans of energy drinks and coffee, with his ankles and one wrist chained to the bed using his leather cuffs and rope. He could feel the coolness of the hammer's handle, the weight of the branch. The wet, sticky feeling on his hands would never quite rub away. The world revealed itself to be a dark place, and that darkness preyed on his crumbling walls.

"Don't you dare fall asleep."

He was a monster.

"You *have* to stay awake."

Liana and Nikolai continued to take turns bringing him his lecture notes and homework, but most of them lay untouched where they'd slipped them under the door. Nikolai knocked and called to him each time. Felix closed his eyes and bit his trembling lip to keep himself from responding, to block out his voice. All he wanted was to open that door and throw his arms around Nikolai. But he couldn't. It was his turn to protect him.

Hearing him come back day after day, sounding so heartbroken and sad, tore Felix apart. He cried harder those nights.

"Don't fall asleep."

Per Felix's request, when they came together, Liana never let Nikolai inside. Sometimes he could hear them arguing about it beyond the door. There would be a lot of shouting, many accusations, and too much pain in their voices for him to bear.

One night Nikolai couldn't handle it anymore. "Why?! Why won't you let me see him?"

Liana's voice was as impassive as a wall. "You just can't. Stop asking."

"I can *help*!"

Papers shuffled underneath the door. "No. You can't."

"Let me at least try! He's my friend too, you can't cut me from his life like this! Let me see him!"

Liana snapped, "He's in love with you, dipshit. Seeing you will only make it worse."

Nikolai stopped coming after that. And to Felix, the world had never felt so cold.

Police System to Screen Prank Calls "Not Fast Enough," Shopkeeper Says After Student Break-In

Nikolai poured every ounce of frustration into his dance. He didn't care if his pose was sloppy or if nothing flowed into a perfectly choreographed routine. He just needed to move. His feet came down hard and bounced right back off to spin. He threw himself into the air as if it could dislodge the stones weighing down his heart. He landed badly, and a lightning bolt of pain shot up from the ball of his foot through his calf. He hissed and stumbled against the mirror. He stayed there for a while, massaging his foot with one hand and leaning against the cool glass, letting his gasping breaths fog up his rosy reflection.

Felix loved him.

The thought kept coming back and making him dizzy with the implications. This introverted boy, with his keen eye for striking stories and his stunning, silent bravery, liked him.

He knew he should be flattered. Instead, he felt guilty. Having a crush on someone should be a thrilling experience: something cute to look back on. But Felix had felt none of that. He'd suffered.

Nikolai couldn't stop thinking about the look on Felix's face that morning in bed. He'd been terrified. He'd looked so sick with himself Nikolai thought Felix would vomit. That was a week ago. He hadn't visited Felix since finding out about his crush.

Besides, he had no idea what he *could* say if he did see him. Replying to his confession was out of the question. He wasn't even supposed to know about it.

The only thing he did know was that the thought of Felix being the killer was ridiculous. Hearing the muttered accusations between classes was so infuriating that if he heard them while walking Felix across campus, he might blow up and scare him.

It physically hurt being apart. The updates from Liana didn't satisfy him, as that hole in his chest would only be filled by seeing Felix in person, but he'd take what he could get. Liana made it abundantly clear he would only make matters worse. Maybe that was true.

But he couldn't sit around doing nothing. The last he heard, Felix hadn't left the dorm to get groceries and his cupboards were growing cobwebs. Liana was too busy to go shopping for him and didn't dare leave campus in case he needed her. The shops should be open after afternoon classes. He decided to stop by Liana's with fresh groceries.

He glanced out the practice room window and spotted her on the grounds heading to an afternoon class. He scooped up his backpack and phone and dashed out before she could get too far.

He caught her just as she was entering the language arts building. "Wait up!"

She gave him an odd look. "Where's your coat?"

"What're you talking about?" He puffed and patted his flimsy, sweat-drenched t-shirt. "It's in the practice room." He'd been in such a rush he'd forgotten. "It doesn't matter. How is he?"

Her shoulders sagged. She continued to trudge up the steps. "He looks like a zombie."

He jogged after her. "Is he eating? Sleeping?"

"Probably not. He's drugged up on so many energy drinks that I'm surprised he isn't vibrating. I convinced him to attend his classes today, at least the mandatory ones like the test he had."

Finally, some progress! Nikolai was about to express his delight, but she slumped against the railing.

"He flunked it. He said he didn't know a single answer. It was on historical photography! He should have aced it!"

Seeing her groan under her breath dropped a lead weight in his chest. He'd rarely seen her show her anxiety so openly. Felix was precious to him, but Felix was Liana's childhood friend. It was hard enough twiddling his thumbs on the sidelines, so it must've been agonizing for her being unable to do much else than ensuring Felix got through the day.

He wished he could put him in a bubble and protect him from his own mind.

"He's going to be okay. It'll get better." He tried to sound optimistic.

"I hope..." She paused and leaned away from him. "You stink."

"I know. Where is he now? Still in the arts building?"

The need to ask if he could walk Felix back to the dorms was strong but the self-preservation that came with not wanting to be kicked down the stairs for the suggestion was stronger.

"He's back at the dorms." She shot him a glare, as if knowing what he was thinking. Nikolai quickly backed off with his hands up in submission.

She continued, "I snuck him a pair of real handcuffs from Police Foundations because he was so scared of breaking out of his bonds yesterday." She dug her fingers into her scalp, and Nikolai could have sworn he heard her voice crack. "I feel awful for leaving him chained to his bed like that, but it's what he wanted."

"Liana…"

"It's all this stupid Executioner guy's fault! There are better ways to protect Felix than to let him believe he committed those horrible crimes! He's convinced he's responsible, and it's tearing him—" She couldn't finish.

He plucked the lint in his pocket to avoid looking at her. "Have you heard from the police?"

"Yeah. Apparently, they don't like being called useless turds."

He looked up. "You did that?"

"Of course! If they'd catch the real killer already, Felix wouldn't be beating himself up like this!"

Nikolai placed his hand over hers and forced a smile. "I know. It'll happen. It's just a matter of time."

She sighed and squeezed his hand back.

"By the way, how did you get the cuffs?"

She cracked a grin. "I know a guy."

"Limber?"

"Ambidextrous."

He laughed. "That's where my investigation ends. Let me know if there's something I can get Felix. I'm gonna stop by the store and get you two some food tonight."

Liana thanked him and waved goodbye. As the old building's thick double doors closed behind her, his phone rang. A jolt of hope that it might be Felix nearly made him drop the mobile, but it vanished upon seeing his parent's name flashing on the screen.

He answered. "What is it?"

An angry Russian rant welcomed him. "What embarrassment! If you're determined to stay at Hell's college, the least you could do is dance correctly! We saw yesterday's recording on school's news page! You looked like flailing goose!"

The familiar, prickling barbed wire of anger flushed through him at his father's berating voice. He waited for the feeling to settle into the dry, blazing heat of the desert sun that would sharpen his voice and his rumble in his chest. It always came when dealing with them, and it always itched for hours afterwards.

This time was different.

"You whined and whined to dance at that wretched place, and *that* is result? How do we show faces in public? What if neighbours see?"

This rage was a tsunami. Waves of emotions backhanded him and stung his eyes with tears. Years' worth of pent-up feelings rose with so much power that he gripped onto the railing for support.

"I don't care if the neighbours see. I don't care if the whole of Russia sees. You know why? Because it has nothing to do with them. It is my life, and I have decided I am going to spend it dancing because it makes me happy. I realize, deep, deep down in that cavern you call a heart, you are concerned for my well-being, and you want me to succeed in life. However, I am not an accountant, I never will be, and you need to cope. Take a lesson from a damn kids' movie: if you don't have something nice to say, don't say anything at all. If you cannot do that and insist on remaining a toxic, abusive leech, I will cut all ties just like you did when I was sixteen. And this time, I'll make it stick. Goodbye."

He hung up. Somewhere, in the back of his mind, his younger self cheered.

The class was supposed to be working on their upcoming performance in groups of six. Key words: *supposed to*. Put a bunch of anxious, "I'm-so-tired-coffee-runs-through-my-veins," jittery art students in one room with black walls, a black floor, a black ceiling, a gigantic mirror, and one stuttering overhead light, and they'd do anything *but* whatever they were supposed to. A girl with straight ginger hair got spooked by her own shadow and screamed. That caused the two girls closest to scream and the poor man lifting the ginger into the air to nearly have a heart attack and drop her in favour of protecting his ears. Nikolai sighed and watched as two groups came to comfort the fallen girl and the poor man before they began to argue over whose fault it was that the ginger had fallen.

He wasn't the only one observing. In the corner, a group of performers huddled together, mimicking eating popcorn at a theatre, and clung to each other when the light flickered again.

Nikolai envied the one team still working—or trying to. They fumbled, stepped on each other's feet, and didn't dare perform the jumps but scuttled along regardless. His team had long since forgone practicing to gossip amongst each other, leaving Nikolai to practice tying knots with a tie he'd brought from home and watch college TV by himself. He wanted to read one of the books he'd borrowed from the library, but he'd read them all. He made a mental note to get more soon.

A man yelped when the light flickered, claiming his partner teleported. A pair cheered as their friend twerked on someone trying to hold a handstand.

Finally, one of Nikolai's teammates babbled something interesting. "The police can't figure it out! It just stopped!"

"It's been, like, a week. Do you think we're safe?"

To his left, another group member snored.

"Thank you for that riveting contribution."

A guy with cactus-like spiky green hair said, "He can't be done that quickly. Remember the way he killed those three assholes? It was brutal! There's gotta be more from him!"

The girl beside Nikolai played with her sweatband, reminding him of Felix. "Maybe the killer skipped town?"

He swore he knew their names. At one point. Right now, it just wasn't coming to him.

Cactus shook his head. His hair, amazingly, didn't sway. "There's way too many names on those 'Kill Me Next' polls. He hasn't left."

Nikolai hated those polls. The first one got taken down, but no matter what, more kept popping up. Why people would encourage this horror was beyond him.

They'd even made a new type. Now you could vote on who you thought was the Executioner. He swore the school was going to divide into factions.

Cactus grinned and slithered next to an unsuspecting girl. "Maybe he's waiting for the perfect moment. Choosing the right victim. A final duel between him and the police where he'll *strike them all down*!"

The girl jumped with a small cry and shuffled away from Cactus' cackling.

So many heads, but so few brain cells...

"Someone shut him up before I do," muttered Nikolai. The girl with the sweatband smacked Cactus upside the head.

The group in the corner huddled together again under the next light flicker, but were less frightened this time, all immersed in whatever was playing on one person's phone.

"In all seriousness," Nikolai said, calling his group's attention, "are the police stumped?"

The first girl piped up. "Yeah. The murders were so close together, you know? One after another. And suddenly... nothing."

Sweatband Girl shrugged. "Maybe he got it out of his system? Got the guys who he wanted gone?"

"Stab! Stab! Stab!" said Cactus.

Nikolai's phone chimed in his pocket just as a couple of the people in the corner gasped and pointed at something on the tiny screen. "They don't even have a suspect?" he asked, pulling it out.

"Trust me, sweet cheeks, it would have been on social media. That isn't gonna stay hidden."

The guy on his left snored in presumed agreement.

Nikolai unlocked his phone. It was an invite to watch a Facebook Live broadcast. He clicked the link and waited for the page to load. It was Felix. He was slumped under a stone walkway overhang, surrounded by people with their phones out. Jackson and Michael were there too, but they didn't look happy about it.

Felix's complexion was as dull as ditchwater, doing nothing to help the bags under his eyes. His once warm, shining brown hair stuck up oddly on one side, as if someone had grabbed a fistful. What was going on?

Jackson lunged and punched Felix across the face. Nikolai jumped and nearly shouted right there. He clamped a hand over his mouth and watched Felix clutch his camera to his chest. *You idiot!* he wanted to yell. *Protect yourself, not the plastic!*

Michael kept to the wall, looking ready to vomit, but didn't stop Jackson from hauling Felix upright like a doll and hitting him again. Nikolai inhaled sharply. *What the—why was this happening?!* Felix slammed back down onto the unforgiving pavement. A string of bloody saliva hung off his lip. The crowd inched closer. Phone cameras flashed. *What was wrong with them?! Why wasn't anybody stopping it?*

He bristled as he recognized three art journal club members in the crowd. They made no move to intervene. Just watched. They were supposed to be Felix's friends!

Jackson's lips moved. Nikolai heard no sound. *Volume, moron!* He fumbled to unmute and gave the stretch of Jackson's pale lips a voice.

"Look at me!" He dragged Felix to his feet by the lapels of his shirt, making Nikolai bite back a snarl. "You think this is funny? Sending us this shit?" He tossed Felix to the cement like a trash bag, snatched a wad of papers from Michael, and threw it in his face.

The camera shook. It got hard to see what exactly the papers were, only that Felix recognized them immediately and scrambled away. The camera zoomed in. It wasn't paper, but polaroids. Dozens of polaroids of Emilio's body. Up-close pictures. Nikolai swallowed around a bitter taste.

"I didn't do this! I didn't send these!" Felix tried to explain.

But Michael was tired of being a bystander. He grabbed a fistful of Felix's hair and shoved his head down, forcing him to look at the pictures. "Liar!"

Felix shut his eyes tight. "I didn't do it. I swear I didn't do it. Please let me go."

Michael didn't have the same rage Jackson did. His bulging eyes and gritted teeth reminded Nikolai of when he was a child, scared to death over the tales of Baba Yaga his parents wielded to keep him in line.

"What did I tell you? Run across the street like that again, and Baba Yaga will break your legs and roast them over a fire," they had told him.

"Eat your dinner or Baba Yaga will have you for dinner."

"Listen to your Mama or Baba Yaga will visit you tonight."

Michael looked like a man who had caught a glimpse of Baba Yaga and would give his life to unsee it.

"You didn't do it? Look at them!" He thrusted Felix's head down. "It had to be you! Who else would be sick enough to do this?!" Felix cried out in pain, and Nikolai clenched his phone at the sound so hard it almost flipped in his grip.

Felix didn't do it. There was no way he did. If they'd just *listened* to him, they'd understand.

Jackson kicked Felix in the ribs. Nikolai could hear the impact through his phone speakers. The dance group in the corner flinched with him.

He had to stop this. He could barely hold his phone still as Felix groaned and curled into a ball on his side. He didn't recognize the archway. The audience blocked any landmarks that could have hinted their location.

Jackson spat on Felix's face. Nikolai's blood roared in his ears. He brought the phone to his nose trying to glean anything from the background.

"It wasn't you? Bullshit!" Jackson scoffed, nudging Felix's bruised side with the toe of his boot for emphasis. Felix cried out. "You're the only loser that carries around a stupid camera like that!"

"Wait, wait. Don't. Please, don't!"

To make his point, Jackson scooped the instant camera from around Felix's neck and hurled it into the stone wall. It shattered. The group in the corner winced sympathetically.

"That's it." Nikolai marched towards the dancers and thrust his phone screen in their faces just as Felix yelled in protest at the next crack of plastic. "You're watching this too, aren't you? Tell me where they are."

They looked at each other in alarm, guilty for witnessing the bullying and doing nothing. They shrugged. Not guilty enough.

Nikolai yanked the guy whose phone played the live video by the collar. "Where. Is. He?"

He dangled on his tiptoes, wide-eyed. His quivering lips gave way to no sound. Only a graveyard would've been quieter than the room was now. Everyone stared. Felix cried out through the phone speakers. Nikolai twisted the shirt in his hand, earning a gurgle.

A girl with braids near the wall spoke up. "They might be by the old greenhouse. Y'know, the one by the eastern dorms? I saw vines on the stone and around the archway. That's the only place I can think of that looks like that."

Nikolai let the boy down. "Thank you."

She nodded. "Good luck."

Felix lived in the eastern dorms, so it made sense why he would be by the closed-down greenhouse. Michael and Jackson must have intercepted him on his way back from classes and dragged him into being their next circus act.

By the time he found the greenhouse and the archway where the livestream was filmed, the crowd had already dispersed and Felix was nowhere to be seen. Michael and Jackson, however, were engaged in a heated discussion next to one of the many blood spatters, pointing and shoving each other. Right now, that was all Nikolai needed.

"Hey!"

Michael and Jackson turned around and cursed. Nikolai pounced.

There was nothing graceful about violence, no code or honour as fairy tales would have people believe. Nikolai bit the arms that grabbed him, kicked the boys between the legs, and punched while they were down.

All he could think of was Felix, the pain that had strained his voice and how his body had contorted to protect itself. It wasn't fair. It wasn't his fault!

"How—dare you—touch him!"

He kicked Jackson into the wall and whirled on Michael, baring his teeth in a snarl. Michael jumped out of the way, wiping his bloody nose, and put his hands up in submission.

"We weren't supposed to hurt him," he croaked, slowly backing up. The broken camera crunched under his shoe. "I told him. I warned him the Executioner would come if he did. We were going to talk to him, that's all. But Jackson." He glanced at his wheezing partner's bloody knuckles. "The Executioner's gonna kill him. He's gonna kill him." He shook his head, muttered an apology, and ran away.

Nikolai didn't feel the fist that connected with his jaw or the tackle that swept his feet from under him. He rolled them both over and punched harder. Again and again, until Jackson could do nothing but react to the pain, just like Felix had.

Felix must have felt so alone, surrounded by all those people who never lifted a finger to help.

I should have been there.

"Nikolai! Get off!" Liana sprinted towards him. She grabbed his shoulders to pull him off. "Stop!"

"No!" He shoved her and fought to get a grip on Jackson's clothes. "He hurt Felix! He deserves it!"

Liana wrapped her arms around his torso and yanked him as hard as she could. "You've done enough! You're going to kill him!"

For the first time, he actually saw Jackson. His face was littered with cuts and welts. Strings of blood stretched across the expanse of angry skin. He couldn't open one eye. Blood was smeared down his neck from trying to protect himself. He lay coughing and gasping for fresh air, not bothering to get up.

Nikolai fell back against Liana. "I saw the video," she said, panting against his back. "Sorry I'm late. It took me a while to figure out where this place was."

He watched Jackson cough up a red bubble. "You're just in time."

Nikolai disentangled himself and gathered all the camera pieces. He doubted he could fix it, but he wanted to try. He walked back and stood over Jackson. Jackson tried to squirm away but seized, grasping his side, and went rigid.

"You're never going to bother Felix again," Nikolai said. It wasn't a threat. It was a statement.

Jackson struggled to nod, and Nikolai walked away hand-in-hand with Liana.

Jackson ended up at the infirmary. His wounds weren't going to kill him, but he sure acted like it, according to some peeping students. Still, he didn't say who had beaten him up.

Felix wasn't there. He must have fled to his dorm room. Every bone in Nikolai's body screamed to barge down the door and take care of him, but Liana stamped that flame out quickly.

"He wants you to stay away from him, remember? He's learning to deal. Seeing you will only tear apart his efforts."

Nikolai huffed where he sat hunched over on the counter like a child as she wiped away the dried blood on his upper lip with a wet tissue in the men's bathroom.

"Besides, you have an upcoming performance, don't you? You need to focus on that. Get busy. The busier you are, the less time you have to worry."

"I can't even go see if he's okay? Look through a window?"

She poked his nose and smirked at his pained yelp.

"No peeking. If this is what Felix needs, we will respect his wishes."

"Yes, Mom. Why are we in the men's bathroom?"

She dabbed some blood from a cut on his cheekbone. "Because if we do this in the women's, you'll get beaten with a broom for being a pervert. I, however, am fine here."

A man walked into the bathroom, saw Liana, and made a U-turn, muttering apologies.

"See? This isn't unfamiliar territory to me."

Nikolai took the opportunity to bat her fingers from his nose. "You'll see him, then, right? Make sure there are no broken bones?"

There was a yelped apology from the women's bathroom and the sound of a very confused, very flustered man scurrying away."

Liana pinched his ear and scolded over his whining, "Of course I will! What kind of question is that?"

"Ow. Pain. Ow. Liana. Pain." He rubbed his sore ear. "Y'know, I'm grateful you're here. I could do with a little less harsh loving, but still. Thanks. For everything. Taking care of him while I can't. Stopping me from injuring that jerk any further. Honestly, I'm feeling pretty useless right now. But you? You're a superhero."

She smiled fondly. "I'll always be around for my boys. Now, you get on to class. We can't have both of you failing."

"He's *failing*?"

"Shoo! Shoo!"

Liana was right. Working on his performance choreography made it easier to deal with being away from Felix. It sucked all of his energy, sure, but it also took his attention away from the ache in his chest. And in his face.

He danced with his group the entire day. One look at his bruised jaw and cut cheekbone after seeing him storm out of class motivated them to actually work. It wasn't his intention, but at least he didn't have to wrangle them.

He quickly became exasperated with the cautious glances, however. To lighten the mood, he tried to get to know them and make them laugh.

He learned that Cactus Guy did have a name, though Nikolai teasingly refused to use it. Sweatband Girl's name was Evangeline, and she had amazing spinning jumps. The crew loosened up after a while, and soon Nikolai didn't have to force himself to relax. They bantered light-heartedly while working themselves to the bone to make their performance perfect.

During the breaks, lunch hour and dinner, Nikolai tinkered with the camera parts. He got most of it back together. The lens was smashed, and a lot of the outer shell had to be duct taped back together, but with enough online diagrams and visits to photography professors and engineering students like Riley, it didn't look half bad.

He caught a look at his injuries in the mirror as he slid under Cactus's wide stance and swung to his feet. He wondered how Felix was doing, if any of his injuries were serious. He toyed with the idea of visiting the infirmary in case Liana checked him in. He quickly boxed the thought away when Evangeline let herself drop three metres from the ground and braced himself to catch her properly.

"You worked yourself to death back there!" Evangeline commented breathlessly. She winced at her choice of words and muttered an apology. Nikolai lazily waved it off.

The others gathered their bags and lumbered out the studio doors, chugging water bottles. Nikolai lay on his back on the floor like a starfish, trying to catch his breath.

"I hope I didn't push you guys too hard."

She made a show of downing some water, already heading out the door. "What? Work hard? Us? Nah! You gonna lock up?"

"When I suck my soul back into my body."

She bid him goodnight and disappeared into the hall with the rest of the dancers. He took his time towelling off and changed into clean clothing. He forced himself to slowly drink his water as he turned off the lights and locked the door on his way out.

The autumn air felt wonderful on his hot skin. His body felt pleasantly heavy. If it weren't so dangerous, he'd be content to fall asleep under a tree.

He wasn't the only one. As he walked through the cluster of campus shops that students affectionately called "the Market" to get to his apartment, he spotted someone leisurely strolling ahead. This person had given more thought to the sleeping outdoors thing, since he was actually dressed for bed. He had a matching shirt and pants with cute sleeping sloths all over the fabric. *Strange for him to be out without a coat,* though,

Nikolai thought, watching the person turn the corner out of sight. *Whatever. I shouldn't forget the food.*

There was a shortcut to the big brand grocery stores through the Market. It cut through student housing backyards, but as long as Nikolai didn't kick over their trash cans, it wouldn't be a problem. If they got spooked thinking he was the Executioner and called the cops on him, even better. They'd be delighted to escort this poor, tired college student and his groceries to the safety of Liana's place. Maybe he *should* kick over someone's garbage.

Hang on. Didn't he know someone with sloth pyjamas? Didn't Liana buy Felix a pair as a joke one year?

He jogged over and looked past the shop the person had disappeared behind. Nothing but crushed beer cans and store trash bins. Odd. He kept walking.

He saw him again—or someone—three stores down, bending over to pick something long and thick off the ground. How did he get there so fast? Before Nikolai could get a good look, the person ducked into an alley between two coffee shops. Nikolai quickened his pace, ready to call out to get his attention. It was too dangerous to be out alone!

Hypocrite.

He heard a thud. Someone groaned. Nikolai peeked into the alley and saw two people crouched on the floor, almost as if cuddling. Oops. He spun back around and rubbed away the blush creeping across the back of his neck. Those two were fine, doing something a little different than cuddling.

He could make a detour to the grocery store. Not a problem.

He cut across a small, wilting garden, and there it was again: that thump. There was no accompanying scuffle, no harsh breathing. Silence.

His stomach knotted. He should've heard something, right? He wasn't that far from the two, and it wasn't like they needed to be too discreet. People weren't shy about hooking up in the alleys since everyone knew the cameras were pointed at the shop doors. So why was it so quiet?

Against his better judgement, he tiptoed back to the alley and peered around the corner. He hoped he wouldn't see somebody half-naked.

A figure stood over a prone body, lifted a plank of wood over their head and swung it. The dim light of a shop lamp caught the corner of the wood in the arc and gleamed off the dripping blood.

Felix was in the area. Was he the one holding the plank? Or the one on the ground? Nikolai cursed. It was too dark to tell.

He dropped his bags and dove to catch the plank. He realized too late that he wouldn't be able to, so he twisted, hunkered slightly, and braced himself. The wood hit his back so hard it forced him to his hands and knees over the body. Searing pain exploded across his shoulder blades and deep into his muscles. His knees ground into the gravel.

He bit his tongue to muffle the cry of pain and gasped to control the tears that sprang forth. He heard the plank clatter and feet slapping the pavement, but when he managed to lift his head...

"Felix?"

There he stood in the shadows a couple yards away, in his adorable white and brown sloth PJs, with a ripped cloth knotted around his wrist. Was he the one who'd attacked? He had to have been. He was the only one here. But Felix could never! Maybe it was self-defence?

Oh shit. Did I just protect the Executioner?

From so close, Nikolai finally got a clear view of the body, and his hands chilled. It wasn't the killer. It was Jackson, knocked out cold—or so he hoped. The side of Jackson's head bled profusely. Bits of torn flesh stuck out amongst his sticky hair.

Nikolai stumbled onto his feet, ignoring the protesting cramps of pain. "What do you think you're doing, Felix? You could have killed him!"

Felix's face was devoid of emotion, his eyes unfocused and glassy. The beating he'd received looked worse in person. There was no telling if Jackson had added any new injuries since the broadcast.

He saw the pyjamas better under the light; once an innocent set, they were now stained with blood. Had Felix snapped?

"Say something," Nikolai pleaded in a whisper. "Did he attack you again?"

Felix picked up the plank and readied to swing, muttering about home runs. Nikolai's heart thudded to his knees.

"Wait! *Stop!*"

He grappled the wood from his hands and tossed it to the other end of the alley. Felix calmly turned to fetch it.

He recognized this oblivious, dazed state. It was the same as when he'd woken to find him dancing in the rain.

"Hey, wake up. You're asleep! Wake up!"

He gripped Felix by the shoulders and spun him around. He shouted his name, but Felix only twitched. He ducked under Nikolai's arms.

"Wait, no! Stop!"

Nikolai grasped the back of his nightshirt before he got too far and tugged him back. They both tripped over Jackson's legs and pitched sideways into the wall. Nikolai jerked Felix securely against his chest as his own head whipped into the brick.

He groaned and blinked stars from his vision. He flexed his hands against Felix's lower back to get the feeling back in his nerves. Felix squirmed with the touch like it tickled and inhaled sharply.

Felix propped his chin on Nikolai's chest and squinted at his face, actual thoughts swimming behind his eyes. His voice was groggy like it usually was when he woke, and he did that nose scrunch Nikolai always liked. "Niko—Wh-where?"

Felix was back. It was a relief, but Nikolai did not relax.

He and Liana were wrong. Small, innocent Felix was the Executioner. He'd actually killed...

They were in a lot of trouble.

Felix looked around in rising panic. Nikolai had to tighten his hold around his waist when his knees buckled. Felix made a strangled protesting sound and pushed away like Nikolai's touch burned him, barely catching himself on the opposite wall. Nikolai ignored how that made his heart twist.

"N-no. I'm—where?"

The lost look in his eyes made Nikolai want to wrap him in his arms and protect him from the world, but it didn't matter what he felt. He needed to take care of this before anyone opened their window and saw them.

He steeled himself for more rejection and stepped forward, pointedly not looking at the blood seeping into the ground. "We're in an alley in the Market. I need you to focus."

He tried to keep his voice level for the both their sakes. If he freaked out, then Felix would lose it, and it would all be over. Someone would call the police and they'd take him away.

"The Market," Felix echoed. He gazed at the night sky, jaw slack. Then he saw Jackson's body and looked like he choked on a mixture of a scream and a sob.

"He's alive! He's still breathing. But I need you to tell me if he saw you. Did you hear me? He's alive. Just tell me if he saw you."

Felix stared at the blood pooling around Jackson's head. Felix's hands, the soft skin of his palms still dented from gripping the wood, shook.

Nikolai's grasp on calm began to slip. "We don't have much time. I need to know if he saw you. Felix? For God's sake, *listen* to me!"

"I didn't mean to," Felix moaned. "I-I didn't—I'm sorry, I didn't mean to." He reached for Jackson's body and teetered.

Nikolai cursed. He wasn't hearing him!

He gripped Felix hard by the shoulders and crowded him against the wall. "Listen to me! Did he see you? *Did he see you?!*"

Felix yelped. Nikolai hated the tears pooling at the corners of his eyes. "I-I don't know! I don't know! He could've, maybe not! I don't know!"

Nikolai released his punishing grip now that he was paying attention. He brushed Felix's sweaty hair away from his face, running the other soothingly down his side. "Okay. It's okay, just sit here for a second. I'll take care of it."

He gently lowered Felix's small, trembling body to the ground. He snatched up his coat from where he'd dropped it and wrapped it around Felix's shoulders.

"I was eating ice cream," Felix muttered miserably. "I was chained up, and had the alarm for every hour and everything. How did I even get out of the dorm?"

Nikolai rifled around Jackson's pockets, pulling out his keys, wallet, and phone before removing his watch. He wiped his prints off and tossed them in the nearest trash bin.

Felix's wide puppy eyes followed him up and down the alley. "What're you doing?"

"I'm making this a robbery instead of another Executioner attempt." He wiped off the end of the plank Felix had been holding and rejoined him. He knelt and held out his hand. "What do you say we get out of here?"

The offer promised more than an escort home. As Felix's clammy hand slid into his, he entwined their fingers. *They aren't going to catch you*, the action assured. *I won't let them.*

They got halfway through the Market before hearing footsteps.

Students? No, nobody would be out this late. If it were Friday or the weekend, then maybe. Tuesday night didn't exactly scream "nightlife party time." Police, then? A faint brush of light brightened a stop sign two blocks ahead. Nikolai dragged Felix behind a bookstore stall and covered his mouth.

Nikolai peeked around. He could've been wrong, in which case he'd be embarrassed. But the universe's sense of humour decided to throw them to the hounds.

Two policemen rounded the corner, talking quietly to each other. Their flashlights bobbed every other step. Nikolai eased back.

"Police?" Felix whispered.

"Yeah. Two of them on patrol."

"We should be fine, right? We're just two students coming home. As long as they don't find the..." He looked shamefully at his bare feet.

As long as they didn't find the body, two college students walking around campus in the dead of night wouldn't seem too strange. If they were discovered, they could lie their way out of the situation.

The body.

Felix couldn't say it. It'd be implying—admitting—to a fourth murder. That Jackson hadn't survived.

"Whether they find Jackson or not, we shouldn't let them spot you," Nikolai said.

"Why?"

He pointed to Felix's bloody cuffs and the spray on his shins. His front was ruined after wiping his sticky hands across his belly. The borrowed coat did a brilliant job of hiding none of it.

"Oh."

The murmur of voices grew louder. Nikolai risked another glance. The cops were just over a block away.

He lowered his voice further. "I don't think any of Liana's tricks can get those stains out. I love the sloths, but as soon as we get back to your place it's got to go. Dead giveaway."

Felix glared at the pun.

"I'm coping, okay? We're lucky you didn't step in—" He motioned to the blood smears. "—more of that, and leave footprints."

He could use himself as bait and draw the police away. He wasn't the one covered in blood. He checked his clothing. Scratch that. Cushioning Felix's fall earlier had transferred the mess.

So he couldn't go up to the cops and chat. No problem. There were other ways to get people's attention. He knew the Market's twists and turns like the back of his hand. It was risky, but for a chance to turn them around, he'd take it.

He turned to share his plan and saw the tired droop of Felix's eyelids. "I'd rather distract them myself and give you time to sneak away, but...."

He lightly smacked Felix's cheeks when he yawned. "Obviously, I can't leave you alone. Stay down."

He could discern their conversation now, complaining about drawing the short straw for the night shift.

"Josie's mad enough that I'm gone weird hours of the day," one cop said. "Now it's all hands on deck to catch this murderer, and I'm stuck out here walking in this creepy neighbourhood at zero-dark-stupid. I swear, one more night shift and she's going to go live with her mum!"

Time to improvise.

Nikolai grabbed a small rock, checked to see if the cops were looking, and threw it down the road between two coffee shops. The rock skipped. It rolled. It stopped in the open.

The flashlights bobbed closer. Nikolai's skin crawled. It hadn't worked. No trash or noisy bins to strike and draw them away.

"The moment I see that psycho, I'm shooting him. Law be damned. I want this over with."

"Even if it's a kid?"

"Whoever tore up those poor boys ain't a kid. I don't care what age he is. A kid is innocent. The Executioner is a freak of nature and needs to be put down."

They'd kill Felix? No questions asked? He'd thought they'd just arrest him! Felix mirrored his fear and huddled closer.

The voices grew louder.

Think, Nikolai, think! They could crawl, keeping the stall between them and the cops as they passed. That could work, if the policemen didn't hear the gravel shift under their feet, lean over the stall, or spot two obvious moving shadows. The flashlight began to eat up the night's dark protection.

He pressed Felix further into the darkness in a feeble attempt to hide him. Time was running out. He had to come up with something! Anything!

They were sitting ducks, waiting in terror for the monster to sniff them out of hiding. They could run, but they wouldn't get far. A gun would be trained on them in moments.

One of the cops kicked a rock. Felix bit back a pained sound as it skidded under their stall and struck him in the leg. It was the size of a tennis ball, jagged and chipped. Nikolai dove for it. He pitched it as hard as he could down a path away from them and flattened just as the flashlight passed over their stall.

His heart pounded so hard he feared the cops would hear.

Don't find us, he prayed. *Don't take him away from me.*

There was a sharp crash and a woman's scream. Two others joined in. The flashlight doubled back. Boots crunched on gravel. The footsteps receded.

Felix stuck his face under the stall and watched the police hightail it towards the screams. "Nice job breaking that house window."

"I was aiming for the trash can."

They encountered no more patrolling officers on their way to the eastern dorms. It seemed the cops didn't see the need to call backup, a win for Nikolai and Felix.

As they circled the dorm complex to reach the main lobby, they noticed one of the windows on the ground floor was open, its bright lights shining onto the grass.

"Is that your room?"

"Probably." Felix grumbled.

"At least we know how you got out."

Nikolai hardly recognized the mess that was supposed to be a hospitable living zone. It was littered with empty energy drink cans, stray headphones, video games, ice trays, ticking clocks, and nests of clothes and blankets. Felix confirmed it was indeed his dorm room and heaved himself inside. He hissed like a rattlesnake at the strain. It seemed attacking Jackson exacerbated his injuries .

Nikolai helped him over the chipped ledge. "Not going through the door?"

"I locked it."

It also had a chair blocking the handle from turning. Apparently nobody had thought to barricade the window as well.

Nikolai climbed inside and made sure to lock the window. Almost immediately, he stepped on an empty energy drink. He had to brush away multiple torn, dangling strings of photographs to get anywhere. It felt like he was crossing a jungle. A post on the bed frame was broken in half, with splinters sticking out at odd angles. The handcuffs Liana had given Felix hung off the wood.

Felix rubbed the scrapes on his wrist and the bone of his thumb thoughtfully. "That's why it hurts."

"You did not get super strength in your sleep and bust the bed frame."

"Bold of you to assume my unconscious self cares about my health. The post is old and not even half an inch thick, anyway." He dragged a hand down his face, not looking like he was in any shape to argue, so Nikolai dropped it and nudged the clutter with his shoe to make a path to the bed.

"You're lucky you didn't break your thumb. I'll help you tie yourself up properly, come here."

"It's not safe for me to be around you. What if I end up—"

"When was the last time you properly slept?"

Felix looked genuinely confused for a moment. "I'm... not sure. What day is it?"

His heart twisted. He smoothed over the bedsheets and patted the pillow. "Sleep. I'll wake you if you start to sleepwalk again, okay?"

"I said it's not safe."

"I don't care."

He extended his hand and smiled, silently begging Felix to trust him. After long deliberation, he allowed Nikolai to guide him into bed. Nikolai stifled a pleased grin and fetched them both a spare change of clothes from the wardrobe.

Then he found the fuzziest socks to warm Felix's feet and bound his ankle to one of the bedposts using some rope, making sure he had room to shift positions. Nikolai switched out the ripped cloth on his wrist for the handcuffs and tucked a scarf he found on the floor between metal and skin as makeshift padding. He was careful of his bruises and any hidden sensitive skin from today's beating.

Felix inspected the knotted rope in impressed surprise. "You've been practicing."

Nikolai blushed and fluffed the pillow under Felix's head, pretending not to notice the flush in his cheeks. He turned off the lights except for a lamp on the desk and sat at the foot of the bed, unsure what else to do.

"This is kinky," Felix joked weakly.

Nikolai chuckled at his poor attempt to alleviate the tension.

Felix's gaze turned grave. "You should go. You saw what I'm capable of doing while asleep. It isn't safe around me."

"Stop it."

"I'm serious. Go back home."

"I'm serious too!" His already cracked walls of calm exploded like a broken dam, and all the anxiety, worry, and fear bottled up ever since the first murder reared their ugly heads to the biting air of reality. "Stop pushing me away! I hate it! You don't get through something like this by isolating yourself. Let me help. Let me stay by your side!"

Felix's breath hitched.

He blinked back tears and avoided his eyes. "From now on, during the day, tell me when you get tired, and I'll watch over you. No matter where you are or what time it is, call me and I'll come." When he didn't respond, Nikolai whispered, "Please. Let me do this."

"Okay," he said weakly.

"Good. That—good. I was expecting more of a fight, honestly."

Silence.

"Oh, uhm..." Nikolai dug through his bag and pulled out Felix's camera. "I tried to fix it. Keyword being 'tried.'"

Felix gingerly took the duct-taped, hot-glued, scratched camera and stroked the plastic in awe.

Nikolai rubbed the back of his neck sheepishly. "The parts are all back together. There are two or three bits we might have to order, according to the internet, or call in a favour from some of the engineering students. And the lens is obliterated, but we can get a new one easy enough. It should turn on. Maybe. It might spark, but I can fix that."

"Thank you." He had the happiest grin Nikolai had seen in a long time. "You know how my mom isn't really the sentimental type? She gave this to me the day after I got my acceptance letter from the college. Despite her toughness, she's the one who encouraged me to go after the starving-artist career I loved so much. She told me she'd be right there, cheering me on, every time I took a picture so I wouldn't get homesick." He traced its lines and ridges. "If I hold it tight enough, I can almost picture her with me, lending me some of her bull-headed strength. I thought after Jackson smashed it against the wall, it was gone forever."

He remembered Felix's scream when the camera had been ripped from his arms.

"Nothing's gone forever," Nikolai said, quickly turning away before the cheesiness made him blush any harder. "You should, uh, go to sleep. Get some rest."

When he turned back, Felix was asleep hugging the camera. Nikolai allowed himself a little smile. He pulled the covers a bit higher around him and settled onto a pile of blankets on the ground.

Felix woke a few times, jerking himself out of nightmares as his handcuffs clattered against the bedpost. Nikolai was ready at the smallest sound of distress with something warm to drink and soothing words, running his hands through his hair until Felix fell back asleep.

Nikolai would be a bit tired come morning, sure, but it was worth it to see Felix's squished face so peaceful on the pillow and the little curve of a smile under his touch.

He couldn't help eyeing the broken post.

Hospitalized but Alive! Survivor of the Executioner, or Victim of Robbery?

The following day, Nikolai kept his promise and escorted Felix everywhere. From the dorms to classes, into which Felix began slowly reintegrating, Nikolai was there with a protective arm around him. It made them both embarrassed and giddy, but neither would say anything about it.

What Felix hadn't expected was how Nikolai even tied his ankles to the desk for him. Nikolai laughed when Felix gasped and glanced around to check if anybody was looking, making it more likely people would.

"Settle down, I'll be done soon enough."

Felix jerked his leg away when Nikolai rucked up his jeans and squawked indignantly when he pulled it back. Goosebumps rose on whatever cold skin he touched.

"I can do it myself, let go."

"But I can do it for you."

Felix sputtered and looked around quickly to see if anyone overheard. "Shh! People will see!"

"Let them."

He beamed victoriously when Felix slumped over his desk with a tomato-red face. He made quick work of the rope he'd brought.

"This is horribly intimate and you're just—You—Ugh..."

Nikolai merely grinned and enjoyed Felix's flustered state while it lasted. He covered the rope with Felix's jeans and patted his leg. "I'll be back after your class ends. See you!"

Felix glared, but he was too adorably red to take seriously.

In the hall, Nikolai's smile dropped. He pulled out his phone and dialled Liana. "We need to talk. Meet me at Felix's."

He was unlocking Felix's dorm room when Liana stormed into the lobby waving a poutine container threateningly.

"I told you to stay away from him! If you don't respect his boundaries, so help me I will—"

"Relax, he gave me his key when I dropped him off at his lecture this morning."

That stopped her short. "He voluntarily went? I had to drag him to take that test the other day. How did you get him to go?"

He had to strong-arm the door against the clutter on the other side. "He's been chained up one way or another from the moment he left the bed this morning. It seems it's the only way he feels safe."

She shook off her surprise and stabbed a finger at him. "Wait, no, don't turn it around. You'd better have a good reason for going near him!"

He held the door open. "You want to come inside."

He closed the door behind them and told her about last night: finding Felix in the alley, Jackson's assault, faking a robbery, and the police's hostility. By the end of it, she wasn't hungry anymore.

"He murdered those boys." She braced against the counter. "I didn't believe him. I thought he was just scared."

"He is, but I don't think he did it."

She tore her gaze from the messy room, expression pained. "I know what I've been saying the whole time but you have to face the facts."

"I am! Look at this." He showed her the broken bed post shards in the trash before she dumped her poutine into it. "Apparently he'd cuffed himself to the bed post before falling asleep. He is not strong enough to break it himself."

She frowned and gave one of the other posts a tug. "Maybe he had a hammer nearby or something?"

"I searched this place top to bottom last night. And I know you wouldn't have left him with anything dangerous."

She shrugged and leaned against the wall, sighing. "I don't know, maybe it was weak to begin with. He's been chaining himself up to it all year. You saw him in the alley. You know what those guys had been putting him through."

"Yeah, but he was sleepwalking!"

Her head snapped up, piercing him with such a sharp look he felt like he was at gunpoint. "You know about that?"

He got the impression he should choose his next words carefully.

"A while ago I found him... dancing in the rain. He showed me his restraints and his scars."

"Definitely one of his tamer moments," she muttered under her breath. "And what do you think about that?"

He felt naked under her scrutiny.

How deep did the bonds between childhood friends go that, despite believing Felix killed three people, she was still defending him? And against Nikolai, of all people? Felix was lucky to have someone like her on his side. How many fake and toxic friends had she sussed out over the years?

He could worry about her opinion of him later.

"I think it just means we've got to watch his back," he said. "Also, it doesn't matter—"

"Yes, it does!"

"No! I don't care if he belly dances or recites Shakespeare in the shower. He's still Felix! You're missing the point! He couldn't have murdered those people because he was asleep. It must have something to do with the person who was with him. They could've been framing him or using him."

She straightened. "What?! Back it up. You saw someone else? Who?"

He threw his hands up. "I'm not sure! I *think* someone else was there! Maybe? It was so dark, I don't know!"

If only he'd gotten to the scene faster, then he could've gotten a better look. Or stopped the attack completely.

He forced the window latch open and shoved the glass up to get some air. "I mean, do you really think our sweet Felix—malnourished and bruised so bad he wheezes—is strong enough to break a bedpost and brutally murder three people? And almost a fourth?"

There was silence for a moment, then Liana joined him, sighing. "People have been known to do unimaginable things when backed into a corner... but no."

"And it's not like sleepwalking turns you into a supervillain with mega strength. He couldn't have busted out on his own."

"What was he doing in that alley, then? It can't be a coincidence he was there."

She leaned too far forward and her hands slipped on the ledge. She jerked back with a hiss. Her palm was cut.

Nikolai winced for her and scavenged for band-aids. "Not surprised. This place is a mess. Part of why I wanted you to come here."

"To help you clean? Wow." She rolled her eyes and thumbed her blood off the windowsill. "Hang on, forget the band-aid. Look at this."

She pointed to a nick in the wood where she'd cut herself. The paint was shaved and chipped, like someone had gotten a blade caught while scraping the paint.

"Pass me a knife," she said.

"I'd say no to that on a good day."

"It can be a butter knife."

"Not much better." He handed her one from the kitchen.

To his confusion, she jumped out the window and had him to lock it behind her. Then she wiggled the blade between the cracks, nudging the lock. It took some effort, but the knife jammed the latch at the right angle and unlocked it. She let out a muffled cheer and heaved the glass up.

"Wow, this place needs better security," he whispered to himself.

She brushed the new paint and wood shavings into small pile. "The scratch marks are from someone jimmying the latch, see?"

"How do you know how to do that?"

"There was a serial killer who only killed people who didn't lock their doors at night. As a kid, it made me wonder if our house could be burglarized, so I tested every place we moved into. Also, Felix used to lock himself to very strange things and needed help getting free."

Her face fell. She looked at the shavings again. "That means someone let Felix out. They probably broke his bedpost too."

He was right. Felix was innocent.

That was not comforting. Someone was trying to lure him. Why?

"You're thinking the actual Executioner too, right?" he said.

"That, or if Felix is the Executioner, it's some fan who wanted their idol free."

Nikolai glared. She put up her hands, backing off.

Or maybe she was partially right. Could it have been one of the Executioner's fans who believed it was Felix and tried to show their devotion?

What was this? A morbid fairy tale? That couldn't be the reason.

Since Felix didn't keep any of the evidence, it was more likely last night was a desperate attempt to directly connect him to a crime scene. Either way, the pair couldn't just sit there.

"We have to tell him. Once he knows he didn't kill those guys, he'll snap out of his depression," Nikolai said, already hopping between piles of cans and clothes and balled-up paper to reach the door.

"You have proof?" Liana drawled, crossing her arms.

"What do you mean? You were the one to point it out."

"It's not enough. Felix is known to be crafty while asleep. He'll still take the blame. We have to present him something he can't deny."

He threw his hands up. He understood that changing Felix's mindset wouldn't be as easy as flipping a switch after being tormented by others and his head for so long, but this was ridiculous! Who wouldn't jump at a kernel of hope?

"What, does he want to go to jail that much?" Nikolai asked.

"No, he's that scared he'll hurt you."

All his strength fled to spark in his chest with such ferocity he was afraid it would burst, his mind wiped cleaned except for...

"You," she'd said. Not "us."

The reminder of Felix's feelings left him reeling. It shouldn't have. He'd known for a while. But he couldn't help it. Everything felt different now that he knew Felix liked him back. It scrambled his stomach into knots and his grasp on everything important went out the window and—

Liana gawked. "Did you just have a gay panic?"

"I didn't. It's not like that. I'm not gay," he insisted, though even to him it sounded feeble. "I just..."

"You're just in love with a man who *is* gay." She blinked, seeing him in a new light. "Holy... how did I not know? For how long?"

"Too long." He gripped the ledge. "This isn't about me, it doesn't matter as long as Felix still believes he's at fault."

"Okay," she said slowly, then went on firmly. "Okay. Well, whatever evidence we give Felix has to be strong enough to make a cop have doubts."

"Like what? The killer's identity?"

She pursed her lips. "At least a small suspect pool."

He sat on the bed, putting his head in his hands with a sigh. 'Not even the cops have figured it out. How are we supposed to?"

"The mental health of someone we love is on the line, we don't have a choice. Let's start with understanding last night. The Executioner likely went after Jackson for beating up Felix. Probably would have done it earlier, but Felix holed himself up."

"To either frame Felix or show his dedication in person," Nikolai said, shuddering.

She slowly lowered herself onto the desk's edge, thumbing her chin. "They have to be someone close to us. Someone on campus who's aware of the daily gossip and news."

"A student? A professor?"

"That's a huge suspect list."

They tried to narrow it down by going through the online polls and threads. As expected, ninety percent was bogus conjecture. Nearly everyone hated at least one of the victims.

"Felix doesn't exactly go advertising where he lives," Nikolai mumbled to himself. "There are many dorm complexes on campus, and they're not close to each other. How'd the Executioner find his?"

Without looking up from the discussion thread on her phone, Liana paused nibbling her nails to say, "If it's a professor, he could probably steal Mrs. Rosewood's dorm manifest. She'd have Felix's accommodations on file. If it's a student, they could've easily followed him home."

"In other words, that's not an angle we can use."

"Nope," she said, popping the P.

He'd have to keep an eye out when escorting Felix home after class. He didn't think the Executioner would approach them, but it didn't hurt to be extra vigilant.

He scoffed to himself. Escort Felix where? Was the place you transformed into a prison really a home? Maybe they could go somewhere else for the afternoon and give him some sunshine. A park, perhaps. He was getting worried Felix would start withering at this rate.

It made him think of someone else who would be holing up.

"Do you know where Michael lives?"

At that, Liana looked up, her body curling in disgust. "Why do you want to know that?"

"Felix wanted to warn him he might become a target. The possibility might seem obvious after Jackson's attack, but since Felix is too scared to see anyone, I wanted to do it for him."

She grimaced. "I could ask around. You sure you want to bother finding that slime's den?"

"It's something Felix wanted to do."

She sighed and lifted her phone to her ear. "Let me make some calls."

Not ten minutes later they were on their way.

They stopped a couple of students for directions. One of them pointed to the north side of campus and grabbed Liana's arm before she could leave, asking, "Hey you're the volleyball chick who's friends with Felix. Is it true he's the Executioner?"

"It's true that it takes an equal amount of force to bite someone's finger off as it does a carrot," she replied, and he quickly released her. "No, he's not. And I'd better not catch you spreading any rumours."

"It gets worse every day," Nikolai muttered as they walked off. Liana agreed with a string of expletives.

When they arrived, he stared up at the tall dorm building, similar to Felix's. "How'd you find it so quickly?

Liana smirked. "My teammates. My girls know all." It vanished as they walked up the steps. "One of them has a sibling who had a tryst with Michael. Turns out it was a prank. Mrs. Rosewood found her walking home barefoot and missing most of her clothes."

Poor girl. He couldn't believe boys still got away with that kind of stuff. "And the eggs?"

Liana tucked the carton she'd bought en route further into her backpack. "The call reminded me how much I hate the guy. He'll be finding rotting eggs around his room for weeks."

Nikolai snickered and opened the door for her.

The interior was a near-carbon copy of Felix's dorm complex. They climbed to the sixth floor and knocked on the door. There was a thud and a muffled curse. Nikolai looked at Liana, eyes wide. Was the Executioner already here?

Time for some payback. He tested the knob. Not locked. Liana stepped back, and Nikolai yanked the door open.

Michael yelped next to a fallen duffle bag, staring at the pair like a deer caught in the headlights. All his cupboards were open with their contents thrown about. Liana huffed at all the overturned hiding spots.

Michael braced a hand against his chest. "You scared the daylights out of me! What'd you want?"

"What are you doing?" Nikolai said, watching him shove more clothes in the duffle.

"Packing. Duh. I'm not staying another night in this place." He turned to his drawer, and Liana shoved two eggs under his growing pile of clothes. When he turned back, she was sitting innocently on the floor. "Why're you here?"

"We came to warn you about the Executioner. We think you're next," Nikolai said.

"I don't need any help from you shucks. Trust me: warning received loud and clear. Jackson's lucky he survived."

"And yet you left the door unlocked?"

Michael went to bite back something undoubtedly nasty, then paused and glanced at the door with a curse. He must've been scared out of his wits to have forgotten.

"You don't think Jackson's attack was a robbery?" Liana asked, sneaking another egg into his backpack pocket.

Michael scoffed, shoving a trophy into the duffle. "If that was a robbery, then I'm a toad. No, we got our warning with those photographs of Emilio—" He slapped his hand to his mouth, shuddering. "I'm out of here."

Nikolai supposed it was good news. One less person to bother Felix. Campus sure wouldn't miss him.

"I'm surprised you aren't doing the same," Michael said to him, then rolled his eyes at his confusion and zipped up the duffle. "Y'know. For the club? Everyone knows you yelled at the twerp. The Executioner will make you pay for that."

"How did you know about that?" Liana asked. "You weren't there."

"Word travels fast. Especially with what he said. Now shoo, I've got things to do."

He shoved them into the hall and slammed the door. They stood there, trying to form words.

"I'm... next?" Nikolai said.

He remembered how distraught Felix had been after that night and was besieged by guilt once more. He didn't mean to come off as he did, but his intentions didn't matter. What mattered was how Felix felt. If Nikolai were the Executioner, someone who hurt Felix like that wouldn't have lived through the night.

"I don't get it. It's been days since the club. Why hasn't the executioner come for me yet?"

Liana blew a raspberry, running a hand through her hair. "You're surrounded by people all the time. I suppose that made it difficult. And Jackson bumped himself to the top of the priority list when he beat Felix up. But now that he's dealt with, though..." Her eyes widened. "Michael's right. You're next."

He paced the hall, talking half to himself. "Wait. Okay. Before we get into a tizzy, let's think." He took a deep breath. "Maybe this can help us. Uh."

"If the Executioner were to care and not discredit it as rumours, they had to have seen you yell at Felix in the club. They were there."

"That's *if* they'd seen."

"They're following everyone Felix interacts with. I bet you anything they saw you two that night."

"Good to know we've reduced the suspect list to less than a hundred."

Her phone buzzed, making them both jump. Her concern grew upon checking it. "I forgot Coach wanted to meet us for drills. Look, meet me this evening at your place with Felix. I've got an idea of how to narrow it down."

"What happened to not saying anything to him until we have a list of suspects that'd sway cops?"

"Michael gave me an idea! We have enough circumstantial evidence that I think I can get Felix to doubt his conviction. After that, I know how he can prove his innocence damn near himself!"

Nikolai was going to sneak so many jalapeños into her food for leaving him clueless like that.

After Felix's lecture finished, Nikolai returned to find him nodding off. His head bobbed up and down, gripping the desk edges so tightly his knuckles were white. The skin on this neck was irritated like he'd been pinching it.

Nikolai pushed through the crowd of hungry students and dropped to his knees by his side. "Hey, you okay?"

He brushed the hair from Felix's forehead and gently turned his heavy head to get a better look at him. Felix melted into the touch, pressing closer as his eyes fluttered closed. Then he jolted like he'd been struck by lighting and slapped his hands around to find purchase on something to ground himself. Nikolai hissed as Felix's nails found his shoulders.

"I fell asleep! Oh my God, I fell asleep! Who's dead? Are you hurt?"

Nikolai buried his hand in his hair to hush the frightened babbling and ran his thumb over his cheekbone, beneath the healing bruises. "You're safe, and so is everyone else. It was only a microsleep. Not even a minute long. You're still attached to the desk. Don't you feel the rope?"

Felix fisted Nikolai's T-shirt, breathing heavily but nodded along. "How do you know what a microsleep is?"

Nikolai dropped his bag to begin untying him, grinning. "I looked it up. An hour ago." He didn't address the death-grip, content to let Felix hold on as long as he needed to ground himself.

A crumpled sheet of paper visible through the bag's half-done zipper drew Felix's gaze. It was a diagram of different BDSM knots and loops. Nikolai followed his eyes and scrambled to zip it back up.

"It's not what you think! I'm not thinking of—of that! I'm just learning and teaching myself the ways, you know? Safe ways. Safe knots. Not for that purpose, though!"

Amusement lifted the corners of Felix's mouth. The skin by his eyes crinkled with the smile and Nikolai lost his train of thought.

"You really do have this handled, don't you?" Felix said quietly. "You really want to help me."

"Of course I do."

His unwavering sincerity seemed to render Felix inoperable. Nikolai wished he could record the flashing "ERROR" sign across his face without ruining the moment.

At his pig snort, Felix rebooted and averted his gaze. "I, uh, I should go back to the dorm. Lock myself back up and drink some more Red Bull. Wake up."

"I have a better idea."

Nikolai grabbed their stuff and led him outside. They stopped by the cafeteria, where Nikolai bought him lunch despite his complaints and then dragged him to a patch of grass on the sunny side of campus. Many people paused to glare Felix's way or run from him as if he'd stab them for breathing the same air. Stupid online polls. Felix protested and attempted to pull away, shirking the stares, but was too groggy to do anything other than stumble along.

"I need to go back to the dorms," he said, pouting as Nikolai pushed him onto the grass.

"What you need is some vitamin D and a nap."

Nikolai slipped the handcuffs he'd taken from Felix's bed out of his pocket and cuffed their wrists together. He lifted his hand to demonstrate and grinned when Felix stared bewildered at how his wrist was pulled along. "I won't let you sleepwalk anywhere, so go ahead and relax."

He unwrapped the sandwich and lifted it to Felix's mouth with his free hand. He waited patiently for Felix to weigh the pros and cons and felt pleasantly tingly when he accepted and took a bite.

He made him eat the whole thing, coaxing him until only crumbs remained. "There you go! That wasn't so bad, was it?"

Felix wiped his mouth to hide the pink dusting his cheeks. Nikolai gently guided his head into his lap and ignored the way the confused, yet curious knit of his brows made him want to squish his cheeks.

"Go to sleep. I won't let anything happen."

It didn't take Felix long to pass out. Days of sleeplessness had taken their toll on his body. Felix huffed, blinked once, then twice, and his eyes didn't open again.

Some gazes drifted their way: some curious, but most disapproving. Some people pointed and hissed to each other. Nikolai glared them into silence and went back to tracing Felix's face.

The only colour in his pale complexion was the blotchy bruises on his healing nose, lip, and under his eye. The rest of his face glowed a peachy cream tone under the sunlight—a small step toward getting his rosy cheeks back. A bittersweet feeling squeezed his heart; it was warm with joy in knowing Felix was getting better but hollow with grief that he had become so sickly.

Having him in his lap felt right. He didn't need the heart-racing, adrenaline-pumping feelings Liana found in her favourite romance movies. Felix brought something just as strong and more essential: peace.

Nikolai's house hadn't been a home for a long time. He hadn't expected that to change coming to college. His parents were never going to support him.

It was nice to find that missing support in the dance program, in his "fans" who watched him perform, but it never filled that hole. They didn't support *him*, not really.

Then this unassuming photography student helped Nikolai reimagine what he thought a home could be.

The best part was that Felix hadn't even done anything remarkable. He made everyone feel remarkable by being unapologetically himself: a genuinely good person. Whenever Nikolai was with him, he felt *seen*, and he wanted to laugh at the cliché of it all. When Felix laughed, Nikolai felt like the world's greatest comedian. When Felix complimented him, he felt like he could do no wrong.

A quiet, ever-present sincerity that was dazzling in its own right.

Before Nikolai knew it, the humble soul had a space carved for himself in his chest, and he'd missed it horribly.

He hoped Felix could see a safe space in him, as much as he saw home in Felix.

"It'll be over soon," he whispered, tucking a messy lock behind Felix's ear.

Thankfully, the rest of the day was uneventful. Nikolai practiced with his dance group and excused himself every couple of hours to escort Felix to classes. Cactus teasingly whined about Nikolai spending more time with his assumed girlfriend than focusing on their performance, but Evangeline had his back every time he left and kept the crew on track until Nikolai returned.

He'd always enjoyed being around Felix. He'd always been excited to hang out, even if they only did homework together. He thought that was what it was like to have a best friend. But after everything that happened, the fear of losing Felix to some monster unravelled the hidden truth behind it all. After Liana had made him aware of it, he couldn't wait to see Felix again.

Nikolai jumped out of formation when his phone buzzed. It was Felix saying his classes were finished.

"I'm heading out!" Nikolai declared over the music and his crew's ensuing grievances. "I'm done for the day!"

"Our Nikolai doesn't love us!" cried Cactus, draping himself dramatically over Nikolai's shoulders. "He's gone to play with his girlfriend! Are we naught but a mistress to you? Second in line to the throne of your heart?"

Nikolai made a face as the rest of the group laughed and shoved him off. "You should be in theatre with that kind of act."

He and Cactus had certainly warmed up after being caged together for hours upon hours of intense practice. They all had, but Nikolai needed to go, and Cactus latched onto his back again with the passion of an octopus.

Cactus whined, "But if I were, our love would be blocked by insurmountable obstacles, created by the gods!"

"You mean buildings and concrete?"

The group laughed and cut the music, taking this as a cue for a break.

Cactus pressed the back of his hand to his forehead. "How ever will I convince you to leave the princess and stay with your knights?"

Evangeline gulped water from her bottle. "At least he *has* a princess."

"Oi!"

The group laughed again at Cactus' offended expression. Nikolai took the chance to slip from his arms and gather his things.

"I have a girlfriend!" Cactus said.

"Your anime pillows don't count!" said a dancer with curly red hair.

Cactus corrected himself. "I can get a girlfriend!"

Nikolai headed for the door while the others were distracted. Evangeline opened it for him with a smile, saying, "Go get your princess. I'll deal with them."

Nikolai rubbed the back of his neck. "He's just a friend."

Evangeline smiled wider and ushered him out. "Then your friend is very lucky. Now, go before they notice!"

He ran to the photography building as fast as he could. He buzzed from his fingers to his toes. It had only been four hours since they'd parted, but it felt at least triple that. Just thinking of Felix rocking on his heels by his desk, waiting for him to untie his ankle from the desk leg, and that shy smile when Nikolai entered the lecture hall made him giddy.

He pushed open the wide doors. "Sorry I'm late, Felix! I got held up at the practice room."

Felix and another man were looking out the window. The giddiness soured.

Felix's smile was as warm and soft as his hair from the morning shower Nikolai had forced him to take. The other man stood a head taller and a foot closer to Felix than Nikolai was comfortable with. He was all easy smiles, a gentle soul with a relaxed demeanour that Nikolai could see himself getting along with, but the way that gaze slid Felix's way like a magnet told him friendship wasn't likely.

"Nikolai, this is Sergio, a friend of mine. He was keeping me company until you arrived. Did practice go well?"

Sergio stuck out a hand in greeting. *A friend? Where had this friend been while Felix was getting the crap beaten out of him yesterday?* Nikolai ground his teeth and shook his calloused palm briefly. He let go before he yanked this new person a good several yards away from his friend.

"Don't I recognize you?" Nikolai said, pocketing his balling fists.

Sergio waggled his index in thought. "It was at the club, right? Weren't you the one who yelled at Felix?"

"And you were the one who swept him off his drunken feet. Good to meet you, Prince Charming." He mentally cursed his dance crew for putting so many fairy tales in his head. "Felix, wanna head out? Liana wants pizza for dinner, and we should order it before the delivery men get too scared of the dark."

"We're having pizza?" Felix echoed. Sergio and Nikolai swooned, noticed each other, and looked away.

"Yeah, since things have gotten—" Nikolai chose his words carefully. "—better with the three of us, we thought it'd be nice to get together."

"Oh! That's nice! Sergio, would you like to join us?"

Nikolai cursed Felix's hospitable nature.

Sergio looked surprised by the polite offer, and when he figured out it was genuine—Felix didn't want him to be left out—it quickly smoothed into a gentle smile. "I'd love to, but I have to get to work. I didn't think you'd be here. I've been passing by all week and haven't seen you once."

"You have?" Felix said. "That's nice. I've been uh, I've been..." Nikolai mouthed "out of commission" behind Sergio's back. "I've been out of commission the past week!"

Sergio frowned. "You've been sick?"

"Yes," said Felix, a tad too slowly.

Blissfully ignorant, Sergio made an "ah" sound. "That explains the eye bags. You look like a zombie. I'm glad to hear you're on the mend!"

Felix thanked him and went back to looking at something out the window.

"Well, I won't keep you from a night of pizza fun!"

Felix nodded but didn't move. Nikolai raised a brow at Sergio. The man shrugged.

"Are you okay?" Nikolai asked.

"We should go out the back."

Sergio chuckled nervously. "Is there some big prank going to happen out front? Do you see a bucket of flour hanging or something?"

Felix tugged on the hem of Nikolai's shirt and nodded to the view below. His hand was so tiny bunched up in his clothes. Nikolai's ego swelled with pride over how Felix grabbed him and not Sergio. He mentally slapped himself.

There was no mistaking the navy-blue uniforms at the front doors. They questioned everyone who entered and exited. Nikolai eased Felix's shaking fist out of his shirt.

"It's just the cops!" Sergio sighed in relief. "I thought Michael and Jackson would be down there."

"Jackson's in the hospital. Robbery gone wrong." Nikolai pulled Felix away from the glass and rubbed his shoulders to calm him.

"Sucks to be him. Why're you shaken up, Felix?"

"Cops make him nervous."

He made a sympathetic noise. "I get that. Boy, do I ever. But you didn't do anything wrong, right?"

"No, you didn't," Nikolai said firmly before Felix could utter a sound. Felix met his calm eyes, tense as a brick under his palms. "You did nothing wrong, so you have nothing to worry about."

"Nothing wrong with three bodies? You believe that?" he whispered as Sergio grabbed his backpack.

Nikolai's hands ran over his shoulders, down his arms, and back up. "I do. You aren't a bad person."

"You guys coming?" Sergio asked from the door.

Nikolai took Felix's bag to keep it from aggravating his injuries and led him out, keeping a hand on his lower back to keep him from trailing behind.

"Keep your chin up," Nikolai whispered into Felix's hair when the officers came into view. He did his best to ignore the smell of grass and pines that still clung to the locks—he wondered if he'd find a crushed leaf in those tangles—and nudged him forward. "If you act like you did nothing wrong, they won't think anything's wrong."

An officer stopped Sergio up ahead. Felix stiffened.

"Relax," Nikolai rumbled.

Felix shot him a look that said, *"As if that will help!"*

Another cop stepped in their way.

"Officer," Nikolai greeted. "What can we do for you?"

Thankfully, she didn't look like the pro wrestler from Emilio's crime scene. This woman's face was long like her body, which loomed tall and thin like a spruce tree but had the strength of a hundred-year-old redwood.

"I'm Officer Lappet. This is Officer Gascon. We're investigating the recent attacks on campus. Currently, we're asking students who were known... *associates* of Jackson Adcock's if they have an alibi for the time of his attack. Somebody said we could find Felix Griffiths, Nikolai Avilov, and Sergio Donato here." She glanced at her notepad and to their faces. She lingered on Felix's bruises. "I'm assuming you're them?"

"Alibi?" Felix repeated weakly. "You think the Executioner did that?"

Sergio was still hung up on something else. "Wait, Jackson's last name is what, now?"

Nikolai met the mischievous glint in his eye. Maybe this guy wasn't so bad after all.

Officer Lappet ignored him. "That's one lead we're following, but we found his belongings in a nearby trash can. It's looking like a possible attempted robbery. The guy tried to pass it off as the Executioner's attack, got spooked, and ran off. Nothing's concrete, which is why we need to know where you three were last night from 10 p.m. to 3 a.m."

"No wonder you only got here now. My name is Sergio. I was working at the tech shop down the road. I had the night shift."

"A tech shop has a night shift?"

"It's a 24-hour support shop. You'd be surprised at how many sobbing customers we get at 3 a.m. 'I spilled coffee on my laptop' or 'I have twenty minutes to submit my paper and it won't send.'"

"I'm Nikolai. I was dancing with my crew until super late. I was too lazy to go home after, so I spent the night at Felix's."

She looked at Felix for confirmation. He gulped and nodded.

"Funny how you and Felix Griffiths have been each other's alibi twice now," inputted Gascon, a stout man who looked like he had stopped growing taller at fourteen. "Your names have been popping up a lot."

Nikolai slung an arm casually over Felix's tense shoulders. "What can I say? We're close!"

Officer Lappet didn't look convinced. "If you're Felix, we've been looking for you all day. I'm told Jackson gave you those injuries."

"Yes, ma'am."

Sergio frowned and scanned his cuts and swelled lip anew, as if he'd seen the bruises before and was surprised by the additions. He hadn't seen the video the other day, then, Nikolai realized.

"That must have made you angry," she said.

"I..." Felix's voice withered. Nikolai lowered his hand to gently rub his back. "I was mostly scared," he admitted, slouching into Nikolai's hand. "He broke my camera and threatened me. There's nothing I can do against that guy. I know if he wants to hurt me, he will."

Officer Lappet must have been a mom; one quiver of Felix's split lip before shrinking at the memory of the beating, and she backed off. Officer Gascon took it as another sign.

"You two are oddly friendly," he sneered.

"We talked about this, Gascon," Officer Lappet said with a glare.

Nikolai's grip tightened. He forced himself to relax. "That's generally what being close means."

Officer Gascon brushed his jacket aside to put his hands on his belt and tilted his pudgy hips forward, gun and baton on display for all to see. "Do you two normally sleep over at each other's houses? I seem to recall another time you both had a sleepover while an innocent boy was slaughtered in a ditch."

Nikolai switched his hold to Felix's left hand, arm stretched across his front to slowly push him away from the officer's malicious gaze. Felix did not complain. Sergio's eyes narrowed.

"I remember. It was a tragic night," Nikolai said.

The officer glanced at their joined hands. "Awfully convenient for the two of you to be together during that 'tragic night,' as well. If one of you were a girl, I wouldn't ask. But, tell me, do boys your age normally spend so much time together?"

Sergio piped up from the sidelines. "This school has a strict no-bullying policy."

The man didn't spare him a glance. "I am confirming information, not bullying them."

"Ah, that's right. My bad. You're being homophobic."

Oh. Nikolai liked this one.

The twitch of a grin Officer Lappet suppressed said she did too.

Gascon's jaw dropped into his flabby chin at the accusation. "I am not! How dare you!"

Sergio blew some dirt off his nails. "I'm only stating facts. As you said, if one of them were a girl, you wouldn't think twice about them spending time together. You'd even hand them a condom, wouldn't you?"

"Excuse you, young man—"

"No, excuse *you*, officer. Your masculinity may be delicate and fragile, but don't go assuming ours is too, you paranoid little cishet troll."

Officer Gascon advanced, hand flying to his baton, but Sergio stood his ground. Officer Lappet snatched her comrade's wrist in a bruising grip and wrenched him back with surprising force.

"Don't you dare touch a hair on his head," she hissed.

When he sputtered to excuse himself, she twisted his arm and marched him toward the parking lot. "You have done enough. I don't care if he calls you the delicate flower prince of Hell. You never attack unless it's to defend yourself from a physical threat. That is a *young boy*! Just you wait until our superiors hear about this!" She called over her shoulder, "Don't leave town, you three."

They watched the officer get punted into the passenger's seat of the police car, still arguing, and Lappet drove them away.

Felix stepped out from behind Nikolai. "That was brave of you. Thanks, Sergio."

Sergio waved it off, but Nikolai noticed the quirk of a smile. "It's time to stop letting jerks like that walk all over us. Learned that from you, actually." The way Felix's ears blushed was adorable. "Anyways, I've got to get to work before I'm late. You guys have a safe walk home!"

As Sergio strolled toward the market, Nikolai asked Felix, "Are you still good for tonight?"

That ass of a police officer hadn't been like the ones ready to shoot them from last night, but he had been threatening enough. If Felix wanted to go somewhere else to calm down, Nikolai would take him wherever he wanted.

But Felix gave himself a little shake and said, "Yeah, I'm fine."

Not too far away, Sergio paused for a moment and turned. "Hey, Felix? You found a good one." He nodded at Nikolai and grinned at their beet-red faces. "Good luck. I hope you get better soon."

"Wait up!" Nikolai ran over and stuck out his hand. Sergio stared at the appendage like it would explode. "I'm sorry about before, and the club. I said some nasty things that I didn't mean, and I was completely out of line. You're a good guy. You didn't deserve that."

Sergio broke into a huge grin and slapped their hands together in a firm shake. "Apology accepted. I get it. Tensions run high sometimes. Whoever's in the way is in the way." His attention slid toward Felix. "Take care of each other, eh? Make sure neither of you turn black and blue like that again."

"I promise."

Nikolai took Felix back to his apartment. They ordered pizza with extra cheese and watched old comedy shows online while waiting for it and Liana. She arrived seconds after the pizza man and scared him by shouting, "Yeah! Food!" from directly behind before he could ring the doorbell. Nikolai tipped him for the scare.

It was the best evening they'd spent together in a long time. Liana and Nikolai competed to see who could eat the most pizza in under a minute. Felix enabled them with the timer. They laughed, choked on cheese, made fun of teachers, and groaned about homework like old times.

They regaled each other with colourful accounts of their week away from each other. They held Liana back from filing a complaint against the homophobic policeman by sitting on her and muffled her threats of violence by stuffing a pizza slice into her mouth before Nikolai's neighbours threatened to call said cops.

It felt good. He felt like they were back to normal.

But they still had something to talk about.

Liana folded her hands in her lap and said to Felix, "We have to discuss something you're going to find difficult to talk about."

He snatched her crust. "It isn't algebra, is it?" The joke didn't take away how his voice wavered.

She pursed her lips. "Look, I don't know how to smooth the way into this so I'm going to go ahead and say it. We did some digging. You're not the Executioner."

He put down his food, pushing back. "Don't try to comfort me and feed me lies. I know what I've done."

"Except you don't."

"I have the motive, the means, and the opportunity. No, you..." Felix tugged his hair, causing most of his low bun to come undone. He turned on his heel. Nikolai thought he'd walk straight out, but he spun at the door and pointed at them. When he finally wrestled out his voice, it was shredded. "Don't try to convince me now. It had to be me."

Nikolai wanted to both coddle and shake him. He took a deep breath. He had to be firm. Felix was hanging on by such a thin thread that any comfort could be interpreted as them sparing his feelings instead of believing the truth. "You're acting like you *want* to be responsible."

"Of course not! But if you're wrong and I put my guard down, I risk being responsible for another person not making it home when I go to sleep!"

"You won't do that."

"I woke up ready to bash your skull in with a mug! What if I hadn't woken up in time? I can't wake up in an alley covered in blood again!"

"You were in that alley because the Executioner lured you there," Liana said.

"No, don't—"

"Shut up and listen to me. You were not physically capable of getting out of your room. The night Jackson got attacked, someone unlatched your window from the outside. I tried it myself. It's possible."

"I don't think even I could break a bedpost with my bare hands," Nikolai said.

Felix blinked rapidly as if that would help him process. "I could have used a hammer."

"Where was it?" Liana asked. "We searched your room. The best weapon you had was a butterknife."

Felix curled in on himself, tugging his hair. "I don't know! I could have tossed it away on the grounds!"

There was firmness, and there was Liana. "Ease off a little," Nikolai said to her. She ignored him.

"Wrong. I locked you in there when this began under your instructions to not leave you with anything you could weaponize. You could not have broken that post." Her phone buzzed. She ignored it and leaned forward, elbows on her knees. "You may have had a lot of reasons to want those guys gone, Felix, but you didn't do it."

Felix peeked, lip quivering. Liana stared him down, unwavering. The longer she stood her ground, the more Nikolai could see Felix's defences chipping away.

"Did you hear me? You didn't do it. Which means you will not hurt us. We're safe. We're not going anywhere."

Felix slumped against the wall and pulled his knees into his chest. A single tear fell down his cheek. "I didn't kill them...?"

"But I've got a plan to lure out who did." Her phone buzzed again. "Not now," she grumbled and tossed it out of her pocket onto the floor. "*Liber-no*" flashed across the screen before it went dark.

Nikolai blinked. "What does that mean?"

She waved it off. "Volleyball joke. Riley's our team's libero, our defence specialist. She asks me to keep attacking her receives even after practice so we've got this inside joke." She paused, staring at the phone. "Our defence... shit."

Felix went stock-still. "No... That..."

She paled. "Yes."

Nikolai put up a hand. "Confused."

Felix whispered, "Her sister had to drop out of school and be institutionalized."

"Because of those jerks," Liana said. "That's plenty motive... and she knows where you live. She's dropped me off there enough."

"Motive? You guys think *she's*—" Nikolai nearly got whiplash from the suggestion. "Hang on, did you have any games the night of the murders? She have an alibi?"

Liana slowly shook her head. "She never showed an ounce of sympathy for the victims. She's... she's strong enough to have broken their... their skulls too." She swallowed. "And she saw you yell at Felix. She was with me when I gave him my card for the taxi."

Nikolai swore and rubbed his mouth. The more he thought about it, the more it made sense. "She became the Executioner to get revenge."

Felix looked heartbroken. "Liana, you—"

She held up a hand. "Don't ask. You know exactly how I'm doing." Her jaw was set tight. Nikolai didn't think they wanted to know everything it was holding in. How could she be okay when someone she trusted was responsible for such unspeakable acts?

Nikolai asked, "Should we tell the police about this?"

Felix chuckled weakly. "Who do you think they're going to believe? A tournament-winning scholarship student or me?"

Liana straightened. "You said the cops were sniffing around you, right?"

He nodded, and a hint of a snarl escaped her. She shook her head, regaining her composure. The ironclad control she had over herself gave Nikolai goosebumps.

"Not good. If we bring it to the cops, we'd better have irrefutable proof. Catch her in the act."

"Absolutely not. I'm not dragging any other innocent person into this mess," Felix said.

"You won't be," Nikolai said, looking at Liana. "Not if the plan is what I think it is."

"You beat me to the punch. You sure you're alright being bait?"

His stomach dropped, but he said, "I'm already on her hit list. If that can be useful, I'll do anything."

She nodded tensely. "I can modify the details to set a trap and trick a confession out of Riley. Felix can record it."

Felix flinched. "Absolutely not! Nikolai, you're not putting yourself in danger like that!"

He said, "What other option do we have? Wait for another piece of evidence to find its way into your dorm and hope the police don't come knocking at your door before we can get rid of it?"

Liana pressed her fist against her mouth in thought. "To control her timeline we'd need Felix to wish you dead in public. The question is where?"

"Stop!" Felix threw a cushion at them, almost hitting the pizza box were it not for Liana's reflexes. "Riley has butchered three people! You are not throwing your life away on a half-baked plan!"

Liana said, "Nikolai *is* next. The best way to keep him safe is to control her timeline."

"No, he can leave campus. Go home."

The suggestion stung, but it looked like it hurt Felix more to say it.

"I know how much this dance program means to you. This place is your escape, and you'd have to go back with your parents again and pay to redo the year. But you can't dance if you're dead. If you're next, you need to leave."

Nikolai couldn't help but chuckle.

"You think this is funny?!"

"Yes." He delighted in Felix's flush and balling fists. The passion was refreshing after watching him waste away for so long. "Dancing might mean the world to me, but there's something more important to me now. I can't leave you to face your problems on your own again."

Felix's jaw snapped shut.

Liana muttered, "This is so cute I'm going to hurl."

"Please don't. I just vacuumed yesterday." Nikolai sobered seeing the tears in Felix's eyes. "The police aren't looking in the right direction. We're the only ones who know it's her. She is going to keep killing unless we do something."

Liana may have known how to calm Felix since childhood, but Nikolai prided himself in knowing Felix too. He knew what mattered most to that big heart he wore on his sleeve. He knew Felix wouldn't be able to live with himself for not at least trying.

His chest swelled when Felix took a deep breath, wiped his eyes with a sniffle and said, steady and firm, "It's busiest around six in the afternoon outside the cafeteria. Liana, can you get Riley there tomorrow?"

"Sure thing."

Nikolai said to Felix, "When you yell at me, you have to really make it seem like you hate me. Be harsh, blame me for everything, whatever you have to do. Don't hold back."

He squirmed but nodded. "I can say something like, 'How dare you—'"

"Don't practice it now. It can't seem rehearsed. My reaction has to be genuine."

"Okay. Then I'll put the final nail in your proverbial coffin by..." He bit his lip. "Wishing you dead."

Just imagining it made Nikolai swallow the lump in his throat. He would have to steel himself for the real deal. "I'll head to the car park afterwards. There's never many people there."

"And I'll pretend to ditch Riley to comfort Felix," Liana said. "We'll follow you with a camera and my bat. Don't worry, we won't let her get the jump on you."

The dim light cast a glow over Felix's pale cheeks and the dark circles under his eyes. He curled his hand into the doorframe. "This ends tomorrow."

No more deaths. No more late nights worrying about each other.

They polished off the pizza and resolutely avoided voicing the hundreds of things that could go wrong with the plan. If they said them aloud, that'd make them real. They finally had a chance. They weren't going to jinx it.

Liana claimed to be too lazy to walk home and passed out on Nikolai's couch. She probably didn't want to be alone after discovering her friend's lies. They tucked her in with a spare blanket and retreated to Nikolai's room, where they stared at the bed for a solid thirty seconds.

Nikolai said, "Do we..."

"Should I sleep on the floor?" Felix asked.

"No, I should sleep on the floor."

"Why would you?"

"I don't know."

They lapsed back into silence.

Felix busied himself with fluffing his pillow. "I can handcuff myself to the bed's feet. All I need is a pillow to sit on. I can stay up by myself tonight."

"We've been over this. You're sleeping. On a mattress."

"What about you? You need to sleep, too. I don't think you got any last night watching over me."

"We'll both sleep."

"Together?" Felix squeaked.

Nikolai ran a hand through his hair. "Why not? We've done it before, right?"

Felix nodded robotically. "Right."

"And it went... fine."

"Except for when I tried to mug you in your sleep."

Nikolai held back a snort at the pun. "You were probably dancing again, but I'll chain both your hands up if it makes you comfortable."

He used the same handcuffs from lunch to lock his wrists to the bedpost near his head. Then, he dug around his closet for a pair of mitts and gingerly slid them onto Felix's hands.

"Circulation. They're not covered by the blankets. Might get cold."

Why was speaking so difficult? He'd been excited to be around Felix after so long apart! ... Up until they stepped into the bedroom. Now, he felt as jittery as an elementary student on their first day of school.

Felix noticed Nikolai's fingers trembling as he tested the chain and peered up at him in concern. Nikolai nearly had a heart attack right there. He stared back, captivated by those big, twinkling eyes. A creak in the mattress from where his knees dug in by Felix's hip reminded him of his task. He tried not to think about how he was hovering only a foot above his best friend.

"I don't want to be cruel to you tomorrow," Felix whispered.

"You have to."

"I know, I just... I won't mean any of it, you know that right?"

Nikolai might've been playing the bait tomorrow, but he couldn't help thinking of how terrified Felix must be. Yet, here he was, worrying about Nikolai's feelings instead.

"You mustn't believe anything less than how much I..."

His heart skipped. An invisible force pulled him an inch closer. "Than you what?"

Felix's eyes dipped to his mouth, then darted back up. "Appreciate... you."

"Appreciate huh?"

He gave a feeble glare, then softened. "Thank you. For not giving up on me."

With his wrists bound beside his ear, his body open and trusting, Nikolai couldn't help but wish the world would stop turning. He wished he could borrow Felix's photographic talent and capture this sight forever: the tousled hair and the flush across his cheeks. Nikolai longed to be the only one to see him like this.

"Is everything okay?"

He shook himself out of his trance and dropped onto the bed. He pulled the covers over them and half-buried his face in a pillow to avoid the question. "You should sleep. You probably still haven't caught up on rest."

As proof, it took Felix twenty seconds to fall asleep.

Conversely, Nikolai was kept wide awake by his erratic heartbeat. It surprised him that Felix didn't hear it. When he was sure he wouldn't turn around to find the whites of his eyes staring back, he rolled over.

He mentally traced the curve of Felix's brow and the globes of his full cheeks. He memorized every bump and scab and found that the more he looked, the calmer his heart became.

He raised a tentative hand to Felix's waist and hovered over the blanket. They liked each other, so this wouldn't be a problem, right?

He gently rested his hand on Felix's side before he could chicken out. Felix sighed in his sleep and shifted closer so Nikolai's arm wrapped around him.

Nikolai bit his lip to contain the sound that threatened to escape. There was so much trust here. So much faith that Nikolai hardly knew what to do with other than to treasure it with every fibre of his being. There was no greater honour.

This was what he wanted to remember: Felix's scent, the warmth of his body, and his touch. Nikolai tucked it all away safely in his memory. No matter what happened in the morning, he wanted to remember how happy they'd been tonight. Felix was curled asleep in *his* bed, snuggling into *his* touch. There was no better way to fall asleep.

Victim's Statement Chills All Night Life Activities

Nikolai woke up to the familiar, irritating tune of his phone's alarm and a strange buzz in his butt pocket. He fumbled around and flung the offending object across the room, where it clattered at Liana's feet by the doorway.

"And you wonder why your screen is cracked," she mused.

He groaned and buried closer into the warmth pressed against his front. The warmth grumbled. He frowned.

Liana unlocked his phone and turned off the alarm. "Your phone's been going off for five minutes now. Get up."

Nikolai rubbed his eyes and waited for the lump under his nose to come into focus.

"I made toast. Do you want milk or water with it?"

"My milk went bad," he replied in a sleepy rumble that stirred the bundle of blankets against him. "I don't own a toaster. How did you make toast?"

"I make miracles with a stove and a frying pan. Come on, we might be catching a murderer this evening but that doesn't mean we can be late for morning classes." Her footsteps retreated in the hall.

Felix popped his head out from underneath the duvet and glared at the disturbances but didn't bother to open his eyes for the full effect. Nikolai almost laughed. He expected a freak-out like last time, or maybe some very awkward explaining for their cuddling. Instead, Felix scrunched his nose like an unhappy rabbit and dropped back onto his pillow.

"Good morning," Nikolai said, chuckling.

"Good night," Felix groused.

"Do you have class this morning?"

Felix rubbed his face into the pillow in what he assumed was a "no."

"Okay, I'll be right back."

Nikolai untangled himself and hurried into the kitchen. His fridge didn't have much that wasn't expired. He found a lonesome apple on the bottom shelf that wasn't growing anything fuzzy. He grabbed a cup of water; put two pieces of toast, a leftover slice of pizza, and the apple on a plate; and scurried back before Liana could question him. He arranged the food on the floor within Felix's reach, unlocked one of his hands, and reattached the handcuff to the bedpost.

"There's some breakfast on your left, you should be able to reach. I'll leave the key with it. Make sure to eat when you get up. Your phone is there, too."

Realizing Nikolai was leaving, Felix patted around the bed with his free hand until he brushed against Nikolai's shirt and clutched it tight.

Nikolai's heart both melted and sped into a ball of anxiety. With what they had in store, he felt an overwhelming need to soak up every moment. He wanted to say, "screw the day," and jump back into bed to cuddle, but he knew Liana would drag him by the ankle to class to keep his grades up.

He eased Felix's hand under the sheets and tucked him in. "Go back to sleep."

"You sure you're up for tonight?" Liana asked in the doorway, her usual mischief gone. He ached seeing traces of grief there instead.

"Don't have much choice, do we?"

Her phone chimed, and she gasped at the screen. "Your alarm was set a half-hour late! My prof is gonna kill me! Toast is now on-the-go!"

He changed his shirt and lingered by the door. He needed one last look. He wasn't sure why. He glanced to find Felix already watching him.

"Be careful today," Felix murmured.

"You too."

Class went by achingly slow. The professor's droning voice and the students posing question after question melted into one unattractive sound. Time was always an alien concept in classrooms. Nikolai remembered being in detention in high school and swearing on his life that the second hand on the clock had moved backwards once. It was no different in college. Three hours could pass by in thirty minutes. One hour could stretch on for four.

He'd been texting Liana under the desk to prepare. After class, he'd go straight to the courtyard. During her breaks, she found the police tape blocking the path to the parking lot was gone. There was a straight line from it to the courtyard.

He forgot what subject he was supposed to be studying. He looked at the pie chart in his textbook and saw Felix's smushed face. It reminded him of how he had pouted this morning over the thought of getting up.

He could still feel Felix's weight against him. Liana was right, he was a goner. He always had been. Felix had claimed the seat in his heart long before Nikolai discovered that cheese was his favourite pizza topping; that he liked smaller, quieter workrooms; and how he preferred British sitcoms to American ones. Nikolai longed to be back at his apartment. He pictured the scene perfectly: Felix huddled in a blanket fort to banish autumn's cold, giggling over something stupid like the way Nikolai's hair sometimes spiked like a pineapple when he woke up. Felix's long lashes would brush against his rosy cheeks. His hands would be warm, teasingly shoving Nikolai off the bed and hogging the blankets.

They would be risking all that potential this afternoon. They were risking their lives.

He checked the large clock ticking slowly above the podium. Two-and-a-half hours. The professor hadn't missed a beat explaining how politics affected classical Greek dance composition.

Only two and a half hours until they faced the actual Executioner. He couldn't tell if he wanted time to speed up or stop completely.

He debated sending Felix a text. They hadn't officially... discussed *them*, and he was terrified this was his only chance. He knew his odds going into that courtyard and making it out of that parking garage. Riley had murdered people in more visible spaces.

No, Felix had to get ready. Be alert. Nikolai couldn't dump his feelings at a time like this.

Liana texted. She was off to meet Riley at the gym.

When the sun began to set, Felix set off to the infirmary. He still had an hour to kill, and he swore his ribs were trying to take him out before that. Jackson was supposed to be recovering there after being discharged from the hospital, but Felix didn't care if they bumped paths at this point. He wanted painkillers.

It felt weird wearing a camera around his neck that wasn't his mother's gift. But they needed something that could record.

The fifteen-bed infirmary was in the campus's main building. A kind-hearted woman at the front desk took one look at the blotchy bruises on his side and ushered him through the curtain to the rows of empty beds. The lack of patients instilled a strangeness in him he couldn't shake off as she fetched him painkillers from one of the "labs/storage" rooms and poked around his sides. Maybe it was because of what he was going to face this evening, or the general unease of one of his bullies not being where he expected him to be.

"Where is everyone?" Felix asked, holding his shirt up so she could stick a heating patch over his side. It felt like someone microwaved his ribs.

"In their dorms. Nobody wants to stay overnight here anymore. Not that I blame them. What on earth happened to you, child? Should I contact Mrs. Rosewood?"

He groaned in relief, already feeling the patch work its magic. "Everything's fine. Staircases are nasty."

He thanked the nurse and called Liana when she returned to the front desk.

"Did you guys warn Michael and Jackson about being on the Executioner's hit list?"

"Hello to you, too. We talked to Michael already, but we didn't bother with Jackson since he's safe in the infirmary. Plus, I might punch him if I see his smug face. Why?"

A spark of panic made him push the dividing curtains blocking some of the beds at the back of the room aside. Jackson wasn't there.

"Just curious. See you later." He hung up and walked to the front desk. "Excuse me, have you seen Jackson lately? Average guy? Looks like he got run over by a tractor?"

It took her a moment to remember. "Oh! That poor boy! Yes, he discharged himself earlier today. Are you friends? If you see him, remind him no screens or stressful physical activity with that concussion."

He held back a sigh of relief, thanked the nurse, and left.

Riley hadn't gotten him yet. That was good. It was also reassuring he didn't sustain any life-threatening injuries.

Jackson was lucky to have come out of the alley with nothing but a concussion. Riley would have killed him if Nikolai hadn't interrupted.

His legs chilled.

That's right. Nikolai had interrupted. Riley hadn't finished the job. Then Jackson had been surrounded by round-the-clock nurses in the infirmary. When was he discharged? Sometime in the morning?

Jackson could finally be caught alone again.

It took Felix a lot longer than he liked to find out where Jackson lived. He raced into the dorm building and up the stairs. Blistering pain raced up his side, forcing him to slow down.

What if he was too late? At the landing, he made himself jog. He scoffed in dismay seeing Jackson's door. Who would leave it wide open after having just been attacked? Did he think himself unbreakable?

"Jackson, it's me, Felix—" He ducked in time to miss a flying cartoon figurine.

"Get away from me you sicko!" Jackson shouted, emerging from the bathroom and scooping up a toaster next.

So, he's fine.

His room was wider than Felix's; there was a bathroom opposite the entrance and room on either side of the door to walk.

Jackson's face was black and blue, his cheeks marked with scrapes. He had a bandage on the side of his head.

Felix put up his hands, half in submission, half ready to catch the next projectile. "Woah, woah! I'm not here to hurt you! Calm down! I'm here to warn you!"

"You should've thought twice about breaking in here! You can turn right back around and shove your threats down your pie hole!"

"Breaking in? No, I'm not the Executioner! I promise! I'm here to tell you to get off campus before tonight!"

Jackson faltered. "Why?" He saw Felix ease up and jerked the toaster menacingly, making him flinch and put his hands back up.

"The real Executioner isn't done with you. We've already warned Michael. We're going to take her down tonight, but you need to be as far away as possible."

Jackson paled, and for a second, he thought he'd gotten through. Then Jackson shook his head and stepped back. "Hang on. Don't you try to trick me! You were there in the alley! You tried to kill me!"

"No, that was her! I was asleep! I sleepwalk! You have to listen to me—"

A low giggle leaked from behind the open door against the wall. Spiders crawled up Felix's spine. The boys stared, paralyzed, as the unsettling giggling grew louder. A hand curled around the creaking door and slowly pushed it into its frame.

He wasn't the one who'd broken in.

Riley laughed, full bellied, clutching her middle with one arm. "You were asleep that entire time? Oh, that's precious! I had a full conversation with you but I thought you were in shock!"

Jackson glared at them both. "What the heck? What are you doing in my room, you creep? Get out! Both of you!"

A knife glinted behind her leg. She was blocking the exit.

Escape out the window?

Jackson didn't live on the first floor.

Felix stumbled out of her path. "Jackson, run! She's the—!"

Before he could blink, Riley grabbed a bowl off the counter and smashed it against his temple, still chuckling. "Asleep, who would've thought?"

Pain exploded. The world tilted sideways. He thudded to the carpet with a gasp.

Jackson didn't get the chance to curse. Riley dove and buried her knife into his stomach.

"Sad that I can't take my time with you. You certainly deserve it." She smiled at his shocked expression and twisted the handle. "I'll have to make do with this."

The new wave of agony broke Jackson from his stupor. He cried out and shoved her into the wardrobe, immediately bowing and clutching his stomach. "You... little..."

"I don't suggest you finish that sentence," she said.

Get up. Help him. Stop being useless.

Felix's mind and body felt like they were on a second's delay from the real world. He tried to get up. His arms slipped from underneath him like he'd missed the floor. "Go," he said to Jackson. Was it the blood trickling into his ear causing his gasping voice to ring?

Jackson staggered for the door. Riley sighed at Felix.

"Sorry about this," she mumbled before kicking him in the head.

His teeth sang. He was pretty sure he blacked out for a second because, when he blinked the spots from his vision, he found himself on his side, watching Riley's legs close the distance to Jackson.

Go. Scream. Get to a neighbour.

His ears rang too loud to hear them, but he saw Jackson's body jerk and blood splash all over the entryway's floor. Felix passed out.

Shock... Disbelief... Grief...

Everything hurt.

It was not an unfamiliar feeling at this point. It wasn't welcome, but at least it meant Felix was alive. His head was as heavy as a bowling ball, and he felt like he'd been next to a club speaker that suddenly got turned to max volume.

With great effort, he lifted his head and wrenched his eyes open.

He wasn't in Jackson's room anymore. He was sitting against a pillar in a dark store aisle. The moonlight from the windows allowed him to make out a hanging sign that said "Tools."

Riley sat with her elbows on her knees a few yards away, toying with a tire iron. His camera lay next to her foot.

She glanced up at his groan. "Oh, good. I was worried I'd kicked you too hard. What's your name?"

Wait—*Riley*. He gasped and choked. His mouth was so dry he swore he tasted sand. "Jackson?"

"Oh dear."

"No, you—What did you... to Jackson?"

She chuckled. "Got me worried there. Don't worry, he's dead. He won't bother anyone anymore."

He'd been too late. Felix dropped his head. His body fell forward with it. Before he could panic, his wrists caught behind him and halted his fall. He blinked and craned his neck to see. It took his fuzzy brain a moment to process. His wrists were tied behind him with rope, the rest of the cord wound around a pillar.

"How many fingers am I holding up?"

"Two." He wanted to hold up his middle finger and ask the same. "You brought me to a... hardware store?"

Not one in the Market. The few items on the shelves had been knocked over. Everything had a layer of dust. The store window had no glass to disperse the moonlight. He tipped his head back and blinked hard through the throbbing pain to get rid of the flickering dots before his vision went completely white. He had to focus.

"The village."

She'd brought him to the village scheduled for demolition. Had she been watching him even during the photo shoot?

More importantly, the village was far from any rescue. He was in so much trouble.

Appease her. Buy time. Call the cops.

Buying himself time to escape meant keeping her happy, and all he could think of was a string of panicked expletives that he felt best stifled.

She leaned back on the crate, releasing her tense grip on the tire iron. "Looks like you don't have brain damage. Well, not severe enough that I can tell. Coach taught us to spot the signs. You should go to a hospital later, though. To be safe. You've had a rough week."

"And whose fault is that?"

He needed a filter. He blamed the goose egg growing on the side of his head.

She narrowed her eyes, raising the hairs on his arms. "See, now that's something we have to talk about. It seems you have the wrong idea about all this. Warning Jackson. Trying to set me up."

"A misguided idea, thinking back."

Where was his phone? He couldn't feel it in his pocket when he shifted. Did she take it?

"Yes, it was!" She leaned in, teeth flashing with a snarl. "Did you think Jackson was off to repent? Bullies like him don't learn. They make people's lives a living hell and feed off of their suffering, and when they get bored, they find another target. And another. They don't *stop* until someone makes them! Despite what the media says, I'm not the bad guy here."

"No... you saved us by killing the bad guys."

She sighed. "Exactly." She put her hands together and rested them against her chin. "So, I need to know whose side you're on. You've seen me deal with them. You remember the alley. I really want you to understand."

The threat of "or else" hung between them like a charged thundercloud.

If he agreed too readily, it'd be suspicious. He had to warm up to it. How was he supposed to warm up to murder?

If only Liana were here, she'd know how to deal with Riley. He mentally kicked himself for the thought. If she were here that'd mean she was in danger as well. It was good he was alone.

Then, what would Liana do?

Keep Riley talking. Empathize.

"I wanted them gone so bad," he croaked, and found it was the truth. Deep inside, a sick part of him sobbed in relief each morning, knowing he was free from another day of torment. That relief curdled to the point of sickness remembering why. "They made school a nightmare. I hated them with everything I had... I could never side with them." He swallowed. "But why didn't you scare them into apologizing instead of killing them?"

Her smile fell, and his gut turned to ice. He'd stalled with the wrong question.

"Apologize?" she echoed quietly. "After everything they did, you think they should have gotten off with an apology?"

"No, of course not! I just—I'd liked to have gotten one y'know! They—and they didn't even get a chance to!"

She got up so quickly the crate clattered over. "I gave them chances! Warnings! More than they deserved! But they aren't the kind of people who take responsibility! You tell them your feelings are hurt and they will belittle you! Those scum knew nothing else than how to terrorize innocent people."

"Like your sister."

For a moment, there was nothing, and Felix considered saying his final goodbyes.

"Did you know she used to sing like a bird?" she said, barely audible. "She lit up the entire room with her voice. Now... She hasn't spoken a word since. She can't even go into crowded rooms anymore."

"That sounds awful," he whispered.

"All thanks to those worthless sacks of meat!" She kicked the crate so hard it sailed across the aisle. Felix flinched as it shattered against the wall. He could easily imagine it being his head.

Don't talk about the sibling. Got it.

He toed a loose rusty nail over with his shoe and wiggled it to his hand so he could scratch at his bonds. He raised his voice to drown out the scratching. "The administration didn't protect her. Their punishments weren't severe enough. So you took it into your own hands. It wasn't enough because it's like you said: they wouldn't stop."

Riley scoffed and flung her arm toward him. "I mean, look at you!" For a moment Felix's hands froze, thinking she'd caught on. "You're black and blue! I left Jackson and Michael alone after killing Emilio because *surely* they were taking his orders. But they proved me wrong and hunted you down after class when you'd done nothing wrong! Just like my sister! Like every one of their victims!"

Shivers wracked his spine. She'd really stalked him everywhere.

"I was going to end him in that hallway right then." She flexed her hands, as if imagining strangling Jackson. "How dare that waste of space think he was important enough he could put his hands on someone for no reason. Then you told them the Executioner was protecting you." She waggled her finger, sucking her teeth. "I thought you were starting to get the picture then." Fury flashed across her face. "I see now that was a lie."

Liquid ice shot through his veins. His brain sped so fast to save himself that he stumbled over his words. "I was happy! So happy! When you sent them those polaroids of the bodies, you were warning them off, weren't you? Man, I'm sorry I was sleepwalking in that alley. You were trying to show me firsthand what you were doing for all of us. You put in all that hard work, and the one moment of recognition you wanted, I missed it."

He slumped and played for a guilty expression. "You're right. They would have kept escalating until I was hospitalized." He tasted bile. "Thank you for stopping it."

"I knew you'd get it."

He almost sagged against the pillar.

"So I got this next one for you."

She leaned around the end of the aisle and returned dragging a limp body by the collar. Felix's breath caught when they reached a patch of light.

He's not dead. He can't be dead.

"Oi. Wake up." She dropped Nikolai with a concerning *thud*. Felix had never been so relieved to hear someone groan in pain before. He was alive. Blood caked Nikolai's ear from a wound on his head, but he was alive. Felix glanced at the tire iron Riley was passively twirling. How long could they stay that way?

She put her boot on Nikolai's back. "What say you to some revenge of your own?"

"What?"

"He verbally assaulted you. Humiliated you. He hurt you just like Trevor. Like Emilio. Jackson. Aren't you hurting? Don't you feel angry? Don't you want to punish them?"

"I—well—"

"I told you, reporting these jerks doesn't work. The authorities don't care about us. What, you want to go whine to Mrs. Rosewood? Let me tell you how that's going to go. They'll look at Nikolai's perfect grades, his sterling reputation, the promise of awards his dancing will give the school, and let him go with a slap on the wrist. Just like the others."

He ignored the ache in his wrist and scratched faster. Was there anything left to distract her with?

He scanned the room quickly. The store had a low ceiling littered with holes, letting you see the offices on the second floor.

"I—I can't possibly..."

"Too soon, huh?" Riley sighed and turned to Nikolai's defenceless form. "Don't worry, I'll do it for you then."

Almost free!

A rock fell through one of the holes in the ceiling and smacked Riley in the shoulder.

She looked around. "Did you...?"

A stapler careened down next, followed by a binder hitting Riley's lower back. She gasped and jumped out of the way of an entire computer monitor.

"Who—"

Felix saw a flash of dark hair through the gaps.

Riley saw it too. "I'll deal with you after, bitch!" She whirled back on Nikolai, raising the tire iron.

Felix ripped his arms free of the last threads and tackled Riley into the shelves. Vertigo slammed him with a wave of nausea so bad he almost vomited. Thankfully he'd cushioned himself against her body. Wood and trash crashed around them.

He scrambled to Nikolai's side and roughly patted his face. "Wake up! Come on, hurry!"

Nikolai inhaled sharply, blinking. He was sluggish following Felix's shoves to sit him up.

"You little..." Riley screeched and covered her head as a huge stone smashed into the debris where she was about to roll over.

"Hey! Hair-for-brains!" Through the gap, Liana had armfuls of projectiles poised. "Keep away from my boys!"

Riley snarled, and Liana began launching. Dust exploded.

Felix scooped up his camera and yanked Nikolai the rest of the way to his feet, pain tearing down his side. "Hurry! Up!"

Whether it was the insistent hands or the panic in his voice, Nikolai startled to his senses and was on his feet running out the doors with him.

"What's going on?" Nikolai shouted.

"Jackson's dead! You were next! Riley's really not happy!"

"Was that Liana?!"

"Yep," he wheezed. "Saved our..." He stumbled, hand slapping over his mouth, and Nikolai caught his elbow.

Bruised ribs were not conducive for running and his stomach was rolling dangerously. He was not pulling another tackle stunt without a miracle. They had to hide. Nikolai was already steering them into the ramshackle house across the street.

Riley's angry scream echoed behind them, along with a crash. Felix spared a glance before closing the door behind them and saw she'd pushed an entire shelving unit over and was marching into the street.

He emptied his stomach. He used to hate it as a child, but now he was grateful for how it hit an internal reset button. His head still pounded, and he felt like he was on fire, but he could think. He definitely had a concussion.

"Are you okay—"

"She's coming this way with the tire iron," Felix gasped out.

Nikolai cursed and scanned the place. The house was empty and too dark to find a hiding spot. "There." He pointed to a shattered window facing the neighbouring house.

Felix climbed out first. He tried to keep quiet, but his side shrieked with pain when he tried to put his weight on his arms. At his gasp, Nikolai gently boosted him over and followed. On landing, Nikolai pointed toward the back. They shuffled between the two-foot gap between houses.

When Riley kicked open the door, he swore he felt the wall shiver. They froze. She stomped around the main floor.

Don't look out the window. Don't look...

Her footsteps went up the stairs.

They continued shuffling and snuck through the neighbouring house's back door and into darkness's safety.

"Shouldn't stay long," Nikolai whispered.

"Don't want to."

Felix crawled to the front door and peeked through the crack, searching for signs of Liana.

Did she know Riley was out of the store? He saw no movement in the other buildings' windows. Did she escape?

Fingers on his chin turned his head. When he fussed, Nikolai cupped the back of his neck. "Your head is bloody. Let me look at you."

Felix let himself be prodded and angled into better lighting while keeping an eye on the street. "It's just a concussion," he whispered.

Nikolai huffed and released him, not looking pleased. "Nothing we can do about it right now. It's too dark to see the wound clearly, but it seems to have stopped bleeding."

Great. He just felt like he'd showered in blood, is all.

"You too."

"What?"

"You got hit in the head, too. You alright?"

"Oh, yeah. I think it was that tire iron." He touched his scalp. "Doesn't hurt too bad, though."

"It will," Felix grumbled, earning a breathy laugh.

An almighty crash snapped their attention to the hardware store. Liana had jumped out the window onto the platform of the neighbouring building's rusted fire escape. It was a tall store with eroding bricks and no windowpanes or readable signs. It would have also been a clean getaway had the bolts not broken on her landing. She grabbed the second story window's ledge as the staircase collapsed beneath her.

Felix stiffened, wanting to rush for her but knowing he had to stay back, even as his best friend dangled.

Because lo and behold, Riley had heard it too.

"Having a bit of trouble there?" she called, stalking across the street swinging her tire iron.

"Yeah, I can't decide between sending you rat-poison muffins or poison ivy tea for your prison moving-in gift."

Liana grunted as she heaved herself up, kicking her legs until she could hook an elbow over the ledge. She swung her leg and got her ankle over, then slowly slid inside. Felix made a mental note to thank Coach for the intensive strength training.

"I'll tell you what, we can decide together!" Riley said, entering the building.

With the fire escape gone and Riley coming in front the main entry, Liana was trapped.

"We have to help her," Felix whispered.

They snuck onto the street and circled the building, carefully avoiding Riley's line of sight. There was an awning around the back, but it was too high to jump off of without breaking a leg.

"That's alright, just get her attention," Nikolai whispered.

"It's a pity you stuck your nose in our business, Liana. Now you'll never beat my receives streak," Riley said, voice faint.

Felix had no idea where Liana was hiding on the top floor. He tossed a pebble through the broken window above the awning, hoping she'd hear it before she answered the taunts.

Liana's eyes and nose peeked over the window edge.

Riley said, "Just come out. Whatever sneak attack you're planning will be as weak as your spikes."

Liana's mouth opened—she caught herself and settled for a glare.

Felix waved his arms to get her attention again and pointed to the awning. She recoiled, eyes bugged out.

A slow grating sound came from inside, jarring his ears like nails on a chalkboard. Was Riley dragging the tire iron?

"Come out come out wherever you are..."

A crash. Liana jerked. She glanced at the awning again.

Nikolai bent his knees and patted his sturdy, thick thighs. He held out his arms to catch her.

Come on!

Another crash made them all jump. It sounded like furniture being thrown.

"I didn't know you were such a coward. I guess all your bravado in the gym was just for attention," Riley said.

Liana climbed over the ledge and slowly scooted onto her bum down the awning. She hesitated at the edge, then let herself fall off. Nikolai caught her with the same effortless strength that stunned Felix every time he witnessed it on stage. Liana covered her mouth to muffle her surprise. They jogged around the corner and down the street out of sight.

They did it. They got out. Felix leaned against a bricked bakery. His legs were shaking.

"You alright?" Nikolai whispered to Liana.

"Surprisingly." She grabbed his shoulders, barely containing a breathless laugh. "I can't believe you *caught* me. I can't believe your legs aren't broken."

"How did you know where to find us?" Felix asked.

"Hitched a ride in her car. When you didn't show up for our plan, we went looking for you. When Nikolai then disappeared, I figured she'd found him first. There was no way she could have transported you both herself, so I checked the parking lots nearby. Would you have known it: I was right and saw her loading you two into her car."

"Have I mentioned I love your brain?" Nikolai said.

"Is her car still here?" Felix pressed.

"Yeah, it's this way."

Felix would have loved to run, but the debris-littered ground made their steps crunch. One of them sliding into a wall would have alerted Riley.

They jogged as quietly as possible, ducking into stores and listening. They kept bumping into each other in the shadows and stepping on each other's heels, but nobody dared suggest using a phone flashlight.

When Riley discovered Liana had disappeared, her enraged scream swept the leaves with the wind.

"Please let the keys still be there," Nikolai muttered.

"Shut up before you jinx us," Liana said.

Riley had parked the car around the block behind the hardware store, amidst chunks of a house's crumbled wall she hadn't been able to drive around.

Luck was on their side. The doors were unlocked. That's about where their luck ended, though.

"I can't find the keys," Liana whispered, crawling around the front seats.

"Hotwire it," Nikolai said.

"Do I look like a mechanic?"

"After everything those true crime shows taught you, you never learned how to hotwire a car?"

"Excuse me for never having planned to break the law!"

Felix slid down to slump against one of the wheels. After all that, they were to be stopped by a set of keys?

"How far's town? Twenty minutes?" Nikolai asked.

"By car," Felix reminded.

"That's a five hour walk through twenty-six kilometres of Canadian woods," Liana said. "You walk in there, you aren't walking back out."

Felix wanted to argue—anywhere was better than trapped in a dilapidated village with a serial killer—except it was so dark he couldn't see the end of the street. They could navigate their immediate surroundings, but the woods would eat the moon's feeble light before it could reach them.

With his adrenaline calming he realized he was shivering from more than fear. The temperature would continue to drop as the night went on.

All they had were thin autumn jackets.

A shuffle in the alley made them clam up and pile into the car to hide. Nikolai and Liana squished onto the floor of the back seat.

There wasn't room for Felix, not without contorting and making an obvious lump. Nikolai looked up in alarm when Felix closed the door on them. Liana shoved his head down.

Felix dropped to the cement and shimmied under the car. It was a tight squeeze that sent shooting pains down his sides, but he fit.

All he could see of Riley was her boots as she stepped out of the alley and approached the car. She circled it.

There was no evil cackle or sadistic humming like in the movies. Somehow, that was even worse. It made room for his heart to pound in his eardrums.

Riley was silent, save for the gravel crunching underfoot.

Crunching that stopped directly behind Felix's ankle.

What was she doing? Looking into the car? How long was she going to stand there?

Goosebumps tickled the skin above his sock where his pant leg had rucked up. He resisted the urge to pull his legs further in. The slight breeze on the exposed sliver felt like breath.

Riley kept walking.

The car door opened, and Nikolai tugged him out. "That was too close. You okay?"

"Yeah," Felix gasped out, already checking his pockets. "Cops. Phone. Who has one?"

Nikolai patted his body and cursed. "She must've taken it when she kidnapped me." Felix's too, it seemed.

Liana said, "I already called when she took you two into the store. The reception's so bad out here that I'm not sure they understood the name of this place. Or if they believed me. Last I heard, there are so many prank calls it's taking double the time to answer real ones."

"How long till they arrive, if they believed you?"

She cringed. "Like you said earlier, it takes an hour."

"Better blast those sirens," Nikolai muttered.

"What are we supposed to do? Hide and hope help comes?" Felix asked through gritted teeth.

Hide. Cower. Call for help. His entire life, that's all he'd ever done.

"That's the smartest option that gets people to the end of the movie," Nikolai said, though he didn't look happy.

Hide. Cower. Call for help. Rinse, recycle, repeat.

Riley murdered Jackson in front of him. She'd gone out of her way to get Nikolai. Now she was hunting them down. And they were supposed to wait?

Felix said, "Riley's already come to the car. She's smart, she'll find us."

"So, you suggest we what? Fight her?" Liana said. "It might be three against one—or two against one," she corrected, slightly apologetic. "But she's got a weapon."

Felix hated she was right. There was no denying it. Even if he weren't beaten black and blue, he would still be a hinderance.

They wouldn't word it like that.

Did it matter? It was true.

He hugged his camera to his chest and scowled at the ground. "I'm sick of this..."

"Trust me, we don't like the situation any more than you do," Nikolai said.

No. He was sick of everything. Being helpless. Being scared all the time. He wanted to do something, but what? He wasn't as sporty as the other two. He had no strength, no endurance. Even breathing hurt. He wasn't a threat.

Maybe he didn't need to be.

"If she didn't have a weapon, could you two take her?"

They whirled to look at him. Then at each other.

"I mean... maybe," Liana said.

Nikolai said, "She's killed three people—"

"Four," Felix said.

"Even worse. She's killed four people, man."

"But would it even the odds?" Felix asked.

Nikolai rubbed the back of his neck. "Having the entire damn volleyball team with us would be better, but... I think so."

Liana narrowed her eyes. "What are you planning?"

"Something really stupid."

Felix stood in the shadows near a boarded-up window in the grocery store, clutching his camera.

He thought of every frustrating thing Emilio and Trevor and all the other bullies on campus had done and how helpless he'd felt in order to keep up his anger. The second he let go of that and paid attention to his shaky knees, he would cry.

Nikolai came out from between the buildings and loudly whispered, "Over here guys!" He exaggerated looking around and tiptoed into the grocer. Once inside, he ran past Felix and dipped behind a pile of crates.

Felix crouched, peering through the cracks between the boards.

As predicted, Riley had followed. She stalked down the same alley and turned into the grocer.

Felix pictured the bodies. The blood in his shower. The polaroids. Nikolai, unconscious.

He stood.

Riley didn't even blink. "Where is he?"

A little closer...

"I wish you could see that I'm doing this for us," she said, still walking.

Felix rooted his heels. "That's far enough."

On cue, Nikolai stood from his hiding spot. Riley paused, lip curling. "There you are." She raised her tire iron.

Perfect.

Liana dropped from the aisle above Riley and landed straight onto her back. They crashed to the ground. Liana wrestled the tire iron from her while she was stunned.

The second it slipped from her grip, Riley bucked, shooting Liana's chin into a shelf. Riley rolled for the tire iron.

Felix kicked it. She grabbed his ankle and yanked him off his feet. He landed on his side. Pain exploded across his torso. Every wheeze felt like breathing fire.

Step one: separate her from her weapon. Painful success. Step two...

When he blinked the spots from his vision, he saw Riley on her feet, ducking Nikolai's swing. She nailed him between the legs and danced backwards, looking around. Nikolai dropped to his knees like a sack of bricks.

She spotted the tire iron sticking out from under a crate at the end of the aisle. He'd kicked it too far. He'd aimed for the middle. She met Felix's eyes. Shoot. She'd be out of range. She ran for it.

"Not so fast!" Blood from Liana's chin covered her neck and collarbones. She threw a box, clocking Riley in the face, and sending her into the shelves.

"Now, Nikolai!"

Nikolai shouldered the shelving unit. It was sturdier than expected and only rocked. Riley cursed and scrambled back onto her feet. She'd get away.

Felix lunged, ignoring the liquid lava coursing through his veins. The floor spun when he moved, making him bash his face into her shin, but he wrapped his arms around her leg.

Riley lurched. "Get off!"

Another *thump* and the shelves rocked again.

Liana shouted, "Stop! Felix is—"

"Do it!" Felix barked, surprising them all.

His yelp mixed with Riley's as the shelves came down. Like dominos, one unit knocked into the next and flattened them both. Felix covered his head and choked on the clouds of dust.

He didn't feel her move. Did it work? Did they knock her out?

He waited, squinting to see Riley face-down under the shelves a few feet away. She remained still.

It was over.

"Felix, you okay? Did we do it?" Nikolai called, coughing.

He was so caught up in the swell of emotions his voice came out strangled. "Yeah. We did it. I'd like help getting out."

A relieved sigh. "Understandable. Where do we... over here?"

His eyes watered and stung from the dust. He wiggled like an inch worm through the small, triangular tunnel of space he had, trying to avoid jabbing himself with the camera around his neck.

When he heaved himself free, he saw the other two crouched at the opposite end. "Over here."

A hand wrenched the back of his collar and something sharp pressed to his throat. "Don't move."

He obeyed.

The other two froze as he felt Riley crawl up his body to loom above him.

"You know, I didn't want to do this. If you'd—don't step another inch, or I'll kill him! I swear, I'll slit his throat right now!" Riley screamed.

Liana stopped tiptoeing.

"Hurting him will go against everything you stand for, you know that. Put the glass down," Nikolai said, using that soothing, honey-sweet voice.

"Don't you give me orders!" Riley snapped. "The one person who should've understood—the *one* person who knew me and my sister's pain, and you corrupted him! You turned him against me!"

Her hand shook. The glass edge cut into his skin. Felix hissed.

"You're hurting him," Liana said.

"Shut up! Sit over there, on that fruit stand!" She jerked her chin towards the opposite end of the store. "Nikolai, sit on your hands in the freezer section." They hesitated. "Do it!"

They did as they were told. Now they were both visible and too far to charge in time.

In time.

Every cell in his body focused on the cool glass against his throat. His pulse thrummed against the edge. She was going to kill him.

He wasn't strong enough to throw her off. Her weight ground his bony hips and knees into the ground. His arms were free, but he had a feeling she could stab a lot faster than he could grab.

Nikolai's gaze darted around the store, searching for anything to help. It was useless. They had no more tricks. Liana's fingers curled into the rubble around her, an angry tear rolling down her cheek.

Felix looked at his camera, then met Liana's eyes. "Hey Riley?"

"What?"

"Say cheese, bitch." He flipped his camera snapped a picture.

The bright camera light flashed her eyes. She gasped and released his collar to shield her face. Liana cocked her arm and spiked a rock into the back of her head.

A pinching pain laced across his throat. His gut dropped. Warmth coated his collarbones.

Nikolai skidded into view on his knees. Was Liana screaming? The world flopped as Nikolai flipped him onto his back and pressed against his neck.

As if his ears popped with the shift in position. Sound exploded around him.

"You're okay! You'll be okay! Stay calm!" Nikolai blabbed through hitching breaths. His fingers squelched as they flexed around the base of Felix's neck.

"Riley?" Felix rasped.

Liana crouched over him. "Don't talk! She's unconscious. She—she nicked you. But it's okay! We can fix it!"

He shivered. He wasn't even that cold. He just couldn't help it. That was probably the shock.

Oh, wow. This was real, wasn't it?

He expected to feel fire . Agony. Blind terror.

He felt nothing.

Liana brought his hands to her mouth, breathing hot air over them. He must've been colder than he thought. "When are they getting here?" She pulled out her phone and dialled. She choked back a sob and tried again. "Connect, dammit!"

Nikolai was still murmuring assurances, whether for Felix or himself, he couldn't tell. Either way, the rumbling undertone made Felix smile.

Seeing it, Nikolai's calm facade cracked, and he jerked his chin away, whispering brokenly to Liana, "I—it won't stop bleeding. What do I—I don't know..."

She stabbed the numbers again, squeezing Felix's hands with her free one. "Just keep the pressure! Hold on, Felix."

The last thing he wanted was to give a cliché "dying speech." But when he opened his mouth, by some cruel cosmic joke, he found he couldn't talk anyway. He almost wanted to laugh. Tears ran down his temples. He tasted mould.

Fatigue coaxed him to close his eyes. He struggled to keep looking at his friends. If he couldn't say anything, he wanted to look at them for as long as possible.

The moonlight caught the strong line of Liana's jaw and shoulders. Even covered in dirt and smears of blood, she held a stunning figure. He hoped she'd laugh a lot.

He looked up into Nikolai's shining eyes. Tears clung to his dark lashes. Had they always been so long?

He ached to speak. He wasn't ready to die. His eyes drooped as more of his strength bled through Nikolai's fingers.

A faint siren blared in the distance. Liana screamed, "Over here!" as her footsteps receded.

Felix didn't know what face he was making, but Nikolai leaned down until all he could see was his wobbling smile. "It's okay. I'm right here. I'm not going anywhere."

That was the last thing he heard.

The Executioner Caught at Last! Shocking Campus Discovery!

Felix woke clammy, stiff-necked, and with a heavy tongue tasting of old socks. His nostrils felt like he'd snorted antiseptic.

If this was the afterlife, it sucked.

He squinted against the bright white lights. He was in a hospital bed in a private room. The trash was full of coffee cups.

Nikolai was asleep on the foot of the bed with one arm pillowed beneath his head and another outstretched like he'd been touching Felix's hand. He had a couple bruises and some bandages. His hair was messy and damp.

Tears pricked Felix's eyes. This was a nice view to come back to.

He wanted to laugh but found his throat ached too much. No, not his throat. His neck. It was heavily bandaged. When he lifted his hand an IV tube came with it.

Had he been here all night? What time was it?

Nikolai stirred. He inhaled sharply and jolted upright, hands flying out. When he gripped the bedsheets instead of Felix's hand, he scrambled and looked up and...

Their eyes met.

"Hi there," Nikolai whispered.

The traitorous beeping heart monitor sped up. "Hi," he croaked back.

Oh good, he still had his voice.

A soft voice approached the room. "He's still here, alright. I finally got him to shower. Told him Felix might think he was hurt if he was still all bloody when he woke." Liana gasped as she entered. "You're up!"

She placed two fresh coffees on the bedside table and prepared to launch herself, then thankfully thought better of it and gently hugged him.

He didn't have to wonder who she'd been talking to for long. To his surprise, his mother marched in. She crushed him in a hug so tight he almost thought she was trying to suffocate him. His father tiptoed in and was more mindful of his injuries.

Apparently, he'd been lucky. Riley had missed his vital arteries and vocal cords.

He'd been out for two days. The media was going nuts. Jackson's body being discovered the same day the police were called to four students requiring ambulances at the nearby demolition site? No assumptions were off the table.

"Soon you'll be able to come home," his dad said, stroking his hair. "Away from the stress and worries. It'll be like a long vacation!"

"Mentally and physically recovering from such an attack will be no vacation." His mother folded her hands over her crossed legs, the picture of elegance. "He'll no doubt be called into court to testify if they don't try to pin you as an accomplice. I'll get us a lawyer. The best in the business. They're not blemishing my son's name."

As conflictingly heartwarming as her support was, there was something he needed to address first. "Guys, can you give us a moment?"

Nikolai and Liana glanced at each other nervously, but left the room anyway.

Felix took a deep breath and looked at his mother. He'd faced down the Executioner. Talking to her shouldn't have been more nerve wracking.

Don't stutter. Don't stutter...

"Before that... All of this has made me realize I need help. Professional help. Honestly I probably needed it before all this mess. And not just about the sleepwalking—though there are sleep institutes I would like to consult at the very least."

She studied him long and hard. He swallowed.

Some people harboured a stigma against therapy, and he wasn't sure where she aligned herself. He was going to get help either way, but the scared child inside him crossed his fingers for her support.

"Of course," she said. "It's your brain, you should be comfortable living with it. Nobody deserves any less."

He let out a heavy breath. His dad squeezed his shoulder.

"Before we launch any plans, let the boy recover," his dad said, smiling warmly and opening the door. "I think there's a restaurant that does take-out around here."

Liana pulled her phone from her pocket to check a text. Wait, that was Nikolai's phone. Why did she have his phone? "I'll show you if you can stop by the tech shop. I've got to pick something up."

On the way out, his dad hugged Nikolai, an amusing sight since Nikolai was a foot taller and didn't know where to put his hands. His mother gave them a firm nod instead.

"Everything alright?" Nikolai asked, lowering himself to sit at Felix's knees.

"Yeah, I think it will be."

Some hours later, a familiar tall cop and her homophobic partner stood in the doorway.

"Mr. Griffiths, are you healthy enough to talk to us?"

Felix cleared his throat with a wince and struggled to sit up. "Yeah, how can I help you?"

The woman entered, pulling out a notepad and a pen. "I'm Officer Lappet, and this is Officer Gascon, if you don't remember us. We wanted to ask you some questions about what happened."

Oh, he remembered them. He wondered what they thought about the campus's killer-by-popularity-vote having wound up a victim.

"Liana, Nikolai, and I figured out the Executioner—or, Riley—was going after bullies. I went to warn Jackson, but..." He remembered the slick sound of Riley's knife cutting up Jackson and shuddered. "She was already there. She stabbed him and knocked me out. I woke up in that hardware store."

They didn't look surprised to hear about Jackson. They nodded, and she jotted something down.

"Did you find him already?"

"Yes," said Officer Gascon. "What time did you go there?"

"Around this time of day."

"Mhm. And the hardware store?"

Nikolai said, "He just said he was unconscious. Liana told you earlier, she—"

"Yes, only she witnessed Riley lugging two grown men into her car in a public parking lot. Please refrain from interrupting."

Felix shared a stupefied look with Nikolai and continued. "We were tied up, and Riley was going to kill Nikolai. Liana distracted her from the second floor so we could get away."

"How'd you get that injury?"

"Liana and Nikolai pushed the shelves onto Riley and me to trap her. Riley tried to use me as a hostage, but Liana threw a rock and knocked her out. I think I got it when she fell off me."

Lappet hummed and jotted more down. "Three... jumped victim..."

"Is that what she's saying?" Nikolai sputtered. "That's ridiculous! She kidnapped us! Did you even check the parking lot's security footage?"

When the first murder happened, the police had to get a warrant to look through the campus's footage. The longer the Executioner was active, the less concern the school had for the invasion of their students' privacy.

"You didn't find anything, did you?" Felix said. By their guarded faces, he'd guessed right.

The security camera around the crime scenes had been tampered with the nights of the murder. Riley was an engineering student.

"Is it not enough that Felix almost became the fifth victim? You have three witnesses. How is that not swaying you?" Nikolai said, tone edging on the boundary of anger.

Felix couldn't imagine the stress the police were under. He hated it, but he could understand why he and his friends were under the microscope.

The police had four bodies and a trio of students who'd been each other's alibis the entire time, who had a greater chance of overpowering the victims, and one of them was the campus's favourite suspect.

He couldn't really blame them for thinking: "At last! A link!" when they were called to a bloody crime scene where the players were the suspicious trio and a star team's volleyball player.

The police finally had a narrative, and since Felix had messed up their confession trap, he had nothing to fight with.

"We're looking into every avenue," said Officer Lappet.

"Every avenue my—"

"Camera," Felix exclaimed, then cringed at the jolt of pain lacing across his neck. "What about the picture I took? Where's my camera?"

Nikolai pulled it from his backpack. Felix scrolled through the memory to the photo he'd taken to blind Riley with the flash. He turned the screen towards the police.

They pursed their lips.

"We'll take it into evidence," Lappet said.

Where it wouldn't then see the light of day. He had to admit, without context, it didn't look like anything more than someone mid-fight. It could be argued this was evidence of self-defence over an attack.

Riley was going to get away with this.

"You don't believe us," Nikolai said.

Lappet sighed. "We need all three of you to come in officially. Mr. Griffiths, we will wait until you're discharged."

"Arresting them, are you? Wouldn't it be awful if I blew all your plans out of the water?" said Liana from the doorway.

Felix's dad said behind her, "What's all this?"

"An interrogation without lawyer supervision?" said his mother, her perfect glare sharpened enough to cut glass.

Liana unlocked her phone. "That won't be necessary."

"*... don't have brain damage. Well, severe enough that I can tell. Coach...*"

Felix couldn't believe his ears. It was Riley's voice from the hardware store. Liana's phone showed a close-up of an old dark wooden floor.. The camera shot panned to peer through a gap between broken planks where, below, Felix saw himself tied up, Riley holding her tire iron, and Nikolai unconscious on the ground.

"*I'm not the bad guy here,*" Riley's recorded voice echoed.

"*No... you saved us by killing the bad guys,*" came Felix's scratchy reply.

"*Exactly.*"

It went on until Riley threatened to kill Nikolai next and cut out with Liana's whispered, "Oh, fuck no."

"Why didn't you show us this video when we interviewed you at the scene?"

"Excuse me for being in shock over my best friend's throat being slit." Liana rolled her eyes. "It got water damage from being dropped in a puddle during the fight. Nikolai recommended I go to the 24-hour tech shop to get it fixed. You might actually know someone who works there."

By officer Gascon's flush and the twist of his face, it was the exact store Felix was thinking of: the one Sergio worked at.

Liana handed the phone to Officer Lappet, and Felix's mother said, "I suggest you take that arrest somewhere else."

News Stations Fight for Front Row Seat in Killer's Trial!

As Nikolai hefted the last piece of luggage into the back of the car and Liana shut the trunk, Felix let out a breath.

This was it.

He looked at the news headline on his phone spelling out Riley's indictment.

"YOUNG AND BLOODTHIRSTY! Bloody Executioner's identity revealed!" said one article. "TOO YOUNG FOR MURDER? VICTIMS' FAMILIES DISAGREE!" said another. "Relieved Campus Parties as Killer Is Arrested" was Felix's favourite. Nobody at the college was partying.

He touched the thick bandages over his neck. The hospital had deemed him fit for release. His wound was healing enough to replace the stitches with clear medical tape. It was over.

His mother barked for him to hurry up and started the car. His dad winked, saying, "I'll buy you a little time," and got into the passenger's seat to distract her.

His friends wore sad smiles. Felix's stomach flopped.

"It won't be forever. The hospital found me a sleep institute with a great therapist. I know it's out of the way and doesn't allow visitors, but we figured the farther from the media vultures around the court case, the better, and—"

Liana squished his cheeks. "I'm proud of you. You clean out all your cobwebs and come back when you're ready, okay?"

He pressed his lips together and nodded. She stuck her head into the car window to say goodbye to his parents.

Felix looked at Nikolai and found himself tongue-tied.

All he could think about was those moments in the store when he was bleeding out: how Nikolai held him and promised him...

"Wait for me?" Felix whispered.

It was brief, barely there, but Felix heard Nikolai's voice loud and clear. "Always."

He spent his nights supervised in the sleep institution. At first, it was behind a one-way mirror. As his episodes began to calm, it was by camera.

Every day, he spoke to a therapist.

"As you know, many factors can contribute to your condition," his therapist explained. "Genetics, substance abuse, sleep deprivation, many others." She flipped through her notebook. "Already, you're showing improvement with a regular schedule."

"That's it?" Felix exclaimed. "All I need is to be in bed by ten?"

"Not exactly. While establishing a regular, relaxing routine before bedtime in a safe space with aid from external resources will help, it will not be a permanent solution until we address your underlying issue. Yours, I believe, is stress. Your hectic, high-pressure college life no doubt triggered your sleepwalking. The bullying and constant fear for your own safety worsened it."

Felix caressed the tough skin on his wrists. "But I'm not there anymore and it's still happening."

"You are still walking around, but that's to be expected when you've undergone trauma. We are close to finding the right medications and dosages to keep you in bed. However, your mind is still at war. There is something you are fighting within yourself. Until we fix that, your sleepwalking will always be a problem." She propped her elbows on her knees to lean in. "So, tell me, Felix Griffiths. Who are you?"

He came back time after time until he could truly answer that question and be happy with the answer.

Months After the First Grizzly "Executioner" Murder, Riley Decker Is Deemed Guilty!

The first thing Felix noticed when his parents opened the hospital doors was not the hints of new snow in the air or the first breeze he'd felt in a year, but two blazing smiles beside a familiar truck. That was the real breath of fresh air, which was then squeezed out of his lungs by the hug Liana all but tackled him into.

Felix heard laughter and a familiar *click* that he'd never forget. Nikolai held up a new instant camera. Liana plucked the developing photograph from Nikolai's fingertips, still clinging to Felix's side. She griped about wasting a camera's first picture with his shoddy skills, but Felix wasn't listening anymore.

Nikolai was smiling at him.

"You waited," Felix said breathlessly.

Nikolai nodded, thumbs in his pockets, leaning on the truck like this was any normal day. Like he was picking Felix up from class to watch Liana practice volleyball together. Like the past year hadn't been a daily struggle.

"Who am I kidding?" Nikolai laughed. "I'm about as cool as a hot pocket. Get over here." He opened his arms.

Felix released a shuddering breath and dove into the embrace.

Nikolai smelled like apple tarts. It felt right. It felt like home. His body was soft, warm, and yielded to Felix's enthusiasm as it wrapped around him. The way Nikolai held him, his face buried in Felix's neck, his lips just barely brushing his skin, moulding their bodies together to not let even a breath of air separate them, told Felix everything he didn't say out loud:

I missed you.

I'm sorry.

Don't leave me again.

With Felix's answering squeeze, Nikolai shuddered, whispering a shaky exhale over his skin as if finally realizing this was real, that Felix was back, and pulled him even closer.

The trio parted ways with Felix's parents to get dinner together for the first time in a year. They ate at a horrible burger joint that smelled suspiciously like cleaning supplies. It was perfect.

Sergio was already there with a "Welcome Home" balloon meant for new mothers and the most embarrassing paper hats he could find as a surprise. Felix laughed and made a U-turn out the door. Liana slung him over her shoulder and marched him back in.

"No fair!" Felix said. "When did you get so strong? Don't shove that thing on my head!"

They fell back into step easily, as if nothing had changed. Only now Nikolai refused to let go of Felix's hand.

"I need both hands to eat my burger!" Felix complained, half-heartedly, because Nikolai's palm was warm, and every time he ran his thumb over Felix's knuckles, his skin tingled.

"I dare you to eat with none," said Sergio.

Felix raised a brow. "Do I hear a challenge?"

"We just got him out of a mental institution, it'd be best if we don't go eating our food like cows and getting him thrown back in," Liana said, smiling.

During the time he'd been away, Liana's volleyball team had won another trophy. "I'm tempted to drop Film Studies entirely and make volleyball my career," she said, slurping her vanilla shake.

"I'd say it would require some thinking, and a safety net just in case, but seeing how you play, you could pull it off," Felix replied. His friends stared at him.

"That was a mature answer," Nikolai said, surprised.

"Thanks for not calling me stupid. Therapy is wonderful. What about you? Anything earth-shattering in my absence?"

Nikolai shrugged, stuttering nonsensical deflections. Liana tossed a well-timed fry and cheered when it landed in his gaping mouth. Nikolai glared.

"Don't let him tell you any different," she said. "He was scouted at the last performance!"

Felix gasped.

Nikolai shoved his burger into his mouth. "It's no big deal. I didn't take it."

"Why not?" Felix exclaimed.

"It would have required me to move across the country and I had other plans." He picked at his pickles, avoiding Felix's eyes. "Uh, more important matters to deal with. In this province."

Before Felix could pry further, Liana jumped in. "Your parents mentioned you had a plan for school?"

"Mrs. Rosewood helped me contact the bureau for student accommodations. They'll let me space out my classes so it's less stressful. Did you know you could do that? It's going to take me a year or longer to graduate, but I won't be pulling my hair out anymore."

"So, the sleepwalking's gone?" Sergio prompted.

Felix smiled. "I've got coping mechanisms and medication to keep me in bed and for when my stress rises. I understand how to manage my condition now rather than fear it. Other than that..." Felix bit his lip and glanced at Nikolai. "I've... figured things out."

"This calls for a celebration!" Liana hollered, perhaps a tad too loud for such a small restaurant. "More root beer!"

They celebrated the proper way, according to Liana: with cheap cheesecake and soda well into the night until they were kicked out.

While hospitalized, Felix's parents had cleaned out his dorm before the college could touch any of it. All his belongings were tidily back in his old bedroom, ready for him to move back in. He only needed to hail a cab to his parents' place and sleep there. But he felt the pad of Nikolai's thumb brush over his knuckles and decided he'd rather spend his first night of freedom somewhere else.

"I'm dropping you off at Nikolai's?" Liana double-checked, melting into the driver's seat with a happy burp.

"Are you sure you're okay to drive?" laughed Nikolai, getting in the back seat.

"I'm pleasantly filled with sugar and dairy, my best friend is out of hospital-jail, and I'm spending the night with the owner of this truck." She patted the dashboard, sporting a filthy smile. "I couldn't be better."

Sergio's grin matched hers. When Felix raised a brow, all he said was, "He has a gay cousin."

Liana let them out at Nikolai's apartment with a tight hug and a kiss on the cheek. They waved goodbye until the truck was a speck in the distance.

"It was a nice surprise to see Sergio get on so well with you two," Felix said. "I knew it was possible. I just didn't think it would happen without a little help."

"You can thank yourself for that," Nikolai said.

"How? I was in a hospital."

Nikolai looked at their joined hands. "Exactly. You touch more lives than you think. The three of us missed you a lot. That gave us common ground. After bumping into each other a dozen times, we figured the universe might be trying to say something."

Felix pulled his hood to hide his reddening ears. "That's cheesy."

"Doesn't make it any less true."

They headed into the lobby. "Don't mind the mess," Nikolai said as he let Felix inside the apartment. "Make yourself at home. I need to grab some clean sheets from the dryer."

Nikolai's place hadn't changed the slightest over the year, which was a small comfort. Felix had gotten used to white walls, white floors, and furniture bolted to the floor. He ran his hand along the dusty grey walls, the tattered old couch, and the marble kitchen counter.

Then he stepped into Nikolai's bedroom, and his jaw dropped.

It looked like a bomb had gone off. Nikolai had bought a desk, but that only elevated the disaster four feet off the ground. It was covered in mountains of papers, books, and notes of Riley's trial. There were folders filled with copies of lecture notes from Felix's missed classes.

He pawed through some of the books and blinked to avoid getting misty-eyed. *Sleep Deprivation: Basic Science, Physiology and Behaviour, Sleep Disorders for Dummies.* Several pages were marked with sticky notes.

He'd never seen Nikolai's wall so cluttered. Before, Nikolai had strung posters between furniture as a big middle finger to the landlord for his ridiculous "nothing touching my paint" rules. Now, his posters lay abandoned in a corner, leaving his walls covered by research papers, the handcuffs Felix used to tie himself up with, a calendar with Riley's court dates circled, and polaroid pictures Felix had taken of Nikolai months ago. He wondered where Nikolai had gotten them. His parents must not have packed his dorm alone...

"Sorry. It's messy," Nikolai said from the doorway.

"How did your landlord not evict you for doing this?" Felix half-joked, rubbing his nose.

"Don't worry, I got chewed out. And threatened. Many times. But I told the old geezer where he could shove it."

"And these?" He lifted the corner of the lesson copies. "How'd you get them?"

Nikolai scratched the back of his neck, taking a sudden interest in his shoes. "Didn't want you to get too far behind. I got them in exchange for dancing at side gigs, bachelorette parties, school shows and stuff..."

Felix felt his ears ablaze. Nikolai had been keeping up with the world and his studies... for him.

Which was why he was startled to hear Nikolai whisper, "I'm sorry."

Nikolai looked more haggard in that second than a man on death row, the barriers crumbling now that they were alone to reveal how distraught he'd been, broiling alone in his thoughts and fears.

Tears glistened in Nikolai's eyes. "I'm so sorry. If I was the cause of this or at least part of the cause I should have done more, gotten you help sooner or dealt with your bullies or *something*, because you didn't deserve—"

Felix put a hand up to silence him. The comfortable, rehearsed line came easy. "My name is Felix Griffiths. I have spent the last six months in a psychiatric hospital learning to not only control my body and mind but also accept who I am."

Nikolai stood in place, stunned. Slowly, a small smile shone through. "And who are you?"

"I am a twenty-two-year-old photographer who used to have a tendency towards sleepwalking. Who likes men."

Nikolai's smile burst into a beaming grin that made his heart skip. Nikolai stepped forward and reached for his hand. The laptop in the corner lit up with a ding and read, "One unread message from The Birth-givers."

Felix expected this moment to vanish and for Nikolai to deal with his parents, but Nikolai just continued backing him into the wall. Blood rushed in his ears.

"Aren't you going to answer that?"

Nikolai kicked the laptop into the corner without looking at it. "They're just complaining again. They're not too happy with me right now."

Felix swallowed dryly. "Why?"

Nikolai backed him into the dresser. Felix's breath hitched. He leaned against the wood to look up at Nikolai without losing his balance. He wasn't prepared for the pure awe and overwhelming affection on Nikolai's face.

"Because I told them I'm in love with my best friend."

Felix couldn't help the toothy grin. Nikolai glanced at his lips. The tips of his fingers brushed Felix's calloused wrist—no bracelets in sight to hide them. Sparks of anticipation danced in his stomach.

Nikolai bent into his space and paused. He glanced up as if to check if it was okay, scanning for the slightest hint that Felix might be uncomfortable. Felix nearly rolled his eyes.

Nikolai leaned down again, lips grazing his, and paused again. "Is this okay?"

Oh, for the love of...

Felix laced his fingers into Nikolai's hair and tugged him down to capture his lips in a heart-fluttering kiss. Nikolai made a surprised noise at the back of his throat and braced himself with his hands by Felix's ears. The surprise turned into a muffled chuckle and a happy sigh. He melted into the kiss.

His laptop's notification alert beeped again. Nikolai ignored it and pulled Felix flush against the hard planes of his body. It beeped again. And again. With every notification bell, Nikolai seemed more determined to kiss the daylights out of him, as if he could embarrass the laptop into shutting down.

"You should answer that," Felix giggled between kisses.

"I'll tell them to get lost later," Nikolai murmured against his mouth, hands kneading dangerously lower. "Right now, I need my dose of Felix."

When people had seen Felix's shoebox of handcuffs and ropes, he could usually tell what they were thinking of. It had been funny, so he'd let them. They'd never guess what they were actually for.

Now?

Looking over at the box on the bedside table over Nikolai's bare, kissed, and bitten chest, maybe they'd been a little right.

Acknowledgements

There are many people who helped bring this story to fruition. First and foremost, I want to thank my parents for their endless support. I literally would not have been able to do this without you guys.

A big thanks to the team at Presses Renaissance Press for handling my bumbling questions with grace and lending all your expertise to make this story the best it can be!

I especially want to thank Nathan Caro Fréchette who, despite the allocated time for pitches over, kindly took time to listen to a lost, anxious girl with a story at her first book convention. Who persisted from convention to convention, insisting for that manuscript. You turned the scary world of traditional publishing into something welcoming.

Even to the other authors at Presses Renaissance Press, like S.M. Carrière and Éric and Jen Desmarais. You might not remember me but boothing next to you guys at CanCon, having you cheer hearing I'd pitched to Nathan, made the world of difference. You guys were such inviting, happy souls that I'm so glad to have met that weekend.

About the Author

When she's not practicing martial arts, going to conventions or rolling around in the grass with her golden retriever, Canadian author Heather Chambers dedicates her time to raising awareness through her writing.

She's made her first step with her debut dystopian, nature-apocalyptic novel *Earth Sucks*, published at 19, and its prequel *The Mercenary and the Hissing Woods*. Now, armed with search histories that'd pique the FBIs attention if ever discovered (for writing purposes she swears), Heather writes for Gen Z readers whose voices are swept under the rug.